THE PERFECT MOTHER

BOOKS BY MATTHEW FARRELL

ADLER AND DWYER PREQUELS

What Have You Done

I Know Everything

ADLER AND DWYER SERIES

Don't Ever Forget

Tell Me The Truth

THE PERFECT MOTHER

MATTHEW FARRELL

bookouture

Published by Bookouture in 2022

An imprint of Storyfire Ltd.
Carmelite House
50 Victoria Embankment
London EC4Y 0DZ

www.bookouture.com

ISBN: 978-1-80314-843-4
eBook ISBN: 978-1-80314-842-7

For Curtis,
What a ride it's been so far.

PART ONE

CHAPTER ONE

The phone was ringing.

Laura Anderson knew what the tone was. A FaceTime call. But she couldn't tell where the sound was actually coming from. She rubbed her eyes and followed the sound, tracing the contours of the dashboard on her car, moving toward the passenger's side. She leaned in a little closer and listened.

The glovebox.

She reached over and unlatched the tiny handle. As soon as the door fell open, the ringing got louder. Laura fished the phone from inside, untangling it from the St. Christopher's necklace she always kept in there.

It was an old iPhone, the kind she'd turned in a few upgrades ago, small and black, the screen cracked in the upper right corner. The display indicated an incoming FaceTime call, but she couldn't see who was calling, the number itself hidden under the caption of a prefilled ID named *Unknown Caller*.

Fleeting questions ran through her mind. Whose phone was it? How did it get in her car? She tried to remember the last time she'd had to go into the glovebox, but nothing came to mind. She also tried to recall her last passenger, certain it had been her daughter, Nelle. Could it have been one of her old phones? Or maybe it was Kurt's? No, that was impossible. They leased their phones and always had to turn in the old ones to get the newer models. Besides, if the upgraded phones were working, the older phones would be disabled. She then thought that perhaps one of Nelle's friends had mistakenly left it in there, or maybe one of the guys at the tire shop had forgotten it when she'd dropped her car off to get the oil changed.

Laura accepted the FaceTime and waited for it to connect.

"Mom?"

"Nelle?" She immediately recognized her daughter's voice and looked down at the screen. It was still black. "Honey, I found this phone in the car when you called. Whose is it?"

"Mom, you need to listen."

"I've been texting you. You never texted back. I understand if you're still mad, but it's important to let me know you're okay."

"*Mom.*"

There was something in Nelle's tone—something unusual—that made the hairs on the back of Laura's neck stand up. Her voice. It was...

"Honey, what's wrong?"

"Mom, *listen.*"

... distressed.

Nelle was crying. Laura could hear her daughter's voice shaking and the rhythmic sniffling that accompanied an exhale full of dread and snot. But she couldn't see anything through the connection. Just the black screen. "Nelle. What's wrong?"

"They took me."

"What?"

"They took me."

"Who took you? What are you talking about?"

Nelle began crying harder. It was hard to understand what she was saying as the words came with sobs. "You have to listen to what they say. You have to do what they tell you. I'm *so scared.*"

A feeling of dread washed over Laura, the ebbs and flows of a sudden nausea like a wave crashing up on the beach. Was this really happening? She gripped the phone tighter in her hand, staring down at it and seeing nothing but her own face in a small picture window in the bottom corner of the screen. "Nelle, tell me what's going on right now. Who has you? What happened?"

"Mom, I—"

"Nelle!"

There was some kind of interference on the other end as Laura pressed the phone closer to her face as if she might be able to see through the blackness. A part of her tried to convince herself that this wasn't happening. It couldn't be real. She'd just come from a fundraiser at her church where she was being honored for her hard work. People were just clapping for her. Father Glipp had made an entire speech centered around her kindness and selflessness. How could this be happening right now? She was supposed to be driving home to take a nap. And maybe have a bath. How could it be real?

"Hello!"

Her breathing grew short as the knot in her stomach tightened, the nausea intensifying. Her eyes darted up to the road and back down to the phone as panic set in. Should she get help? Should she flag down the next car she saw? Should she call 911 from her own phone that sat in the cup holder only inches from her grasp?

"Nelle!"

"Enough," a voice commanded on the other end. This voice was calm, mechanical, like someone was digitizing it. It sounded robotic. Unfeeling.

Laura held her breath and waited.

"We have your daughter. We want you to come get her."

"What's happening?" Laura could hear hysterics on the edge of her voice. "How do you have my daughter?"

"We know the truth."

"About what? What are you talking about?"

"We loaded an address in your car's GPS. I'm sure you'll recognize it. It's your mother's house."

Laura could feel herself hyperventilating. She struggled to breathe, certain she was going to vomit at any moment. She tried to focus on the screen as her subconscious begged her to step back from such an awful reality. She wanted to hang up and drive away and go find a drink. A drink would make things better. But this? No, this wasn't happening. Couldn't be.

"Come alone," the voice continued. "And if you want to see Nelle or your mother alive again, you might wanna get here before six-thirty."

The voice forced her to stumble back to reality. "I don't know who you think I am, but my mother's dead."

"No more lies. We found you and now we need to talk about what you did to us."

"My husband's a cop. He'll come after you."

"Come to your mother's house. We'll be waiting."

"My mother's dead! I don't know what you're talking about!"

"Six-thirty. Don't be late or everyone dies."

Tears welled in Laura's eyes as she fought with all the strength she had to stay under control. She took a breath and shook her head, steadying herself. "I'm telling you, hand to God, I don't understand what's going on. Do you want money? We don't have much, but I can get you some. Would that help?"

"Stop talking and start driving. Follow the GPS or come from memory. You know where Clare lives. Nelle will be there. We all will be."

"Who's Clare?"

"Six-thirty."

Laura pulled up the GPS and saw the address loaded into the screen: 122 North Shore West Caroga Lake Road, Caroga Lake, NY. Travel time: three hours and six minutes. She did some quick calculations in her head. Three hours was probably doable on an early weekend morning or late night when roads were clear, but leaving at the start of rush hour would undoubtedly push her into heavy traffic on either 87 or the Taconic Parkway and I-90.

"Let me talk to Nelle."

"You already talked to her."

"I need to know that she's okay!"

"She's fine. For now."

"Who are you?" Laura's own voice was completely foreign to her. The calm and steadiness had vanished, replaced by something that sounded choked and raspy.

"It ain't important to know who we are. Not yet. What's important is that we know who you are. That we found you."

"I wasn't hiding!"

"Maybe Laura Anderson wasn't. But Betty Hamms was."

Laura stared at the phone, watching her eyes glass over as she bit her bottom lip. She felt the effects of the pills she'd swallowed and the vodka she'd been drinking mix with her adrenaline and became lightheaded. One hand grabbed onto the steering wheel to keep from falling forward.

"This is a mistake. Please. I don't know who Betty Hamms is. You have the wrong person."

"We don't. You're Betty Hamms. In another life. A life you tried to escape from. But we found you. Took us a while, but we found you."

Laura's tears hit the phone. Her hand shook, creating a kind of vibration of her small image in the box on the screen. The woman who'd been at the church celebration only minutes earlier, the happy wife with the happy life, had melted away, showing the depressed, sad, and melancholy Laura she'd come to know over the years: long blond hair that hid the gray, the crow's feet at the edges of her brown eyes that matched the tiny wrinkles at the edges of her mouth, a mouth that always seem to turn downward.

"I'm not Betty Hamms. I promise. You have the wrong family."

"Throw your personal phone out the window," the voice instructed. "You have this one now. You won't need yours."

"Please, I—"

"Throw it out the window!"

In the background, Laura could hear Nelle start to scream.

"We're the ones in control, Betty. You need to understand that."

"Okay! Okay!" Laura cried. "I'm throwing it out." She took her phone from the cup holder, knowing it was the only link to any help she might hope to have, and rolled down the passenger side window.

"Smash it first."

"What?"

"Break the screen. Smash it."

"Okay!"

Nelle's screams grew louder. Laura pounded the phone against the steering wheel over and over until she heard the screen shatter and felt bits of glass skip across her hand. "It's broken! It's broken!"

More screaming.

"Throw it out the window."

"Leave my baby alone!"

"Throw it out the window!"

Laura did as she was told. "It's gone! I threw it out! It's gone!"

Nelle stopped screaming.

"Do not hang up this phone," the voice said. It was calm again. Measured. "There's a charger in the glovebox along with a mount you can put on your dashboard so we can see you. Plug in the charger, connect the Bluetooth, and set up the mount. Always keep the phone on. This is our way of keeping tabs on you. We can see you, but you can't see us. If you try and call the police or ask for help in any way, your daughter will die."

Laura felt woozy. She couldn't understand how she could be in such a situation. She had just been resting peacefully in her car on the side of the road, longing for her bed and a bath with some wine and soft music to pass the rest of the day. It was startling how quickly things had changed.

"Let's go!"

Laura followed the instructions. Her sight was blurry with tears. A shaking hand reached back into the glovebox and came away with the charger and phone mount. She plugged one end of the charger into her USB port and the other into the old iPhone. She then took the mount, stuck it on top of the dashboard, and after she connected the phone to the car's Bluetooth, slid it into the mount.

"Now start driving. You're running out of time."

Laura wrapped her hand around the gear knob to pull back out into traffic, then stopped.

"I said drive."

"I can't. Someone's coming."

CHAPTER TWO

She watched as a truck with flashing yellow lights pulled up behind her and took up her entire rearview mirror. She stared through her mirrors, wondering if this was her last chance to save her daughter or if it would be the invitation the voice on the other end needed to kill her. Laura rolled down her window as a pudgy man sauntered up to her and bent down.

"Car trouble?" he asked with a smile. "I can help. That's what I'm here for."

She paused, contemplating her next move. As soon as the silence slipped in, Nelle's voice, whimpering and broken, came through the speakers on the car.

"Mom, don't. Please."

"Whoa," the man said. "Who's that?"

Laura wiped her eyes and smiled in return. "Just family. I'm fine. No trouble. I was taking the call and didn't want to drive while I was on the phone."

The man looked at her. "You okay?"

No. Pretty far from okay, in fact.

Laura knew the moment she asked for any kind of help,

Nelle would be killed. She knew this in her bones, as a mother. There was nothing she could do.

"I'm fine," she said into the phone, then turned back to the man. She wiped her eyes again. "We had an unexpected death. Just found out."

The man's expression changed as his smile faded. "Oh, well, I'm sorry to hear that."

"I appreciate you stopping, but I'm going to get back on the road. Head home."

"You have a nice day. I really am sorry for your loss."

"Thank you."

She watched him walk back to the tow truck and broke down as he pulled away. She chose to do nothing, and in doing so, had either saved her daughter's life or sealed her fate.

"Mom!"

"I'm here!" Laura sobbed.

Nelle was sobbing, too. "You have to do what they say. You have to come. Or else they're going to kill me. That's what they said. I'm scared."

"I'm coming, baby. I'm coming now."

"I love—"

"Three hours," the voice said.

"Why are you doing this?" Laura asked.

A pause. Static.

"You need to pay for what you did."

CHAPTER THREE

Tires squealed as Laura yanked the car into the left lane and passed a slower-moving Honda Civic on her right. She pressed the accelerator, gripping the steering wheel, her knuckles white around the soft leather, her mind still trying to swim to the surface. She moved back into the right lane as Broadway became Route 9. All of the grogginess had been replaced by adrenaline that kept her focused, alert.

"I'm telling you," she said aloud. "You've made a mistake."

"No mistake."

"My name is Laura Anderson. My maiden name was Trotz. Laura Trotz. I grew up in St. Petersburg, Florida."

"Your name was Betty Hamms before you changed it. You grew up in Bastrop, Texas. You graduated from the University of Texas with a nursing degree."

"I didn't."

"You landed a job in the ER at the Dell Seton Medical Center in Austin. It was in that ER where you met our mother. Then you killed her."

The statement hung in the air, the static of the connection the only sound but for the tires that droned underneath her.

"I didn't do any of that!" Laura cried. "You have the wrong person!"

"You coming up here to your mother's house will clear things up. She can have a look at you. Tell us what we already know."

"My mother's dead."

"No, ma'am. She's very much alive."

Another thought began to creep into Laura's mind. What if she called their bluff? They wouldn't hurt Nelle. Not when they wanted Laura. She could pull into the shopping center that was up ahead in about a mile. There was a liquor store there. She could buy herself a treat and let the day fade away like she'd wanted to do all along. She could take the rest of her pills she kept hidden in the armrest and forget about everything. She could forget about the strange voice on the other end of the phone telling her they had Nelle, and she could forget the name they called her and the people they told her she knew. All she wanted was to be curled up in bed, nestled in the gentle embrace of an Ambien or two, sleeping away the day and the bad thoughts about her fight with Nelle the night before and the fact that she should've been watching out the window while Nelle walked to the bus stop that morning. Why hadn't she been watching her? A good mother would've kept an eye. What had she been doing while Nelle walked to the bus? She knew, but didn't want to admit it to herself.

She looked down at her forearm and could see the two scratch marks Nelle had given her the night before as she'd pushed Laura into the vanity and yanked herself away at the same time. She could remember the moment when their simple argument had morphed into an actual altercation, but the subject of the argument itself remained foggy. She'd had a few drinks before dinner and her exact memory of what happened hadn't stayed with her afterward. Thin wisps of memory hung onto her subconscious like cobwebs, but the details had no hard edges, nothing to grab onto. What had happened last night? Did it have anything to do with what she was going through now? She couldn't recall.

Laura wiped her eyes with the back of her hand so she could see through the world that was blurring in from the edges. The single lane opened to two and she stepped on the accelerator again, passing the slower cars that kept her in place. The lanes were narrow and twisting, her Volkswagen Passat forever teetering on the verge of losing control. Every curve of the road was a question of whether she'd come out of it alive.

"I shouldn't be here right now," she said. "I should be home throwing a load of laundry in the washer and starting dinner. Nelle should be bouncing through the door with her ear pods in so she can avoid telling me how her day was." A tiny laugh slipped through. "We'll get in a stupid argument about homework or her messy room, and she'll pretend I'm some kind of monster because that's what fifteen-year-old girls do to their moms. Then my husband will come home, and we'll have dinner, and he'll get her talking. He's good at that. Getting through Nelle's tough exterior. He can make her melt. Every time."

More tears.

"She's only fifteen. Please. Let her go."

"You lied about what happened to our mother. You're a liar and you think there are no consequences. But there are. We're here to show you that."

Laura took her eyes off the road and stared into the phone. "You have the wrong person."

"We don't. You think I can't hear that accent you try and hide. I can hear it plain as day. We got the right person for sure."

"Just give me my daughter back."

"Come up and get her."

The Passat's tires screamed as she rounded a turn so fast, she had to yank down on the steering wheel to keep the car from crossing into oncoming traffic. When the momentum shifted, something moved in the trunk. A heavy weight slid from one end to the other.

"What was that?" she asked aloud, her head turning around for a moment.

The voice didn't reply.

"What's in the trunk?" she asked again.

"Insurance."

Panic bubbled up. Breaths came short and sharp. Laura's lungs burned as her throat began to close. She took her foot off the accelerator and pulled into the right lane to keep from crashing.

"Tell me... what's in the... trunk."

"Gordon Avenue is coming up on your right," the voice said. "Pull off there."

"How do... you know where I am?"

"We're tracking your phone."

Laura turned right as she was told. The interior of the car was suffocating. Her windpipe felt as if it was no wider than a straw. She tried to concentrate on her breathing as she stopped at the curb in front of a typical suburban home—a white colonial with trimmed hedges edging the property—and grabbed at her chest, ripping the buttons on her blouse, trying to claw her way to her heart and lungs. She was wheezing, the air she was trying to take in too thin.

"Get out of the car."

"I... I need a minute."

"You don't have a minute. Neither does your daughter."

Laura opened the door and flopped one leg out onto the road. She could feel the fresh air blowing in her face and that made a bit of a difference. It took some strength, but she climbed out of the car and leaned against it, her breath coming back slowly, her lungs and throat reluctantly opening back up.

"Pop the trunk," the voice instructed.

"Please. I... I don't want to."

"Open the trunk. You wanted to know what was in there. I'm going to show you."

Tears filled her eyes again, slipping down her cheeks. "I don't think I want to know anymore."

"Go. You're running out of time."

Laura looked at the clock on the dashboard. 3:45. She should've been home already. If she hadn't passed out on the side of the road, she might've been climbing into her bed for that quick nap or taking that relaxing bath. She knew none of that would be happening now. No nap. No argument with Nelle after school. No dinner where Kurt would make them all lower their guards so they could be a family again. Everything was different now, and unpredictably terrifying. She desperately wanted to go back to the way things were just a few minutes earlier. She wanted the life she was familiar with. Her friends. Her church. Even if it was all a facade, it was hers.

Laura bent down and pressed the button near the fog light switch. She heard the pop of the trunk coming unlatched and stood up, waiting for the next command, trying to buy a little more time.

"Take the phone with you so I can see what you're doing."

She plucked the iPhone from its cradle on the dashboard and held it out in front of her as she walked around to the back of the Passat and took a final, ragged, breath. Her trembling hand opened the trunk.

At first, all she saw was the thick plastic covering that seemed to have been repeatedly wrapped around something large, the excess plastic pushed and crushed into the trunk so it could be closed. Upon closer inspection, she saw some of the plastic was stained red. It was blood. Had to be. She was certain she could smell the salty metallic aroma of it, and she choked back the vomit that was trying to push its way up. Inside the plastic, she could make out the faint features of the person. It was a female, white. The hair was dark, somewhat wet and matted. It fell in front of her face, covering it almost completely. There was no visible wound that she could see, but details were hard to make out. It was like she was staring at this person through a thick layer of ice. She instinctively reached inside to dig through the plastic and look for a pulse, but the sound of an approaching car made her slam the trunk closed. She watched as a white work van passed, and then she slid onto the ground, biting her fist to keep from screaming.

"Do you know who that is?"

"I don't want to know."

"You can't tell?"

"Please."

"The girl in your trunk is Stephanie Parson."

She could hear the mechanical voice echoing through both her phone and the speakers in the car, the identification of the girl reverberating both physically and within her very soul.

"No," Laura choked. "No, please. Tell me you're kidding. Tell me you're trying to scare me or something. Not Steph."

"She was walking with Nelle this morning. We had no choice. I couldn't take Nelle and leave Stephanie. We took them both. The girl's your problem now."

Laura knew the voice was still talking. There were warnings about going to the police with a body in the trunk and how no one would believe her if she was caught with Steph's body. Something like that. She missed most of it, her mind having caved in on itself as she crawled around to the driver's side door on her hands and knees, her stomach tying itself in knots, the thought of such a vibrant young woman, almost a daughter by proxy, being killed and stuffed away like that. It was too much. She thought about Steph's parents and how they weren't even aware of how much their lives had already been altered. The sharpness of the mechanical voice's words seemed to dull and the warnings turned into warbled sounds of nothingness. She suddenly didn't care if a car came around the bend and stopped for her. She'd have nothing to tell them because she was fading away. Going... going...

Laura opened the door and fell back into the driver's seat. The voice was still talking. She heard none of it, and instead, leaned over and threw up into the street. When she was done, she closed the door, put the car in gear, and drove back toward Route 9. This was all suddenly real. Lives actually were at stake, and if he'd kill Steph, there was no question he'd kill Nelle. She had to get moving.

Two hours and forty minutes remaining.

CHAPTER FOUR

MARCH 27, 2000

The emergency room at the Dell Seton Medical Center had been quiet for most of Betty's shift. There had been the usual visits that coincided with a Saturday night—broken bones from a drunken fall, cuts and bruises from a fight, respiratory infection from a flu that had been ignored for too long, a pulled lower back from lifting furniture—but these patients were quickly tended to and sent on their way with pain scripts or sutures or casts that friends and family would sign over the next few months. There was nothing too serious, and for that, she was thankful. This wasn't a mockup of a hospital setting at school, nor was it a rotation where the real nurses did the work and the students assisted while trying their best to stay out of the way. This was an entirely new world, and in this world, she was *the real nurse.*

It was almost ten o'clock. Two more hours until the midnight team came in. Betty had discharged a man who'd presented with chest pains and shortness of breath. That was scary, but she'd handled it. After a battery of tests, Dr. Decker, the attending ER physician, had determined it was an acute case of indigestion and wrote the patient a prescription for powerful antacids. Now she was helping a nurse assistant, Charlene, exchange the sheets on the bed with a new set of linens.

"How long you been here now?" Charlene asked as she unfolded a top sheet and spread it on the bed. Her hair was tucked up under a cap and her flawless brown skin practically glowed in the overhead lighting.

"Six months," Betty replied.

"Oh, you're still a baby."

"Trust me, I know."

Charlene chuckled as she folded the sheet at the corners. "Don't worry about nothing. The days start to blend in together and before you know it, you're pushing twenty years like me. Keep your head down, learn what you can when you can, and you'll be fine."

"Thanks."

"We're all heading to the diner after shift if you wanna come. I got the next two days off and I need my disco fries to set me right."

Betty took two pillows from the bin and placed them on the bed. "Thanks, but I need to get home and catch up on some sleep. I have a clinical paper due that I have to finish. Between these shifts and my classes, I've only been stealing a few hours of sleep here and there. I need real rest."

"You still in school?"

"Going for my MBA. Figured I'd get it over with now before things in life get really crazy."

Charlene sucked her teeth. "Girl, I hope you know I don't feel sorry for you. Only a fool signs up for her MBA right when she starts her nursing career. And your first job is in the ER? You're crazy. A glutton for punishment. In fact, I'd call you a fool, except I like you too much and I don't talk like that about people I like."

Betty pulled the top sheet on her side and tucked it under the mattress. "Thanks. I think. Just trying to plan the best I can."

"Nothing wrong with a little planning. But you also have to make sure you can keep up with all of it. The three hours of sleep. The constant craziness of the ER. All the codes and procedures and drugs and protocols you need to learn. Not to mention—"

Betty held up her hand, laughing. "No more, please! I can't take it."

Charlene was smiling. "I want to make sure you got your priorities right. Giving up disco fries to get a master's degree. I don't get it."

"That decision is harder than you think," Betty said. "Disco fries are one of my favorite things on earth."

Tricia Parks, one of the senior nurses, opened the door to the room and nodded toward Betty. "You got a phone call."

"Okay, thanks."

"Take it at the main desk."

Betty handed her sheet to Charlene and walked out into the hallway, picking up her pace as she made it to the central nurses' station. The receiver was off the phone's base, waiting on the desk next to one of the printers. She leaned over and picked it up, turning away from the others.

"Hello?"

CHAPTER FIVE

Laura took a right onto Broadway and returned to the busy road. Traffic surrounded her, forcing her to maintain a slower speed than she wanted to as two lanes merged into one. She could still taste the vomit in the back of her throat, and all she could think about was the thud coming from the trunk, knowing it was the body of a teenage girl sliding from one side of the car to the other, lifeless and limp. She realized how easily it could've been Nelle or Kurt and felt shame in her relief that it was Steph and not one of her own.

Steph and Nelle had been best friends since they met in kindergarten. Two little girls who happened to be running for the same slide on their first recess of their scholastic lives had formed a bond that had lasted over a decade. They were inseparable, closer than sisters, sharing everything from secrets to life milestones and everything in between. Now Steph, who Laura affectionately called her second daughter, was gone. But it was more than that. It was the way she'd died. Murdered. And for what? Because she was walking alongside Nelle and these sons of bitches couldn't leave any witnesses? It wasn't fair. Steph didn't deserve that. No one did.

"Please," Laura said. Her tongue was dry and caught on the back of her teeth. "Let my daughter go and I won't try and find you. I won't press charges or get the police involved. I don't know who you are, so there's no way I can identify you. I'll throw this phone in the river and we can all move on."

"Nelle ain't our focus," the voice replied. "Neither is your mother. You are. We can't end anything yet. We're just getting started."

"I keep telling you, my mother's dead. Why won't you listen?"

"You gotta pay for what you've done."

"I haven't done anything."

"You have and you know it."

The road became two lanes again and Laura pushed on the accelerator, maneuvering around a box truck taking up more road than it should've been. Steph's body slithered to the right this time and Laura thought about her parents. How would she be able to face Elma and Doug and try to explain what happened? How could she sit with them knowing she was the reason their little girl was dead? Laura knew how deeply and irrevocably a child's death could impact the parents. They'd never be the same again. How could they?

The entrance to the shopping plaza was coming up on her left. Without thinking, Laura jerked the wheel and made a sharp turn across oncoming traffic, suddenly speeding down the ramp and onto the road that led to the string of stores.

"Where are you going?" the voice asked.

"I..."

Laura turned right and made her way toward the parking lot, quickly backing into a spot near the retaining wall, next to a bus stop, and put the car in park. She stared at the liquor store that was directly across the way. Tim's Liquors. Like an oasis in the desert.

"Why are you stopped?" the voice asked.

"I need a minute."

"You don't have a minute."

Her pulse quickened as she stared at the tinted storefront. The neon signs named all the brands she knew so well. Maybe if she explained that a quick treat would help her focus and get up to Caroga Lake faster, he would let her pop in and grab a bottle for the ride. She just needed a drink to set her mind right. The Hydro Flask was empty and there were too many things spinning out of control. Nothing could fix it better than a quick treat. Despite the adrenaline and chaos, she could feel herself fading. Plus, running in would only take a second. Grab a bottle, get out.

"Betty."

"Don't call me that."

Laura licked her lips and leaned up in her seat. She tried to do the math in her head. If she took five minutes in the store, she could more than make that up once she hit the highway. If there was no traffic, she could do eighty or eight-five the entire way and this detour would be nothing more than a memory. Better to waste a little time now than be too sluggish to do anything once she got up there. She just needed something to set her head straight.

"Betty."

Laura blindly reached into the center arm rest and felt for the plastic sandwich bag under her sunglasses case. With fingers that had done it more times than she could count, she opened the zip lock and pinched a Xanax between her index finger and thumb. She slipped it into her mouth and ate it as if it was candy. Five minutes. She could make it up.

"Laura."

Laura laced her fingers through the door handle and opened the car door enough to hear it pop. She waited, her eyes fixed on the liquor store, her heart beating in her chest. She eased her weight to the left and felt the door give. All she had to do was give it a nudge to push it all the way open and step out. The store was right there. In and out. It would be quick. It was—

"Mom?"

Laura snapped back to reality and immediately slammed the door shut when she heard Nelle's voice. She held her breath and tried to keep the tears from coming, but they'd already filled her eyes and begun slipping down her cheeks. What was she doing? Her daughter needed her. Her life was in danger. Of course there was no time to stop. How could she think of such a stupid thing? How could she be so selfish?

"Mom?"

She shook her head and cleared her throat. What would Nelle and Kurt think of her if they saw her wasting time in front of a liquor store, daydreaming about grabbing a drink while her child's life, literally, hung in the balance? What would her congregation think of her choosing a drink over her child's safety? It was unconscionable.

"I'm here, baby. I'm here. Are you okay?"

"Why did you stop?"

"I don't know. I'm scared."

"I'm scared, too."

"I'm sorry."

"Do what he says. Please. Get up here. They're not fooling around."

"I'm coming. I am."

There was a rustling sound before everything went silent.

"Nelle?"

"No more games," the voice said.

"I'm sorry. I don't know what I was doing. I can't think right now."

"You don't need to think. We'll think for you. Get on moving and follow instructions. Got it?"

The accent was clearer now. She'd missed it in the initial

confusion, but she noticed that it came through when he got angry. Texas. No doubt about it.

"I'm going."

Laura wiped her eyes and put the car in gear, pulling out of her spot and following the service road that would lead her back to Broadway, then further onto Route 117, and eventually the Taconic State Parkway. She knew what she did was stupid and wrong and selfish and petty, but as she pulled further away from the shopping plaza and the hints of a migraine began to show itself in the back of her skull, she also knew that a drink would've set things straight and made her stronger and more focused. But why couldn't she be strong enough to stay focused without a drink? What was wrong with her? Any other mother would've been speeding north with the single goal of getting their daughter back. Why did she need to stop and get a drink first? What kind of a monster was she? The same kind that should've been watching her little girl walk to the bus stop that morning. Where was she? Not where she should've been. Never where she should be.

Two hours and thirty minutes remaining.

CHAPTER SIX

Laura drove in silence, her mind churning over the ridiculous detour she'd taken and the peril it had put her daughter in. She knew what it was called. She'd heard it mentioned in a few of the meetings she'd attended over the years. Alcohol obsession. It was when the compulsion to have a drink overcame every other sense of one's mind and the person was left with that single thought and desire, stamping out everything else. It was that same alcohol obsession that caused her to stop attending the meetings and the private counseling sessions and the weekend rehabs she'd tried secretly attending over the years, and at that moment, when she'd turned into the shopping plaza with everything cascading onto her—Steph's body in the trunk, Nelle's abduction, the strange mechanical voice on the phone—it was the alcohol obsession that had made her want to so desperately escape into a bottle.

She cursed herself for being such a shitty mom and a weak person. She should've been on the highway already, pressing the gas pedal to the floor, flying up to Caroga Lake, traffic laws and other drivers be damned. Her one sole focus should've been getting Nelle back safe and ending this nightmare. But she wasn't the kind of person who could take control like that. Despite the facade she gave off of being one who was always in command, a leader others could depend on, she was a scared little girl still living with her nightmares of the past, still drowning in the guilt from her own mother. The alcohol helped in that regard. Without it, she felt extremely vulnerable.

She could hear the static on the other end of the phone and knew he was there, but the mechanical voice hadn't said anything for the last few miles. She glanced at the black screen and could feel him watching her. Always watching. She took a few more breaths to keep from crying, and as she turned off of Route 117 and drove up the ramp to merge onto the northbound lanes of the Taconic State Parkway, Steph's body slid to the left side.

She rubbed her forehead and tried to think. There was no convincing the voice that they had the wrong person. She'd tried to plant at least a seed of doubt, but the voice seemed so certain she was who they were looking for. Who they'd found. She decided to try a slightly different approach.

"This woman's house you have me driving to," Laura began. "Who is she?"

"It's your mother's house," the voice replied. "You know this."

"I don't. My mother's dead. Who is this woman?"

"Don't play games with me, Betty. I don't have the patience."

"Don't call me Betty. My name is Laura."

No reply.

Laura closed her eyes for a moment. Her headache was really starting to come on. "Okay then, *where* is she? This woman you think is my mother? If you're up at her house with Nelle, what happened to the woman who owns it?"

"She's here," the voice replied. "Alive for now. That could change."

A dark blue sedan settled in behind her. Laura watched it through her rearview mirror as it came up fast and began tailgating even as she looked down at her speedometer and confirmed she was traveling almost eighty-five miles an hour. Red emergency lights suddenly came to life on the sedan's dashboard, its headlights blinking on and off in some kind of strobe light effect.

"No," she whispered, watching the car behind her keep pace. The other vehicles around them pulled left and right, clearing the lanes as they made their way through traffic.

"What's happening?"

"A cop. He's pulling me over. I don't know why. I wasn't speeding. I mean, I was, but I was with the flow of traffic. I wasn't going faster than anyone else."

Laura put her turn signal on and slid the Volkswagen into the slow lane. She watched through her side mirror as the sedan followed.

"Stop looking at your rearview mirror," the voice said. "Look straight ahead and drive the car. Act natural. Be natural."

"How can I act natural? My daughter's been kidnapped and I have a dead body in my trunk."

"Calm down."

Laura began taking short, quick breaths, the pain in her temples intensifying. The Xanax was not quelling the panic attack she could feel rising in her. Her chest tightened, her breath turning shallow.

Don't cry. Don't cry. Don't cry.

She took her foot off the accelerator and let the car coast as she slid onto the shoulder. The sedan followed.

"Stay calm," the voice said. "Show him your license, take the ticket, and go. If you draw attention or he suspects something, I'll hurt Nelle. I'll kill her if I have to. If I even think you're making any attempt to try and get help, I'll carve your daughter to pieces over the phone so you can hear every scream. You got me?"

"Yes."

"No mistakes."

She put the car in park and leaned back in her seat, waiting as the blue sedan stopped behind her. Her hands were trembling and she dropped them onto her lap. She tried to steady her breath the best she could, but she was so scared. Scared and hopeful and terrified and desperate all at the same time.

The driver's door opened and a man dressed in a navy suit stepped out. He was average height and weight. Not fat or skinny. Not tall or short. A regular guy. His gray hair was buzzed military-style and most of his face was shielded from the mirrored sunglasses he wore. His lips were thin and tight. No smile. The suit meant he was either a detective or someone important within whatever department he was from. As he approached, Laura heard the ticking of her hazard lights and saw the other cars slowing as they passed, watching. She was doing the one thing she knew she couldn't do. She was drawing attention to herself.

She rolled the window down and, with the back of her hand, quickly tried to wipe whatever makeup might still be smudged on her face from crying and puking and everything else. She could only imagine what she looked like as the cop bent down toward her.

"Hello," she said, clearing her throat and trying to smile.

The man gave a quick glance into the backseat, then the passenger's seat, then to her. "You okay, ma'am?"

"Yes, I'm fine."

"You look upset."

"Got some bad news at work. Death in the family. I'm on my way home now to meet my husband."

"I'm sorry to hear that."

"Thank you."

"I didn't pull you over to give you a hard time," the man said, the corners of his mouth slightly turning up. "My name is Waylon Derry. I'm the chief for the Westchester County Police Department. Apologies for the lights and everything. Needed to get your attention."

"Oh," Laura replied. "Well, it was a bit of a startle. I thought I was going with the speed of traffic, but I guess we were all probably going too fast."

Chief Derry took off his sunglasses and folded them into the breast pocket of his suit jacket. As soon as she saw his face without the glasses, she noticed how kind his eyes were.

"I'm not trying to get you over for speeding," he said. "Taconic isn't even my jurisdiction. That's the state troopers'."

Laura pulled back a bit. "Um, okay. I've never been stopped for not speeding."

A quick chuckle. "I stopped you because you have a pretty gnarly piece of plastic hanging out of the trunk, whipping around. If that gets loose, it can cause some damage out here. I suggest you secure it before you go any further."

Laura closed her eyes for a moment and had to stifle what would've been a manic laugh. Of course. The plastic covering. Of all things.

"Can you step out of the car and secure the item?"

"Yes. Sure. Okay."

The chief opened her door and moved aside. Laura made a move to step out, then heard the phone crackle.

"Mom, take us with you."

Laura nodded at the phone the best she could, slipping it from its mount and tucking it against her chest, the black screen facing out. She climbed out of the car and felt the brisk spring wind that had taken over the warm sun she'd felt earlier outside the church. It would be dusk soon. Then dark. She should've been home. Cooking, sleeping, having a glass of wine in the bath. It didn't matter which. All of it, any of it, would've been fine. Instead, she was out on the parkway walking toward the dead body in her trunk with a police officer. A chief of police, no less.

"Back here," Chief Derry said.

Laura turned away from the road and followed the chief to the rear of the Passat as the whoosh of the passing vehicles filled the air. He stood in front of his own car and pointed. She looked and sure enough, a piece of the plastic covering that had been wrapped around Steph's body was hanging out of the trunk, much larger than she thought. One corner was almost touching the ground, and she figured it must've kept getting pulled by the wind as she traveled faster. Luckily, she didn't see any bloodstains, just dirt and grime from the roads she'd been riding on. It looked filthy, but no one could see proof of anything else.

"That corner catches the right way and it could get tangled in your exhaust," the chief explained. "I'm surprised you didn't see it when you were driving."

Laura shrugged. There was nothing else to say.

"Pop the trunk and shove it back in there. I'm not here to give you a ticket. I wanted to give you a heads up so you'd be safe, that's all."

"Thank you. I appreciate it."

"No worries."

They stood silent, each of them looking at the other. Chief Derry was clearly waiting for her to open the trunk and secure the plastic, and she was waiting for him to get back in his car and drive away. Neither moved until he spoke.

"Ma'am? I need you to open the trunk and put that away."

Why couldn't she just ask for help? What was the harm in opening the trunk and showing him what happened to Steph while imploring him to save Nelle? She had the address. She could give it to him and he could call for SWAT up that way or something like that. She could let a professional handle a situation she was clearly not equipped for. She could pass the responsibility over to someone other than herself and then she could escape into her bed where she was supposed to have been. Why did she have to save Nelle? Why couldn't this nice man save her?

"Ma'am?"

The voice whispered in her mind.

If I even think you're making any attempt to try and get help, I'll carve your daughter to pieces over the phone so you can hear every scream.

"Ma'am? Are you sure you're alright?

"Right. Sorry. Let me go unlock it from the front."

Laura half-staggered, half-walked back to the car and sat in the driver's seat, leaving the door open. She looked at the trunk release button and wanted so badly to push it and make everything else go away. But she knew that was a stupid thought. They only had Nelle to get to her. If she told anyone, she'd be sealing her daughter's fate. Hoping for any other outcome was dumb.

"You can't open that trunk," the voice said.

Laura looked down at the black screen. "I know that."

"Nelle dies if you open it."

"I know that too."

"Drive away."

"I can't. He'll chase me."

"Outrun him."

Laura chuckled. "I can't outrun the police in a Passat."

"Where is he now?"

"Standing at the back of my car."

"Show me."

Laura quickly lifted the phone up over her shoulder.

"Back up into him," the voice said. "He can't chase you if he can't get into his car. You can pin him against both cars and crush his legs."

"No!" Laura whispered. "I can't do that."

"It's the only way."

"Ma'am," Chief Derry called from behind her. His voice had a bit of an edge now. He was growing impatient. "Let's go. Open the trunk. We can't be out here all day."

"Do it."

"I can't. It's not in me."

"Sure it is. You've killed before. Crushing a man's legs should be nothing."

"I can't hurt someone like that."

"Betty can."

"Ma'am!"

Muffled screams began to emerge from the speakers, quiet and distant at first, then growing louder.

"What is that?" Laura asked. "What are you doing?"

"Mom!" Nelle cried, louder this time.

"Leave her alone!" Laura cried, a bit louder than she should have. Her headache was coming in waves now, swelling from the back of her skull and crashing at the front.

"Take him out," the voice commanded.

"Ma'am! Who are you talking to? Open the trunk!"

"Mom! He's hurting me! Ow! Mom! Help!"

"Leave my baby alone! Don't you touch her!"

"Ma'am!"

"Take him out or she dies!"

"No!"

"I'll kill her, Betty! I'll do it!"

"Mom!"

Time slowed in that moment. Laura could hear Nelle screaming through the speakers as the pain in her head kept crashing from back to front, over and over. She sucked in a breath and held it as she glanced into the mirror and saw the chief standing directly behind her, between his car and hers. It would be so easy. Disable the man and get back on the road. She could do it. She had to. For Nelle.

A curtain seemed to drop over her face as everything around Laura dimmed but for Nelle's screaming and the headache that would not relent. As if she was standing outside the car watching, she saw herself shut the door and grip the gear shifter as she threw the car in reverse and press the pedal all the way to the floor. She focused on a small metal brace that clasped her right shoe shut, then watched as her car hit the chief and kept moving until the impact with his car caused everything to stop. Nelle's screams were replaced by the sound of the chief shrieking as both legs were crushed.

"Now drive!"

The curtain lifted.

Time sped back up again.

Nelle was still screaming. The chief was screaming behind her. Laura was silent, fading, thinking about escaping but at the same time, unable to move fast enough.

"Mom!"

The back window shattered, snapping Laura to attention. She looked in the mirror and saw Chief Derry with his weapon in his hand. He'd fired into the car and missed hitting her, then dropped the gun and fell forward onto her trunk, a low groan emanating from his throat.

Without knowing what she was doing, Laura got out of the car and ran, snatching his gun from the ground, her fingers touching the blood that had pooled on the gravel and dirt. The smell of burning tires, exhaust, and gasoline mixed with the metallic smell of the blood as she lifted her fingers up to her face. She was right back at the playground again. Everything was the same.

"Betty!"

Laura looked up and saw that other cars were beginning to slow down, looking as they passed. She watched a pickup as it pulled off onto the shoulder about a quarter mile up the parkway. People were starting to notice something was wrong. It was time to go.

She tossed the chief's gun next to her purse on the floor of the passenger's side, then climbed in, slammed her door shut, put the car in gear, and spun back out onto the parkway. Her head was still throbbing, but the adrenaline had refocused her and she pressed the accelerator to the floor, weaving in and out of lanes, passing the pickup truck that had begun to reverse down the shoulder.

"There's an exit for Underhill Avenue coming up," the voice said. "Take it. You're going to need to get over to the interstate. You can't stay on the Taconic. You can take backroads. They'll be looking for you on the parkway."

"I killed him," Laura said with no tone or tenor in her voice. She stated it as a fact, too shocked to emit any emotion. Just that one fact, over and over. "I killed him. I killed him. I killed him."

"Get off the exit, fix the sheet in the trunk, and wipe the blood off your car. Things are serious now."

"I killed him. I killed him. I killed him."

Two hours and twenty minutes remaining.

CHAPTER SEVEN

Laura's body shook uncontrollably as she drove on instinct more than anything else. The pain in her head intensified as she tried steadying her breath, taking a deep inhale, and letting it out slowly, but the shaking wouldn't stop. She sped through the backroads, following the directions the voice gave her, her mind replaying what happened with the chief over and over.

That poor man was lying on the side of the road, crippled and dead, as lifeless as the other roadkill that ended up in similar positions up and down the shoulders of the parkway, while she was alive, undeservedly so. Why did she get to live and a man of honor and purpose had to die? It didn't make sense. She'd made the chief nothing more than another deer or possum or racoon or squirrel. Only he wasn't. He was a human being, an officer of the law. Perhaps a father and a husband. Maybe a son or a brother or an uncle. He was more of a person than she could ever dream to be. The whole reason he pulled her over was to make sure she didn't hurt herself or others with the plastic sticking out of the trunk. He was selfless, acting to protect people, willingly putting himself in harm's way to do so. Now he and Steph were dead, and their blood was on her hands. If there was a god, she could find no logic in letting people like that die while she got to live. No good deeds or fundraisers or church donations could ever even out the scales from what she'd just done. She was hell bound. Her soul was irrevocably scarred. That was a fact.

"At the traffic light, make a left," the mechanical voice said. No inflection. No emotion. Only a hint of that Texas accent. "There's a shopping center about a quarter mile up. You can park in the back and fix things."

"I killed that man."

"You did what you had to do for Nelle."

"I'm a shitty person."

"I know that, Betty. That's why you're in the situation you're in. The chickens have come home to roost."

Laura nodded, knowing he was right. She turned left at the light as she was told, then followed small signs that led her to an abandoned strip mall that marked the edge of the commercial district in Yorktown Heights. Hollowed carcasses of what had once been a ShopRite and Kmart stood as empty anchors. Smaller mom-and-pop shops filled the storefronts in between, but most of them had gone the way of their retail elders, the soaped windowfronts having turned from white to brown, a result of inattention and decay. She knew there was a liquor store at the opposite end of the building, but she dismissed the thought from her mind.

Laura crept down the center lane of the empty lot and pulled around back. The rear of the building was protected by a small forest that acted as a buffer between the residential neighborhoods across the road. Loading bays that hadn't been used in years stood abandoned, the sliding doors that had once opened for eighteen-wheelers carrying anything and everything a consumer might want now rusted shut from neglect. She pulled close against the rear wall, put the car in park, and popped the truck.

"I have to go back," she said. "I have to see if he's okay."

"Don't be an idiot," the voice replied. "I have no time for stupidity. Neither do you. If you go back, you'll be arrested, and then Nelle becomes the person we have no more use for. What do you reckon happens then?"

"This isn't real," she whispered to herself. "This can't be happening. Please. Tell me it's a dream. Or some kind of joke. Tell me I can wake up and it'll be tomorrow and I can move on with my life. Tell me I'm asleep. Please."

"Fix the trunk."

"Tell me!"

"Your daughter's waiting. Hurry up."

Laura started crying again as she fumbled for the handle and opened the car door. She stepped out and almost fell over when her legs refused to hold her weight. She rushed around to the back of the Volkswagen, repeating instructions to herself to keep her mind focused.

More of the plastic covering had come loose as she'd raced down the parkway. Laura opened the trunk, but refused to look at Steph's body. She gathered the plastic and stuffed it back inside, frantically pushing it into a ball, feeling the density of Steph's body in the back. When the plastic was secure, she shut the lid and stepped back, her breath coming in heaves that she couldn't seem to catch.

Blood streaked the crushed backend of the Passat. The chief's blood. Laura knew there were towels and rags in the trunk, but there was no way she was going back in there. She also knew she couldn't keep driving around with blood on her bumper and tailgate. She unlatched her bra from under her shirt and pulled it down her sleeve. She used the bra to wipe the blood, then tossed it into a pile of garbage at the edge of the woods. When she was done, she took the bottle of Zoloft from her pants pocket and popped a pill, chewing it quickly as she climbed back in.

"You'll have to take the back roads to 684," the voice said when she shut the door. "I'll help you get there."

"I know how to get to 684," Laura mumbled, her voice barely there. She placed her hand on the gearshift.

"Wait."

She stopped.

"Why did you take the chief's gun?"

Laura looked down at the weapon sitting on the floor next to her purse. "I don't know. I did it without thinking."

She was lying, of course. She knew exactly why she took it. She wanted it so she could get to the house at Caroga Lake and kill the people who were keeping her daughter captive. Kurt had showed her how to shoot long guns and pistols in the past, and he had taken her to the range more than once. She figured if she had the element of surprise on her side, she could aim and fire and eliminate whoever was at that house. She'd placed the gun on the floor because she didn't think the phone's camera could see that far down, and didn't think he'd seen her take it in the first place.

"No guns," the voice said. "Throw it away."

"I can't throw it out here. What if a kid picks it up? Or a criminal finds it or something?"

"Not our problem. Throw the gun away."

"But I need it."

"I'm not going to ask you again."

Laura bit her bottom lip, wiped her eyes with the back of her hand, then reached down and grabbed Chief Derry's sidearm. She held it in front of her, studying it.

"You were planning to bring that along? Exact some revenge for what I'm putting you through?"

"Yes."

"Throw it out. And let me see you do it."

Laura rolled down her window, held the gun so the camera on the phone would capture it, then dropped it against the wall.

"Hey! You okay?"

An old man was hobbling toward her, his dirty arm waving hello, his stained and baggy pants sliding along as he approached.

"You having car trouble? I can help!"

"Drive away. Now."

Laura put the car in gear and pulled out of her spot, driving back in front of the abandoned supermarket and speeding down a side lane until she was back onto Route 35. She knew 35 would lead to Interstate 684. From there, she'd drive north and eventually west, but at the moment, all she could concentrate on was getting as far away from the Taconic as she could. Get away and get up to her daughter.

"You can't win this." The voice was emotionless, artificial, matter-of-fact. "We're watching. We know everything you do. We see what you see. You can't sneak up on us and think you can somehow gain an upper hand. There's no other ending here except justice for our mother. You killed her and we suffered for it. Our father committed suicide because of it. We had to go through our childhoods in foster care, always moving from house to house in the system. You can't imagine what we endured. We know what suffering is. Now you will, too."

"You don't know anything," Laura replied under her breath. "I know suffering. Every day I know it. We're best friends."

She closed her eyes into slits and tried her best to focus on the road ahead.

CHAPTER EIGHT

Detective Roman Estrada shielded his eyes from the sun as it inched its way toward the mountain range in the west. He walked across the three-lane parkway, aware of how strange it was hearing his heels scrape the pavement when there should have been cars and trucks racing by at eighty miles an hour. The Taconic had been shut down in both directions, making rush hour a nightmare for the commuters who were forced to take detours onto side streets through small towns that weren't equipped for such a surge of traffic. But his chief had been hurt in the line of duty, and that took precedence over everything else. To hell with the commuters. He had to take his time, and he would. Duty called for such diligence.

The setting sun cast a burnt-orange glow over the crime scene. Police personnel and emergency workers hopped from area to area, collecting everything they could for a case that was beginning to take shape. New York State police cruisers mixed with Westchester County police cars, all of them parked at different angles in the middle of the parkway. The grass median separating north and southbound lanes was chewed up from arriving backup. An ambulance waited on the shoulder, but

Roman knew it was empty. Chief Derry had already been taken to Westchester Medical Center. A flatbed was positioned in what would normally have been the right lane, the chief's car on top, the frontend dented, streaks of blood visible from a distance. The attack had been violent.

Sergeant Chip Baros, a middle-aged veteran Roman had worked with for years, met him as he approached the scene. Roman brushed his dark hair out of his eyes and rubbed the thin beard that he'd let grow in over the winter.

"Never seen a thing like this," Baros said. He was a big man, a high-school football star who never shed the thickness he'd been born with. He tugged nervously on his utility belt that hung under his gut.

"What'd you find so far?"

Baros ushered him closer to the right shoulder. "Luckily, people still have kind hearts and quick minds around here or Chief Derry might've bled out. A bunch of drivers pulled over when they saw he was hurt and called 911. We got a couple of eyewitnesses, too. Not sure why, but witnesses say he had a sedan pulled over. The bar lights on his dash were on, so it looks like he was making a traffic stop, but this isn't his jurisdiction, so I have no idea what he was doing. No one saw make or model, but they did confirm the driver was female and one person wrote down her license plate. We're running it now. Apparently, something went down and the driver ended up backing the sedan into the chief and then drove away. Crushed both legs above the knee."

"Jesus."

"Tell me about it. He was unconscious when backup arrived. Some good Samaritans tied two tourniquets around each leg. By the time I got on scene, EMTs were loading him in the ambulance. He lost a lot of blood. I don't like it. State police gave us full rein since this is our guy. They're here if we need them, but this is our show."

"Family notified?"

"Yeah. They went to pick up his wife."

Roman pointed to the chief's car on the flatbed. "No dashcam in those."

"Nope. First thing I checked."

"You think the driver could've reversed by accident and then panicked and drove away?"

"Doubtful. The chief discharged his weapon and appears to have taken out one of the windows. We got broken glass on scene. Also looks like the driver took his sidearm. None of those moves speak to panic, if you ask me. Sounds premeditated."

Roman walked to the spot where the impact had taken place. Glass crunched underfoot until he came to the place where the chief's blood had pooled. The middle of the pool was still glimmering with a sickening crimson moisture, but the sun had already begun to dry out the edges. A piece of cloth from his boss's pants was stuck in the blood, a thin edge of cotton flapping in the breeze.

"We retrieved the casing from the single shot fired," Baros said as he stood over Roman's shoulder. "Shouldn't be hard finding a sedan with a dented backend and glass missing."

Roman looked up and focused on the parkway. He spun around once, taking it all in. "They're completely exposed out here," he said. "No cover. Late in the day, so traffic was getting heavy. The focus was undoubtedly on them because the chief's car was lit up. The other drivers would be slowing down and rubbernecking. The fact that this woman was bold enough to back into him in the first place is astounding. But then she stops, gets out of the car, grabs the chief's gun, gets back in the car, and leaves? That's suicide. The amount of people who could've identified her at that point makes the move pointless. I mean, we only know the driver is female because she got out of the car and people saw her. She's trying to get away. Why stop and take the gun? Why expose yourself like that?"

"She must've needed it. Otherwise, like you said, it wouldn't be worth the risk."

Roman turned and faced the same direction Chief Derry would've been facing when the suspect's car backed into him. "Why was he back here?" he asked.

Baros held up his arm to cover his face from the sun. "What do you mean?"

"This was an 11-95. Routine traffic stop."

"Well, maybe. Maybe not. Wasn't his jurisdiction and he wasn't on duty, so we don't really know what it was."

"But if he stopped her for some kind of traffic violation, he would approach the vehicle in question by coming up to the driver's side window with his weapon unclipped and holstered. If he deemed the situation safe, he would snap the holster shut and move on with the request for license and registration."

"Yeah, that's the procedure. What're you getting at?"

Roman rubbed his beard again. "If the chief was following protocol, he would take the license and registration back to his car and check the computer for warrants or violations. After he was done, he'd issue the ticket, return everything to the driver, and return to his car. Nothing that I explained would put the chief in a position where he'd be standing *behind* a suspect's car. So why was he back there?"

Baros was silent for a moment. "I have no idea. If he took her license and registration, he'd have to call the state police to come and process. That never happened."

"Sir!"

Roman looked up to find a young trooper running toward him, dodging the flatbed that was getting ready to pull away.

"We located Chief Derry's weapon," the trooper said. "Yorktown PD called it in after they got the BOLO we issued. Some local guy waved one of their patrolmen down and told him a lady driving a maroon car threw it out of her window in the back of the old Kmart up there."

"Yeah, I know the place," Roman replied. "Good. Go pick it up, and make sure they bag it. I want prints."

"Yes, sir."

Baros watched the young man leave. "Okay," he began. "Now we have a color to go along with a sedan, smashed-up rear end, and no window. Can't miss a car like that."

"You'd be surprised," Roman said as he pulled his cell phone from his pocket. He dialed and waited.

"Westchester County Police."

"Yeah, this is Detective Estrada. I need to coordinate units from all local and state departments in the area. We need all eyes on 684 and the Taconic in relation to the 10-99 issued and the BOLO we sent out regarding Chief Derry. I want everyone patrolling in both directions, up and down. I also need local departments handling the town roads, and I want stationary units down at the Hutch and up on Route 22. Update on the BOLO is that the vehicle is maroon in color. Make it happen."

"Copy that."

Roman hung up and looked at the sergeant. "Only two possibilities," he said. "Either this woman lives in the area, in which case I'll have Yorktown PD and all the neighboring towns scouring for the car, or she kept running and she knows she can't stay on the Taconic, which makes 684 her only other option if she's trying to go north. I figure if she got off an exit that put her by the Kmart, then she has to cross through Yorktown on 35 to get to 684."

"Makes sense."

"Call me when you get that license plate info. I want to know who we're dealing with. If she lives around here, we'll nail her by dinnertime."

"On it."

The sergeant hustled back to his car, and Roman stared down at the chief's blood once again. Anger bubbled up in him. It didn't matter how many homicides or attempted murders or assaults he came across in his career. The senseless cruelty of his fellow man always elicited something visceral in him. As he looked at his boss's blood—his friend's blood—he kept asking himself who would do such a callous and evil thing. Obviously, someone with something to hide. Someone who felt no shame or remorse. Someone who had no conscience. He'd seen a lot over the years, and this was right up there. He wanted the woman responsible with every cell in his body. The chief deserved it, but it was more than that. Roman wanted answers to his most basic question.

Why?

Why would someone do something like this?

CHAPTER NINE

"I'm a good person."

The wind was so loud as it rushed through the back of the Volkswagen. Gusts pushed the car from side to side as Laura fought to keep it centered on the road. Her hands were still trembling, her head still swimming with images, one after the other, the frames taken out and discarded, making the movie in her mind a blur of events without a beginning or end: The lights from the police car. The friendly man at her window. The plastic hanging from the back of the trunk. The crunch of bone and bumper. The screaming.

"I try to be. I work at it. I want to be good. I want to show others that I'm good. I try and be a dedicated mom and loving wife. I volunteer at the church and at Nelle's school. I collect for the homeless and run food drives and coat drives and I coordinate the turkey deliveries on Thanksgiving. I want to be good."

"That ain't goodness," the voice replied. "That's penance. It don't matter what you do to show others you're good. It's a game. You don't care about any of the people you help, just like you don't care about the people in your church. You can't. You're not built that way."

Laura shook her head. "No, I'm good. I'm a good mom. I'm a good wife."

"Okay then, where were you this morning when your kid got abducted? You were home. I saw your car. What were you doing that was more important than standing at the window to make sure she got on the bus okay?"

It was like he was reading her mind, the words digging deeper into her skin, asking the same question she'd been asking herself. She knew exactly what she was doing, but she didn't want to admit it out loud. Her memory came, despite her wishing it away. She was in her bathroom, unscrewing the metal screen on the broken vent in the floor where she'd hidden a bottle of Tito's. The house was empty and she wanted to have a drink before getting ready for the church celebration. That was what she was doing while her little girl was being kidnapped.

"Nelle doesn't like me hovering. She hates when I watch her walk to the bus."

The justification tasted bitter.

"That wasn't the question."

She'd enjoyed that drink, too. The peacefulness of a quiet house and the calm that she felt, knowing no one would be home and she could take her time and savor the moment.

Laura rubbed the scratches on her forearm. "She thinks I'm too involved in her life as it is. We fight about it all the time. She doesn't understand that I'm trying to do right by her. Even when I say the wrong thing or embarrass her or do something she thinks is mean or dumb, it's just me trying to do the right thing. I love her so much. I want to give her the life I never had. I want to make sure she's happy and safe and I want her to know how much she's loved. But she's growing up and I know I have to let her. And she knows we love her. One day she'll appreciate it. For now, she walks to the bus on her own and meets up with Steph. I let her do that."

"Still not answering my question. What were you doing while Nelle was being abducted?"

Laura couldn't say the words out loud. Knowing was bad enough. Hearing the words would be too shameful. Allowing someone else to hear them would be tantamount to admitting how shitty of a mom she knew she really was. She wiped away a fresh set of tears. The voice was right. The volunteering and the church stuff were window dressings. She wasn't a good person. Not the way she needed to be. Maybe once, but not anymore. Not for a long time. She sniffled as she drove. What was she doing while Nelle was walking to the bus? The opposite of keeping her happy and safe. She was sitting on the floor of her bathroom, halfway through a bottle of vodka, making last-minute changes to a speech she didn't want to give. That's what she was doing.

"I need to fix the window," she said, trying to change the subject, unable to stand the introspection anymore. "I won't make it all the way upstate like this. I need someone to put some plastic on it. Take it to a mechanic. Something."

"You can't draw any more attention to yourself," the voice replied. "They're already looking for you."

"I'm more noticeable with a back window missing, and I'm not using the plastic in the trunk. I'm not ever going back into that trunk. Please. I won't make it like this."

There was no reply on the other end. Laura continued driving on Route 35, the suburban homes and clusters of forest passing by in blurs. She looked at the houses and knew that was where she should've been.

"You're coming up on Lake Road on your left," the voice said. "Take that and we'll work back toward Baldwin Place. There's a hardware store there. You can get what you need to fix the window."

Laura saw the road sign and turned left, climbing a steep hill onto more suburban landscapes. As she went, the voice from her GPS kept imploring her to make various lefts and rights or to turn around when possible as it attempted to get her back on track toward Caroga Lake. The computer wasn't aware of the detour or the felony that had caused it.

"Okay, I made the left."

"Follow the road to the end and make a left onto Route 202."

She turned left onto 202.

"After you fix the window, you can take the local roads from Baldwin Place and get back on 684 from there."

"What about the time limit you gave me? I won't make it if I have to fix the window and take local roads. I can't keep getting sidelined and still make it up to the house in time."

"If the choices you made are impacting your ability to get here in the time I laid out for you, that's on you. Choices have consequences. You haven't learned that by now?"

Laura shook her head and swallowed the lump in her throat. "No. You told me not to let the cop open the trunk. You were hurting Nelle. I had to do something. That wasn't my fault. This can't count against me!"

"Turn right."

She turned.

"You left the covering exposed. You got pulled over. Choices, Betty. Choices and responsibility. You chose to shut the trunk without making sure everything was secure. You are responsible for your daughter's safety. Not me."

"I wouldn't have opened the goddamned trunk if you didn't tell me to!"

"Betty, I—"

"Stop calling me that!"

The sign for Johnny's Hardware appeared before the entrance to the small plaza showed itself.

"Park in the back."

She found a spot between two delivery trucks and parked the car.

"Take this phone with you. Stay connected so I can see and hear you. Get the items and get out. If I sense that you're asking for help or trying to signal someone, Nelle dies."

"I know."

"Choices. Don't make any more bad ones."

Laura hopped out of the car and jogged around the front side of the building. The lights in the parking lot had begun to turn on. Shadows grew thicker on the perimeter. It wasn't dark yet, but it was getting late for sure.

The bell above the door jingled as Laura pushed through the entrance. The few people who were inside turned to look, and she put her head down, immediately walking toward the back. The fewer people to notice her, the better.

The hardware store was a basic mom-and-pop operation. Decent size, but in no way a Home Depot or Lowe's. This was a place where the local residents could stop by and pick up a snow shovel or mouse traps, maybe a light switch or some paint.

A young boy, skinny with a mop of dirty blond hair, approached from behind her as Laura craned her neck. "Can I help you find something?"

She spun around, startled. "Sorry," she said, trying to smile. "You scared me."

"Didn't mean to."

"I know. And yes, you can help me. I need a roll of plastic, a pair of scissors, and some duct tape. I have to fix a broken window until I can get a replacement."

"I can get those for you and put them up front, if you want."

"That'd be terrific."

The boy remained where he stood, the silence between them awkward. He kept looking at her as he shifted his weight from side to side.

"We good?" Laura asked. Something in the pit of her

stomach turned and she wondered if a photo of her was already circulating and the boy recognized her from the news. She considered running and felt her body tense.

The boy took a step closer. "I don't mean to be rude or all up in your business," he whispered. "But are you okay?"

Laura kept smiling, forcing her stupid grin to stay on her face when all she really wanted to do was burst into tears and scream for help. She held the phone up to her so the voice would know she wasn't doing anything to jeopardize her daughter.

"I'm fine."

"You sure?"

"Yes. Fine."

"Okay. There's a restroom in the corner there if you want to take a second. I'll have your things waiting up front."

She nodded. It was all she could muster.

The boy left and she ducked into the bathroom, flipping on the light and leaning against the sink to look in the mirror. The woman who stared back was so different from the woman who normally lived in public. She had wide, panicked eyes. Streaks of mascara stained her cheeks and chin. Smudged lipstick. Tangled and knotted hair from the blowing wind as she drove with no back windshield. She looked like she felt: beaten down and hurt, a walking sign pleading for assistance, a beacon of suspicion alerting everyone around her that something was terribly wrong. She had to fix herself.

The water was freezing, but there was no time to wait for it to warm up. Laura put the phone on the back of the toilet and used the dirty bar soap on the side of the sink to wash her face, remove the mascara stains, and get rid of the smudged lipstick. She dampened her hair and brushed it in place the best she could with her fingers. She noticed the scratches on her arm and took a second to study them, still raw and fresh. A curtain of fog came over her as she tried to remember what she and Nelle had been fighting about. Things had seemed so much simpler only twenty-four hours earlier.

Laura finished drying herself off with paper towels, then took a final peek in the mirror. Better. Not quite the put-together wife and doting mother she was used to seeing, but no longer the mess she was when she walked in. This would have to do. She leaned in closer toward her reflection.

"You're a good person."

The reflection didn't respond.

Laura grabbed the phone and emerged from the bathroom, hustling to the front of the store where the boy waited with her items. He began ringing her up as she approached.

"Did you need anything else?"

"No, that's it. Thanks for your help."

"$27.13."

She opened her purse and instinctively reached for her credit card, then stopped. If the police could identify her as the person who hit the trooper, they'd be looking for her. They could trace purchases through her cards and figure out where she was. She'd seen enough shows on TV to know that was how it worked, and although she was desperate for the police to help her, she knew Nelle would die if she sought their help. She slid the card back in her wallet and pulled out the last two twenties she had.

The boy completed the transaction and handed her the change. He placed the money in her palm and stopped. "Much better," he muttered with a smile.

She quickly nodded, put the change in her purse, took her items, and left.

"You're running out of time," the voice said through the phone. "You need to get that plastic on the back windshield and get moving."

"I'm doing the best I can."

"No more excuses. Don't be late."

Laura opened the car door and placed the phone back inside. Her head seemed to be pulsating with the beat of her heart, and her stomach began to hurt. She did her best to ignore the pain and laid the plastic on the ground, unrolled it, and cut a piece she thought would be big enough to cover the back window. Her body shook as she snatched the plastic and the tape and climbed on the trunk.

"You need some help with that?" a voice asked from behind her.

Laura didn't even bother to turn around. "I got it, thanks."

"You sure?"

"Yeah. I got it."

She could only imagine how ridiculous she looked in a skirt and blouse, braless and barefoot, taping plastic on the back of her window, but none of that mattered anymore. She knew that if she wanted to be the person she had to be—strong and willing to do anything to get to her daughter—she needed to get on the road as soon as possible. That had to be her focus going forward. Nelle. Nothing else.

As she worked, she thought about the seeds of things: how certain events could turn into something so completely opposite from their origin. She thought about how she'd met Kurt only minutes after she thought she was going to die. She thought about a boy from her past named Mike Schuccle and how different her life would have been if she hadn't had that crush on him. But without the incident with Mike, she wouldn't have moved to New York and met Kurt, and there would be no Nelle. But there'd still be Donny. Fate had a cruel way of playing its hand. Add one, take one. You can't have it all, Laura thought. There is no yin without the yang. There is no good without the bad.

From the corner of her eye, Laura noticed an elderly woman struggling to take a bag of cat litter from her grocery cart and put it into her the trunk of her car. She turned back to the plastic and taped a corner into place, securing it both inside and outside the frame. As she made her way around the car, she saw the old woman continuing to tug on the top of the bag, her tiny body shaking, the oversized bag refusing to budge.

"I have to help this lady," she said.

"You don't have time," the voice replied.

Laura shook her head. "I know, but it'll just take a second. I can't stand here and do nothing." She hurried over to the old woman. "I can help you with that."

The old woman spun around and as soon as she saw Laura, a look of relief washed over her. "Oh, thank you so much, dear. I asked the cashier not to put the litter all the way inside the cart, but I guess he wasn't listening and I was too busy writing my check to notice. It's so heavy."

Laura yanked the litter from the cart and placed it into the trunk. She couldn't help but think of what was in her own trunk, and the image of what she'd seen earlier turned her stomach.

"Do you have someone at home who can help you get that out?" she asked.

"I do," the old woman replied. "My husband and I have a visiting nurse and she'll be able to get it out of the trunk and into the house. She'd be here with me now, but my husband wasn't feeling well and she stayed back at the house with him."

A quick smile. "Okay, good. Get home safe."

"Thank you again. Have a blessed day and know that you've done a good deed for an old lady. It's much appreciated."

Laura waved and ran back toward her car to put the rest of the plastic on so she could get on the road again. One good deed down. Countless more to go. She feared her account would never be settled, but there was no time for introspection. Not now. Nelle was waiting for her and she was running out of time.

JANUARY 3, 1993

He was dead. No doubt about it.

Betty sat on the curb facing the swing set in the elementary school's playground. She focused on the middle swing and watched as it rocked gently back and forth in the cold winter wind, the sound of a locomotive's diesel engine churning in the railyard across the street behind her. The middle swing had always been Donny's preference. He had this weird theory that if he was the only one swinging on the left or right, his weight might throw off the set's balance and topple the entire structure. It didn't matter how many times she tried to explain to him that the swings' foundation posts were cemented into the ground and it would take a lot more than his seventy pounds to tip the set over. Reasoning with a ten-year-old proved impossible, so whenever the set was unoccupied, she knew he would pick that middle swing.

One of the first policemen to arrive at the scene had placed a wool blanket over her shoulders. She clutched the rough edges and pulled it tighter around her frame. He'd offered to have her sit in the patrol car where it was warm, but she'd refused, opting instead to stay right where she ended up after the man who'd been driving by stopped and pulled her off her brother, placing her on the curb, facing her away from the carnage and onto the playground. In the recesses of her memory, she could still hear the screaming and the calling for help, but she never knew the faces behind the panicked and distraught voices since she would not allow herself to turn away from the swing set. Even when more police came and then the ambulance and finally the fire truck—all with their blaring sirens and rotating emergency lights—she did not turn around. Instead, she watched that middle swing, knowing her little brother would never get to enjoy it ever again. Knowing that fact already proved to be too much.

"Donny! Oh my god!"

Betty stiffened when she heard her father's voice. She knew he'd show up eventually. Even at sixteen, she knew protocol was protocol. The senior officer would ID her brother and then call the local headquarters to have someone deliver the news to her father in person in Austin. He was a lieutenant with the Austin Police Department and worked at their main headquarters on 8th Street, so she figured by the time proper procedures were executed and someone was assigned to drive him—a drive that took about a half an hour—she would've already been moved from the scene. But they must've been going a hundred miles an hour with lights and sirens the entire way. He'd made it in record time.

"Betty!"

She focused on the middle swing for as long as she could before her father's beefy hands took her by her shoulders and forced her to look at him. She recoiled when she saw him. His face was so different. His eyes were large and full of fear, red around the edges. His nose was red too, and his thick mustache seemed to have more gray than blond in it. How had he aged so much in a single afternoon? When was the last time she'd taken a good look at him? His bottom lip quivered and she realized she'd never seen her dad look so weak before. Vulnerable. The anguish in his expression made her heart ache.

"Honey, what happened?"

A fresh set of tears began to well in Betty's eyes.

"I... I don't know. One minute we were walking to the playground and the next minute I hear this crash and Donny's under a car. It happened so fast. I... I..."

"Did you see the car coming up behind you?"

"No, I—"

"On the sidewalk?"

"I—"

"Did the car honk its horn or try and swerve out of the way?"

She began to cry, helpless and confused. "I don't know."

Her father pulled her into his chest. "Shhh, it's okay."

"I didn't know anything was going to happen. We were walking to the playground."

"Then the driver rode up on the curb and hit Donny. I get it. You don't have to relive it now. She was driving drunk. We have her in custody."

"But Dad—"

"It's okay. We know who she is. Her name is Sofia Bennett. The local police know her from being in trouble before. Not like this, though. This'll put her away for a long time. She won't hurt anyone else again. I promise."

Betty turned her head away from her father's chest as he continued to hug her, crying quietly on the curb with her. She peeked around his arm and finally looked upon the scene. She could see her little brother, covered with a white sheet, lying face up, half of his body still under the white four-door hatchback, its front end crushed in from the impact, specks of blood pocking the white paint. Perhaps seventy pounds could do some damage after all.

She nestled into her father's embrace. There was so much

she wanted to tell him, but he kept crying, closing the door on any opportunity to explain what she remembered. She watched as one of the police cars drove by. The drunk woman was in the back, staring at her as she passed. Betty returned the stare, both of them glaring at each other, the hate burning through their souls. Betty could feel her hands ball into fists and she fought the urge to break away from her father, throw open the back-door, and attack the woman like a rabid dog, tearing her apart with the rage and agony and guilt that burrowed within.

But none of that happened. The car drove by and Betty watched it go until it rounded a corner. Then she returned her attention to the middle swing, focusing on it until her father peeled her off the curb and put her into his car to go home. They had to tell her mother that her little boy was dead. Betty wanted to tell her something more.

CHAPTER TEN

MARCH 27, 2000

Tricia poked Betty's shoulder as she was hanging up the phone. "Let's go, we have a car accident victim coming in. ETA under one minute."

"Okay."

"Get the crash cart and get set up. I hear she's in bad shape."

"On it."

Betty quickly brushed the tears from her eyes and hurried down the corridor. She could see Dr. Decker waiting inside the bay doors. He was a picture of calm, gloved hands up and ready, his protective gown covering his dress shirt and tie. There wasn't a hair out of place, his clean-shaven face stoic. He might as well have been waiting for a bus rather than preparing to save a life. He looked over at her and gave a quick nod. He was ready.

The ambulance bay doors opened as Betty passed the nursing station. Two paramedics ran in with a patient on a gurney.

"What do we have?" Dr. Decker asked, quickly sliding next to them to start a cursory examination as they made their way inside the emergency room.

"Female, thirty-four. Hit-and-run. Multiple lacerations. Multiple fractures both upper and lower body. Possible internal

bleeding. BP is 95 over 50. Heartrate is high. 120 bpm. We secured her with a cervical collar and put an eighteen-gauge needle in the A/C. Gave her two milligrams of Dilaudid IV at the scene."

Dr. Decker pointed. "Put her in room two."

"Copy that."

The paramedics pushed the gurney into exam room two, and as Dr. Decker, Tricia, and the other senior nurse, Pat, followed, Betty got to the crash cart. The cart looked like a small metal dresser with a monitor and paddles on top. The six drawers were full of medicines, IV needles, bags, and various other supplies that were already unlocked and ready for use. She wheeled it into the room while the rest of the team focused on evaluation and treatment.

The woman was conscious, breathing rapidly, her eyes darting from side to side. She was groaning, seemingly unable to speak, but it was clear she was in a lot of pain, even with the drugs she'd been given at the scene.

"Name?" Dr. Decker called from over his shoulder.

"Sofia Bennett," the paramedic replied as he backed out of the room.

CHAPTER ELEVEN

They were going to kill Nelle. Laura could sense this was not a bluff. She had to get to her to stop it.

She drove in silence for miles, her lips pressed tight and her eyes on the road, the crumpling of plastic on the back window the only sound within the car. The voice instructed her to go through the town of Carmel instead of using Route 35 to get onto Interstate 684. He wanted her to stay hidden and staying on local roads through small towns made the most sense. Her head ached and the pain in her stomach was getting worse. The taste of the last Xanax she chewed still coated her mouth. Alternating between the Xanax and Zoloft made the need for a drink all the more important to get her head on straight. She just needed a quick one to clear the growing fog and to stop the shakes.

Her body was beginning to fail. She knew it, despite her reluctance to admit it to herself. She gripped the wheel and swallowed the pain, determined to keep going, trying not to focus on the fact that she so desperately needed a drink. Tears welled in her eyes and she wiped them away with defiance. She didn't want him to see her crying again. She just had to stay focused and get north. Her little girl was depending on her and she'd be damned if she was going to let her down.

"How do you know you have the right person?" Laura asked as she passed the town line for Patterson, New York. Her pain was presenting as irritation and Laura couldn't help but speak what was on her mind. "You risked kidnapping one child and you killed another in order to get to me, and despite me telling you I'm not the person you think I am, you hang all your hopes on that fact that I am. How are you so sure I'm the person you've been looking for?"

The ramp for Interstate 84 West appeared on her right, and she carefully merged with the rush hour traffic.

"I want to know what you're planning to do to prove to yourself that I'm Betty. Or better yet, what do I have to do to convince you I'm not?"

She passed a slow-moving truck and got back into the right lane. The voice on the phone remained silent.

"What happens when you finally understand that all of this has been for nothing? What are you going to do when you find out you were wrong? Kill us anyway? Let us go? Offer an apology for your misunderstanding? How will this end?"

She glanced at the phone as the black screen blinked once and the call shut down.

"Hello?"

She looked back and forth between the road and the phone, her throat constricting when the message came across the screen.

Connection lost.

"No!"

Laura pushed down on the gas pedal, watching the bars under the corner of the cracked glass. She was in some kind of dead zone and the FaceTime call had disconnected. The mechanical voice's warnings about ending the call screamed in her mind.

"I'm here!" she cried as she drove even faster. "Please! I'm here! I didn't hang up. I'm here!"

The phone began to ring again. Laura quickly pressed the green button to accept the call.

"I'm here! I'm here! I lost the signal. I didn't hang up. Please!"

Static on the line.

"Are you there?" Laura asked. "Can you hear me?"

"We're here," the voice replied.

"I didn't hang up. I swear."

Silence.

"Let me speak to my daughter. I need to know she's okay. I want to hear her voice."

"No."

"The call dropped. I didn't hang up. Please. Let me talk to her."

"No."

Without considering what she was doing, Laura pulled off to the shoulder and stopped the car. She put on her hazard lights and stared into the phone, one half of her confused and scared at what she was doing, while the other half—the mother half—told her that what she was doing was right. A mother needs to know if their child is safe.

"Let me talk to Nelle right now. I'm not going any further until I do."

"The clock keeps ticking," the voice warned. "No way to stop that."

"I need to know that she's okay."

"She's fine."

"Let me hear it for myself."

"Your daughter's life depends on whether you get back on the road, Betty. You can't play games when you don't hold any cards. You're a smart lady. You should know that."

"Just for a second. One word. A sound. I need to hear her. Please."

"Start driving."

She bit her bottom lip, defeated and angry, then put the car in gear and merged back onto the interstate. She fought the urge to start crying again. How could she do this? She was powerless against these people.

"You never gave us a chance to say anything to our mother before you killed her," the voice said. "We were waiting at home and the hours passed by without her car pulling into the driveway like she always did. My father told us she probably had to work late, but looking back, I could tell he was starting to get nervous, too. He told us all kinds of things to ease our fears, but we could both see that when he smiled, it wasn't real. All that time he was trying to make us feel better, and we were wondering when she'd be home, she was already dead. It's just that no one had told us yet. We never had a chance to say anything to her before you stole her from us. Why would I give you the satisfaction of talking to your daughter whenever you want?"

"You're wrong," Laura said, her voice choking out the words. "I didn't kill your mother."

"You did. All those lies you told. You lied about what happened and then you killed her. But now we've found you and you're gonna pay for what you did."

A few minutes passed without any more conversation. Laura drove on, trying to focus on the road, wondering how this nightmare might end.

"Mom?"

Nelle's voice filled the speakers and a wave of relief washed over Laura. "Nelle, honey! Are you okay? I'm coming. I promise. Are you okay?"

"Mom, I—"

And then the screams. Loud, painful, horrific screams from

her daughter, unyielding in their anguish, and so intense in their pitch. Laura punched the steering wheel, her relief quickly morphing into wails of rage and terror and hopelessness.

"Stop it!" she screamed as loud as she could, her defiance and bravado instantly melting away. "Get away from her!"

But the screaming wouldn't stop. It grew louder and more penetrating.

"Can you hear her now, Betty?" the voice asked, cutting through the torment. "Nelle's alive. You don't have to worry about that. You satisfied now? Can you hear her? You're good now?"

"Please stop!"

"Can you hear her now?"

"Stop hurting my daughter! Please!"

Laura drove on, crying and yelling and pleading for them to stop, but the torture continued for what seemed like miles, pushing her to the edge of sanity. There was nothing she could do. She was alone on the road, completely helpless, forced to listen, unable to turn the phone off. Absolutely trapped.

One hour and thirty-five minutes remaining.

CHAPTER TWELVE

The Anderson house was a crime scene now.

Roman Estrada stood in the middle of Laura Anderson's living room, hands on hips, spinning in place, trying to take it all in. He could see framed pictures of the family lined with precision atop a table behind the couch. More pictures in framed collages hung on the wall behind a small upright piano. School books and folders were piled neatly next to a shoe rack where each pair of shoes and sneakers were placed toes in, heels out. Laura Anderson seemed to keep a very tidy home.

A forensics unit was spilled out around him, collecting whatever they could find that might tell them how an upstanding citizen, and husband of a police detective, with no criminal record, was suddenly wanted for the attempted murder of the Westchester County Chief of Police. The search on the plate number had led him to the modest split-level ranch in Garrison, New York. The house was nice enough, about fifteen hundred square feet. Nothing fancy. It looked like a house a typical middle-class family would live in. Not a killer. Not a fugitive.

Roman walked into the kitchen where Laura Anderson's

husband, Kurt, was sitting, elbows on the table, hands covering his face, one knee bouncing endlessly up and down, his department ID still hanging around his neck. Much like the living room, the kitchen was a mixture of neat and utilitarian with a dash of family love shown by the countless pictures in magnet frames on the refrigerator.

He'd gotten the call while he was still at the scene on the Taconic. Kurt had contacted 911 after he'd returned home to find his house tossed and his wife and daughter missing. The computer monitoring the BOLO had matched the name on the 911 call with the name on the plate registration and Roman was notified. When he arrived at the house, he was greeted by Kurt's superior, Chief Slacks, who gave him all the information he'd collected, including a quick summary of his recorded interview with Kurt. Roman had thanked the chief, then dismissed him.

Kurt jumped up out of his seat when Roman entered the kitchen. His brown eyes were almost black in the lighting. His cheeks were thin, his chin pointed and cleft. He was attractive. In shape. Looked younger than his early forties. But the expression on his face made him look like he'd aged ten years in that one afternoon.

"You find them?"

"Not yet," Roman replied. "How you holding up?"

Kurt began pacing. "I'd be better if someone could tell me what the hell is going on."

"I'm Detective Estrada. Westchester PD. Did they tell you what your wife did to my boss?"

"Yeah. I can't believe it."

"So that doesn't sound like something your wife is capable of doing?"

"Do you think I'd be married to a woman who would knowingly run over someone? No, that doesn't sound like something Laura would do."

"How long have you guys been married?"

"Nineteen years."

"Has she ever—"

"No," Kurt said, cutting him off. "She's never shown any signs of aggression. She's never displayed any characteristics that would lead me to believe she would be involved with something like this. She's not on drugs. She doesn't drink. The marriage is fine. She loves being a mother. Her job is fine. She volunteers at the church every chance she gets. Everything is good." He spun around and stopped. "I know all the questions you're going to ask because I'm usually the one asking them. There was nothing out of the ordinary going on with Laura. Today started like every other day. I have no idea what's going on so somebody better start telling me something."

Roman walked further into the kitchen and sat down across from Kurt who began pacing again, running his hands repeatedly through his hair. Roman studied his subject for any signs he was lying. Subtle movements, like lack of eye contact, short breath, general nervousness. He saw nothing that would make him suspicious. The man seemed genuinely confused and his concern was showing itself as anger, which would be considered normal under the circumstances.

"Based on what happened to my chief, we know Laura's alive," he said. "But we don't know anything about your daughter, Nelle. No one's seen her. That concerns me."

"Yeah, me too. After I got home from work, I found the house dark and the place tossed. Not torn apart, but things were out of place. Kitchen cabinets were left open. Our desk was rifled through. Spare keys were missing. Then I heard a message on our house phone. The school called to report Nelle absent for the day. That's when I knew something was up. I called 911 and when the operator told me she was dispatching units, I walked to the top of my driveway to meet them. I found Nelle's backpack in the grass on the shoulder next to our mailbox. I even tried the Find My Phone app and couldn't locate either of their phones. What's happening?"

"We're working to find that out. I promise."

"I wish I could tell you more, but I was in court all day and came home to this."

Roman let the conversation sit still for a minute. The house was quiet but for the crime scene unit who worked around them.

"We found remnants of a broken mirror in your bathroom garbage. Looks like it came from the vanity in your bedroom. You know anything about that?"

Kurt stopped pacing and nodded. "Laura and Nelle got into an argument last night and Laura accidentally slipped and fell against the mirror."

"She okay?"

"Yeah. Couple of scratches."

"Must've been some fight."

"Nelle's a fifteen-year-old kid testing boundaries. It was a regular argument. Laura just lost her balance or something."

"Did you see it?"

"No. Happened when I was still at work. And no, I don't think that had anything to do with what's going on now."

"Do you think your daughter is with Laura?" Roman asked.

Kurt quickly wiped his eyes as they began to glass. He fell into his seat and stared at the detective. "I don't know. I really don't."

"Think for a second."

"I am thinking. Like I told my chief, if Nelle was with Laura, why would her backpack be on the side of the road? I called the church and the pharmacy where Laura works. Father Glipp said she was there for the ceremony and Mr. Harper said she worked that morning before the ceremony, but no one saw Nelle. None of this makes sense."

Roman looked up at the ceiling. "You and Laura been married nineteen years."

"That's right."

"Would you say you know her well?"

"Of course."

"Any secrets between you two?"

"None."

He looked back at Kurt and leaned in closer, lowering his voice. "You told us your wife isn't on drugs and is just an occasional drinker."

"That's right."

"You sure?"

"Yes. She doesn't use drugs and has, like, a glass of wine at dinner. A few drinks on the weekends. That kind of thing."

Roman exhaled slowly. "I don't want to start tearing holes in the life you think you had, but my men found four bottles of vodka and two bottles of whiskey hidden in Laura's closet behind her sweater rack. Any idea why they'd be there?"

Kurt's lips parted and his mouth opened. It appeared as if he was about to say something, then his mouth closed again and he turned away.

"Six bottles of liquor," Roman continued. "One of the vodka bottles was empty. Another was half full. The other two were unopened. One whiskey was almost done. The other unopened. It looks like she was stashing it. Or hiding it. How do you explain this?"

"I can't."

"Do you know your wife to be a vodka or whiskey drinker?"

"No."

"Looks like she was, in fact, keeping a secret from you."

Kurt didn't reply.

"And you have no knowledge of a possible problem she might have with alcohol?"

"I swear to God, I have no idea."

Roman paused for a moment, allowing Kurt to let the new information sink in. He knew he'd dropped some kind of bombshell with the liquor bottles with the way Kurt's eyes widened and he shifted in his seat. It was obvious Kurt was unaware such a secret was being kept from him. Roman felt awkward interviewing a fellow detective, but he needed to get things out in the open before the union came in with Internal Affairs to muck everything up.

"I know this is hard to digest, but I think it's time to start grasping the idea that you didn't know your wife as well as you thought you did," Roman said. "The way I see it, the strongest possibility is something happened between your wife and your daughter this morning as a carryover from last night. Your wife did something to Nelle. Probably an accident, but maybe she hurt her bad. Maybe worse. The house looks tossed because she turned the place over, looking to quickly pack up and get out. She went to work and the church so people wouldn't get too suspicious too soon. Now she's running with Nelle. Whether Nelle's alive or not remains the unanswered question."

"Laura would never hurt Nelle," Kurt snapped as he slammed his hands down on the table. "Nelle was Laura's entire reason for living. She loved her more than a human being can love another. She's her mother. No way she'd ever hurt her."

Roman held up his hands in surrender. "I'm not saying I'm right or wrong. But you don't know what you don't know. Those six bottles of alcohol hidden in her closet confirm that."

Sergeant Baros thundered up the stairs and walked into the kitchen. "We got two laptops," he said. "I'll bag 'em and see if the tech guys can find something."

Roman turned back to Baros. "Sounds good."

"Jacobs called from the hospital. The chief's still in surgery. He'll live, but there's a question of whether or not he'll keep his legs. The drivers who pulled over and applied the tourniquets definitely saved his life. Not sure if he'll walk again, though."

Roman and Kurt watched the sergeant leave the room. Roman stood up and placed a hand on Kurt's shoulder, man to man.

"We'll find them," he said. "Laura and Nelle. I can promise you that."

CHAPTER THIRTEEN

How easy it would be to kill her. So prone. So vulnerable. It could be over before it even started. But no. That wasn't the plan. They had to stick to the plan.

He stood over her as his vision cleared, his chest rising and falling as he took deep breaths to quell the anxiety. He walked over to the phone propped on the table, a small piece of black construction paper covering the camera, and hit the mute button. He could see Betty clearly. Hysterical. Hurting as much as her daughter. He was breaking her to get to the truth. This was what they wanted. This was what they had worked for. It was something he never knew he needed until it was offered to him: the truth. What they were doing was supposed to be beautiful, but it wasn't. It was...

Hard.

Nelle was lying on the floor, facedown, arms stretched out in front of her as if she was flying, her wrists tied to thick rope wrapped around the foundation columns that separated the living room and the kitchen. She was crying as quietly as she could, trying not to make any more noise so she wouldn't draw further attention, and that alone broke his heart. This wasn't supposed to be something the girl had to endure. She was simply a means to an end, a tool that had to be used. It hurt him to hurt her. He knew what she was feeling. He'd felt it himself countless times. The physical pain was one thing, but the emotional trauma that accompanied it was sometimes even worse. She shouldn't have had to pay for the sins of her mother, but this chapter in his life was bigger than himself. It was everything, and there was nothing he would do to change course.

Small burn marks pocked the back of her calves. The aroma of charred flesh mixed with the burning logs in the fireplace and made for a sickening smell. This wasn't the kind of pain he'd inflicted before. The pinching of her skin was to elicit a temporary scream so Betty knew not to disobey. This pain, and the act behind it, was something more. This was dark.

He backed away and returned the fire poker to the rack, then ran to the kitchen. He opened the freezer and grabbed three ice trays, hurrying back into the living room where he knelt down next to Nelle.

"I'm sorry," he said quietly. "I know this is all confusing and terrifying for you. I promise it'll be over soon. We don't want to hurt you any more than we have to. If it were up to me, I wouldn't hurt you at all."

He cracked the ice tray and spilled the cubes onto the floor. Picking up a handful of small squares, he pressed them against the burns. Nelle recoiled when the ice touched her charred skin and she began crying again.

"I know. Burns are the worst kind of pain, but don't worry. I didn't go deep. These are just flesh wounds." He made tiny circular motions around each wound, watching as the ice melted in his fingers. "I know how you feel. This exact thing happened to me when I was eleven and staying at a foster home. The guy—I won't say his name, because screw him—started with cigarettes when I wouldn't do things he wanted fast enough. We graduated to the tips of steak knives after a while. He'd hold the tip of the knife over the fire on the stovetop and burn me for shits and giggles. He was sadistic. A real sicko. He finally got to the fire poker. Did it twice, and that was it. The idiot didn't realize the social worker would see the scars. Got me moved and he got arrested. Happy ending, right? Not really. Different home, different way they mess with your head when you're an orphan. It's still torture any way you slice it."

Nelle remained on the floor, silent but for the whimpers that escaped her lips as he tried to numb her pain with the ice.

"I wish I didn't have to do this," he said. "I wish I didn't even know your mother, and I wish you didn't have to find out the truth about her this way. I mean, if I never knew your mom existed, that would mean my mom would still be alive, my dad wouldn't have turned into a drunk who killed himself, and my sister and I wouldn't have ended up in foster homes. But, as fate would have it, I do know her. That means my mom's not alive. It means my dad did fall into a pit of blackness where his depression was so bad he couldn't even stay alive for his children and, instead, thought tucking a shotgun under his chin and pulling the trigger was a better option. And it means me and my sister got abused in the system like you can't imagine. So, I know her, and now I know you. Doesn't mean I'm not sorry, though. You shouldn't have to go through this."

Nelle tried to push herself up and cried out in pain.

"Shhhh, easy," he whispered. "Don't move too much. Let me numb the burns. When we're done here, I can give you some oxy to dull the pain. You can sleep for a bit, too. That'll be good for you."

"Hello!"

He paused and looked in the direction of the kitchen, the muffled voice emanating from the very floorboards Nelle was lying on.

"Can anyone hear me? I need some help down here."

"Who is that lady?" Nelle asked. Her voice was quiet, weak.

He smiled. "That's your grandma. Your mother's mother."

"My mom said her mother died when I was a baby."

"Your mom is a liar."

Nelle sniffled and cleared her throat. It pained him to hear her talk. She was so scared.

"How do you know you have the right family? My mom keeps saying you're wrong. That she's not this Betty person."

"Hello! Is anyone there? I need help!"

He climbed to his feet, crossed the room, and snatched a paper bag off the fireplace mantle. "You like candy corn?" he asked.

Nelle couldn't turn to face him. "I guess."

"Your grandma likes them, too. Told me it's her favorite candy. She was eating out of this very bag when I first met her. That's how I know I got the right family. Coincidences don't exist where I come from. Never did."

He dropped the bag in front of the girl, close enough so she could see the label without having to strain herself. "You know Harper's Pharmacy in Sleepy Hollow?"

"Yeah. My mom works there."

"So how would the lady who lives here have a bag of candy corn from the pharmacy your mom works at without knowing your mom?"

Nelle looked up at him, but didn't speak.

"Hello!"

"I'm gonna go see what your grandma wants. I'll be right back and we'll fix those burns some more."

He watched her studying the bag, making the connection between her family and the old woman in the basement. He could see her asking herself his question. How could this old lady be all the way up here and have that particular bag of candy from that particular store? The odds were too astronomical to consider, unless it wasn't chance. He saw it dawn on her and he smiled. She knew. She was getting it now.

Her mother was a liar.

CHAPTER FOURTEEN

Laura stood behind the checkout watching a young boy slowly walking up and down Aisle Three, pretending to peruse the aftershave or underarm deodorant sticks, when it was clear he was building up the courage to buy a pack of condoms. In her ten years of working that exact counter in that exact store, she'd seen the same kind of boy, skulking with the same nervousness in the same aisle more times than she could count. She felt for him, knowing how difficult it must be to make that first purchase when it would've been so much easier to forgo the protection and just roll the dice. She was proud of him, despite knowing nothing about him. He couldn't have been more than thirteen. Definitely younger than Nelle. Too young to be having sex, but it wasn't her place to pass judgment. Besides, kids were different these days. In some respects they were more about the world than ever, each of them caught in their own bubbles of social media. But at the same time, when it came to social issues and social norms, they were smart in a way she never was at that age, and way more mature than she had been growing up. The stigma that came with buying a pack of condoms had dissipated over the years, but it still didn't quell the anxiety a first-timer had when completing this rite of passage. She watched, making sure his fear didn't overwhelm his common sense and force him to pocket the rubbers instead of buying them. She found herself holding her breath in anticipation and let it out slowly, laughing at her silliness as she pulled for the boy to gather his nerve and do the right thing.

"These scripts aren't going to put themselves away."

Mr. Harper's raspy voice cut through Laura's thoughts and she quickly turned to find the old man standing behind the drug counter, his frail arms pitched out and leaning on the glass top in a kind of tripod way, hovering over a stack of about a dozen white bags. Marvin Harper was a third-generation pharmacist and owner of the beloved store that was his namesake, but unlike his father and his grandfather who founded the place, Marvin Harper was always miserable. He was Ebenezer Scrooge to Laura's Bob Cratchit, an older man, frail and gray in body but mighty in spirit, a man who could never be satisfied with a kind smile or simple compliment. A man who'd rather bark an order than compliment a job well done. A man who had yet to be visited by Dickens's three ghosts of Christmas.

"I'm on it, sir," Laura replied, leaning up and snatching the pharma bags one at a time.

Mr. Harper glanced at the watch that was strapped around his skinny wrist. "Put them in the drawers and restock the razors in the case before you go. You don't have much time left, and I don't pay overtime."

Now it was Laura who checked the time on her phone. "Is it three-fifteen already?"

"Almost. Time flies every inventory day. You know that."

"Feels like I just had lunch."

Mr. Harper shrugged and pushed himself up off the counter. "I don't know what to tell you. The laws of physics aren't any different in my store than they are in the universe. You worked your shift and time went on as it always does. Now you need to *hurry up and get your chores done so you can get home for Nelle."*

"Yes, sir."

"Don't be late."

"I won't."

He lowered his voice into a grumble. "And make sure that kid doesn't steal any of those rubbers he's trying to get the gumption to buy."

"I'm on it."

Mr. Harper disappeared back behind his drug desk and Laura quickly pulled the drawers out from the cabinet she was standing in front of, placing each pharma bag in the assigned alphabetical basket as she'd done countless times before. She glanced at the drugs as she put them away, recognizing some—Lisinopril (high blood pressure), Atorvastatin (high cholesterol), Metformin (diabetes), Omeprazole (gastro reflux)—and clueless on the others—Escitalopram, Furosemide, Clonazepam. The medicines had changed over the years and the variety of what a patient could take had grown ten-fold. It was hard to keep up, but the pull to be in and around medicine was a pull she could never ignore.

A bell rung behind her, quiet, unassuming. She turned around to find the boy standing at the register, his finger hovering over the call bell that was next to the lotto tickets, his face red and splotchy, a can of soda, a Snickers bar, and a pack of Trojans waiting to be rung up.

"You find everything you needed today?" she asked as she closed the drawers and approached.

The boy nodded.

"Need anything else?"

A quick shake of the head. "Just these."

Laura pulled the items toward her and rang them up. "You're a good man, Charlie Brown," she said. When the boy looked at her, she offered a wink.

* * *

Laura let the memory dance in her mind. Get home for Nelle. That's all she'd been trying to do then. Now, she was trying to get *to* her. To save her life. To trade lives, if necessary. Whatever it took.

The voice had been silent for a while now, and she hadn't heard Nelle. There had been certain spots along the way when the call's connection faltered, but never dropped. The quiet was too much. She felt worn out, helpless. She had to know what was happening, but at the same time, she was terrified to learn the truth. What if...? No, she couldn't come to terms with that. Nelle was alive. They were waiting for her to get up to the lake. Nelle was okay. For now. She had to be.

Brake lights began to pop on in front of Laura, and she slowed the car down. Yellow hazard lights from large eighteen-wheelers started flashing, alerting drivers behind them that the slowdown was more than temporary.

"We're stopping," she blurted. She could hear the panic in her voice. "Why are we stopping?"

"What's happening?" the voice asked.

"I don't know." Laura craned her neck to see past the cars in front of her. "It's traffic. An accident, maybe?"

"You're running out of time."

"What do you want me to do? There's no exit and nowhere for me to go."

"You're failing your daughter."

"There's nothing I can do!" Laura hit the steering wheel with her fist. "You can't hold this against me."

"Find a way out."

"There is no way out!"

"The clock is ticking."

The traffic was starting to move again. It was slow, her

speedometer hovering at only twenty miles an hour, but at least they were moving.

"It's gotta be an accident. We're stop and go."

The voice didn't reply.

Laura tried to calm herself. She concentrated on her breathing and focused on the car in front of her. There was no use yelling. It solved nothing, and worse, it might motivate the people behind the voice to hurt Nelle again. She had to stay calm. She had to breathe. She could do it.

She traveled for what felt like a half mile, and everything stopped again. This time, she could see the tips of orange lights flashing and a line of white service trucks taking up the left lane. Two of the trucks had cranes extended with men in buckets trimming tree branches that hung over the interstate.

"They're doing tree repair," Laura said aloud. "One lane closed. I'm almost out of it."

Silence.

Her fingers drummed on the wheel until the traffic started moving again. She let a few cars from the left lane come into the right, and as she approached the beginning of the lane merge and construction area, she could see a female flagger with her sign turned to SLOW. Right beyond her, hidden from sight by the first bucket truck in the line, was a New York State Police patrol car, red lights flashing, headlights strobing.

Laura's breath caught in her throat and she clutched her stomach as it lurched and tightened. She pushed herself back in her seat, as if that would get her further away from the trooper. There was undoubtedly some kind of APB out for her. There had been witnesses on the Taconic and they'd seen what she'd done. They'd also seen her vehicle. The dented rear end and missing back window would be dead giveaways. There were mountains on both sides of her with no way to exit the road. She was a sitting duck.

Laura looked straight ahead at the car in front of her. As

soon as she got to the flagger, the woman turned her sign and put up her hand.

STOP.

"Oh my god," she choked. She pointed in front of her, then to the watch on her wrist, smiling, silently asking the flagger if she could please go ahead. But the flagger shook her head and pointed to her sign.

STOP.

"I'm stopped at the merge and there's a police car right across from me."

"Stay calm," the voice instructed. "Act natural."

"He's going to recognize my car. I have no rear window. The back is dented. I might as well have a sign that says I killed that cop on the Taconic. What do I do?"

"Wait."

Laura dared not turn her head, but she did sneak a peek through her periphery. The state police car was pointed right at her. The flashing bar lights and pulsating headlights made it impossible to see the person inside, but she could imagine a trooper sitting behind the wheel, studying the Volkswagen caught in its strobes, matching it against a description that had gone out across all departments.

Passat. Check.

Maroon. Check.

Missing back window. Check.

Damaged rear end of vehicle. Check.

She swallowed the lump in her throat and stared at the female flagger. Her sign hadn't changed and the woman was looking behind her at the crew working, waiting for their signal to allow traffic through again. She didn't look like she was in a rush. Time stood still.

"He's probably calling it in right now," she whispered. "He's got backup coming and they're going to surround me. Then what? We need to go."

"Stay calm."

"How? His car is pointed right at me. He knows."

"Be patient."

"If he comes for me, I'm going to have to kill him. It's my only option."

The flagger turned her sign.

SLOW.

Laura began to drive through the construction zone and glanced at the cruiser as she passed. The lights from one of the cranes caught the interior of the patrol car and she saw it was empty. No driver. No police. Just the lights to alert others of the work going on in the area.

"Okay," she said. "We're moving again. I got through."

"Were you going to kill that trooper if he tried to stop you?" the voice asked. "All to save your daughter?"

Laura was quiet.

"Are you willing to kill for her?"

Her hands tightened around the wheel as she contemplated the question. A few hours earlier she would've answered quickly, not because she necessarily meant it, but because she knew the answer others would want to hear. Now she answered with complete conviction, knowing it was not only the truth, but a distinct possibility. "Absolutely, I would," she said. "I would kill for my daughter. No doubt about it."

"I hoped you'd say that."

One hour remaining.

CHAPTER FIFTEEN

Roman pushed through the front door of Harper's Pharmacy and heard the bell ring above it. The store was about half the size of its big box competitors down the road in Tarrytown and Croton, but there was a charm about it that was unmistakable. Old-school glass counters ran the length of the shop on both sides, displaying razors, first-aid kits, and medicines. A few antique beakers and scales were thrown in for aesthetics, and the combination of old and new worked well at showing consumers how long the business had been around. The center of the store was much more twenty-first century, with shelves packing everything from beauty products and healthcare to snacks and magazines. The floor itself was still original hardwood, worn and sagging. As Roman made his way to the back where he knew Marvin Harper would be waiting, the boards creaked under his weight.

The old man was busy behind the drug counter, dumping pills out onto a scale and sliding them into smaller vials for his patients. He had his bifocals teetering on the tip of his long nose. One false move and they would slip off. Old and arthritic hands worked with dexterity as if they'd done this job so long, they had their own muscle memory.

"Mr. Harper?" Roman asked as he stepped up to the counter.

The old man didn't look up or stop what he was doing. "That's me."

"I'm Detective Estrada. I called you earlier about Laura Anderson?"

"And I told you earlier that I don't know what happened to her. She left early to attend one of her volunteer functions. Walked out the door at noon as planned. Haven't seen or heard from her since."

Roman watched the old man work. Fast. Confident. He looked behind him to ensure the store was still empty, then leaned on the counter. "Yes, I contacted the church where the function was being held. She arrived on time and left when it was over."

"Yet here you are."

"Let's just say we've reached the point in our investigation where I need to know a little more about Laura as a person. I was hoping you could help me with that."

"You're profiling her now?"

"Kind of. Yeah. Trying to get a general picture."

"Well, I don't know her as a person. She's an employee, and it ends there. My family hasn't survived for three generations in this shop by befriending every person who ever worked for us. We keep things at arm's length. Employee, employer. As it should be."

"I understand. Tell me about her as an employee, then."

"What do you want to know?"

"How is she as a worker bee?"

Marvin Harper capped a prescription bottle, slipped it into a small white bag, placed it on the counter, and finally looked up at Roman. "She's one of my best ever."

"How do you mean?"

"Always on time. Always willing to stay late and help, even though she knows I'm loath to pay overtime. She knows her medicine, which is strange considering she's just a cashier, but damned if she isn't up on her stuff. I asked her about it once, back in the beginning, and she said medicine was a hobby of hers, which is why she sought the job here instead of a grocery store or nail salon or whatever. Laura never calls in sick. Always treats me with respect, and she gets to know our customers on a personal level, which is what keeps them coming back. She's a model employee."

"How long has she been working here?"

"A while. I lost count. She put Nelle on the bus when she started kindergarten and immediately got to looking for work. I started her part-time a few days a week so she could be home for Nelle, but as Nelle got older, Laura took on more shifts and more responsibility, and now she's full-time. Basically manages the place."

Roman tried to balance the difference in the person Marvin Harper was describing and the person who'd hurt an officer of the law on purpose, then left him for dead on the side of the road in broad daylight. A fugitive who was currently running from the law, possibly with a hostage daughter, or worse.

"Did she seem distracted or agitated today at work?" he asked.

The old man walked back toward the drug stock and began exchanging old pill bottles for new ones. He was onto his next order. "She seemed like regular Laura. Cheerful. Kind. Normal."

"Do you know if she received any phone calls or if someone had come in to visit her?"

"No idea."

"Any change in her attitude or mannerisms?"

"None."

Roman stood up from the counter when the bell over the door rang. A woman came in, waved a hello, and walked back toward the hair accessory section. "Did you ever get a sense that Laura had a problem with alcohol? Maybe drugs?"

The old man shook his head and opened a new pill jar. "If she has a problem, she's a master of disguise. I never sensed it even for a second. If I had, she wouldn't have been working here much longer. I don't have much tolerance for that kind of stuff."

"What can you tell me about Laura's family?"

"Kurt is a detective with the Pleasantville Police Department and Nelle is a sophomore at Haldane High School. From what Laura tells me, and it isn't much because I really don't want to know, everything seems fine. Nelle is fifteen, so there's a struggle there, but that's kids growing into their own."

"Marriage is okay?"

"As far as I know. I don't pry."

"Money trouble?"

"No idea."

Roman nodded. It appeared Laura had worked a regular shift on a regular day, and other than having to leave early to get to her volunteer group, there was no real material change in her behavior or her actions. That could only mean that something triggered her behavior between the church and what happened on the side of the Taconic.

"Thank you for your time, Mr. Harper. I appreciate it."

The old man didn't look up from his scale. "Not a problem."

Roman turned away and walked toward the door. As he did, he pulled his phone from his pocket and called Sergeant Baros. "How we doing with Laura's phone records?"

"We don't need a warrant because the husband granted us permission. Only a matter of getting them from the cell phone company. Shouldn't be much longer."

"Something happened between the time Laura left her church celebration and the time the chief pulled her over. The daughter's either with her or missing, but since the kid never made it to school and Laura went to work and the church, I'm leaning toward the daughter not being with her."

"Or she's dead."

"Correct."

"Detective, one moment. Please." Mr. Harper hurried up the center aisle.

"I gotta go," Roman said to Baros. "Call me with any updates."

"Will do."

Roman ended the call and put his phone in his pocket. "Yes, sir," he said to Mr. Harper.

The old man's eyes had turned from cold and uncaring to soft and fragile. His face had morphed from chiseled cheekbones and a pointed chin to something made of dough. "I take pride in minding my business," he said as he folded his hands against his stomach. "I don't pry, and I know how to mind my own, but if you're a man of the law and you're asking me if anything strange was happening with Laura, I feel like I should tell you the truth. It's my duty to do so."

Roman straightened up. "I'd have to agree."

"There was nothing strange about anything Laura did today. Everything was fine in that regard, but I'd suggest looking into a Clare Hamms. I have no idea who she is, and Laura won't tell me, yet I fill prescriptions for her every few months. Laura always comes in with a legitimate prescription and takes them home for Clare. Nothing shady as far as I can tell. But kind of strange nonetheless."

"Shouldn't you be monitoring who you give the prescriptions to?" Roman asked. "Getting ID or something?"

"That's not the way it works. As long as the prescription is authentic and from a licensed physician, I can fill it. Doesn't matter who it's made out to. I've pressed Laura on a few occasions and she tells me Clare is a family friend who's staying with them. But other than the days she brings in a new script, she never mentions Clare."

"Who's the doctor writing the scripts?"

"They always come from an urgent care facility in the Bronx. I'll make you a copy of the last one she gave me."

"What meds did you fill?"

"Rivastigmine," the old man said. "You'd know it as Exelon. It's for early-onset dementia. Perhaps if you find Clare Hamms, you'll find answers to more than one question."

JANUARY 3, 1993

Betty stared at the yellow legal pad her father had placed in front of her. He sat across from her at a table in the corner of the hospital cafeteria, arms folded across his chest, his eyes never moving from hers. The other policeman from Bastrop stood in the opposite corner of the room writing in his notepad. Her father had taken her to Ascension Seton Hospital for a quick evaluation in the ER to ensure she hadn't been injured, but she checked out with a clean bill of health and was discharged soon after. There was nothing wrong with her. Not a scratch or a nick or a hair out of place. Why would there be?

From what she could tell, hearing bits and pieces of official conversation from officers trying to keep her father apprised of everything while, at the same time, conducting a murder investigation, Sofia Bennett—the lady who'd hit Donny—was uninjured and in custody at the station. She was apparently still pretty drunk and denying any wrongdoing. Officers had been dispatched to Betty's house to notify her mother who was at home with their local pastor. Betty knew when she saw her mom that would be the hardest thing. Her favorite boy was dead, and Betty knew she should've been watching over him.

How could she come back from that kind of failure? How could she ever be loved by her mother again after such a betrayal? Her stomach turned at the thought of it.

"I need you to write down everything that happened," her father explained. His voice was still raspy and full of phlegm. "This'll be your official statement for the police, so make sure you write everything. Every little detail could matter. Don't leave anything out."

Betty grabbed the pen and tapped it on the pad. "I'm not sure I can do this."

"You'll be fine."

"But I don't really remember anything. I never saw the car coming, and by the time I could understand what was happening, she'd already hit Donny and it was over."

Her father nodded. "I get it, but this woman has been arrested before for drunk driving and public intoxication. She needs help. She's going to go away and get that help, and at the same time, she'll be off the streets so she can't hurt anyone else. Write down everything you remember so we can get her the help she needs."

"Dad, I don't remember anything."

A long growl of a sigh. Her father looked out the window, unmoving, hands still crossed on his chest.

"She killed your brother."

"I know."

"She needs to go away."

"But—"

"But nothing. You're the only witness we have. Do right by your brother and write down what happened."

Tears slipped from Betty's eyes. "What if I don't remember the right stuff? What if I mess it up?"

"You were walking down the sidewalk, right?"

"Yeah."

"To take your brother to the swings?"

"I was also meeting Mike Schuccle. I wanted to go alone, but Mom made me take Donny. She didn't know I was meeting Mike. I didn't tell her because I knew she'd say no."

Her father nodded. "Okay. Then write down that you were walking to the school to meet a friend and to take Donny to the swings."

She did as she was told, then dropped the pen and looked up.

"What happened next?"

"I don't know."

"The car hit Donny."

"Yeah, I guess. It came out of nowhere."

"If you were on the sidewalk and the car hit Donny, that means the woman drove up onto the sidewalk."

"But—"

"Write that down."

"Dad, I—"

"Write it."

Again, Betty did as she was told, stopping at the end of each sentence and allowing her father to coach her through the chain of events that he believed happened. In that moment, she could've changed everything. She could've told him he was wrong and that although she couldn't quite remember exactly what happened, she was sure it didn't play out the way her father was telling her it had. She could've spoken up, but doing so would've only made things worse. The woman was still drunk behind the wheel. She still hit Donny, and Donny was still dead. Neither her version of the truth nor her father's would change those facts. So she kept quiet and continued to write what her father told her to write, knowing that whatever version of the truth was told, the woman's fate had already been sealed. The pen hit the paper and gained momentum as her father recited what had happened in words that would sound like Betty's. She tried to keep up as he spoke, the ink smudging some of her letters, the pen unable to let up from the yellow legal pad. Her father's anger began to narrate and she found herself writing faster and faster. A person doesn't kill a cop's kid and get away with it under any circumstances. This was her statement, but it was really her father's vengeance. Betty was only doing what her father told her to do. Like a dutiful daughter was supposed to. That was love. That was family.

CHAPTER SIXTEEN

Roman knew that each passing moment was a chance for the case to disintegrate before his eyes. He felt like he'd been spinning in circles, getting nowhere. No solid leads. No motive. What was going on? Where was Laura Anderson?

The Pleasantville Police Department sat tucked in a small building on the edge of town, across from a pedestrian bridge that spanned train tracks running north to Dutchess County and south to Manhattan. Roman had called ahead after he was done at Harper's and was told the chief would be waiting for him. By the time he'd reached out, the news regarding his own chief had been passed to all departments throughout the county, so the men in Pleasantville were eager to cooperate. The fact that the wife of one of their own could somehow be involved, and that same detective's daughter was missing, made it an even higher priority.

Chief Slacks was thin and old. His uniform hung from his frame and his hair was thick and gray, matching his even thicker mustache. He wore a holster with a Colt Python as his sidearm. Roman hadn't seen a Colt used on the job in decades.

"Thanks for meeting on short notice," Roman said as the chief hopped out of his chair and extended a hand.

"No thanks necessary," Chief Slacks replied. "I told you at Kurt's house, anything you need, you have our cooperation. I want to know everything you know. I don't care what it takes, we need to find out what's going on and we need to work together before Internal Affairs gets a whiff and wants to come in and take over."

"My thoughts as well." Roman sat in one of the chairs and the chief did the same.

"You get anything new since we last spoke?" the chief asked.

"No, sir. We're pinging Laura and Nelle's phones. Hopefully that'll get us somewhere. We got a few laptops from the Anderson house and we're waiting on cell phone records from Kurt, Laura, and Nelle. We spoke to a few neighbors, but no one saw anything unusual this morning. The Andersons don't use any kind of surveillance at the house, so no recording of what happened after Kurt left for work. A few neighbors have Ring doorbells, but no range to see over toward the Anderson house. Everyone we talked to said the Andersons are the quintessential suburban married couple. Loving. Close. Laura is a model in the community. She volunteers at their church. She's on the PTA. Always chipping in to do whatever needs doing. No knockdown battles or anything that would cause a neighbor to think they were anything but a normal family. Marvin Harper is Laura's boss over at the pharmacy she works at in Tarrytown. He said Laura was acting completely normal right up to the point she left for her volunteer celebration at her church. Father Glipp said nothing out of the ordinary happened there, either. Laura was Laura."

"Yet we have an attempted murder, a chief of police clinging to life, and a missing fifteen-year-old."

"Exactly."

The chief folded his hands on his desk. "Talk to me," he said. "What do you need to know?"

"Let's start with this morning," Roman said. "Detective Anderson was on the schedule?"

"He was technically working, but he was in White Plains testifying in a case involving a reckless driving car accident that resulted in a manslaughter charge."

"Is he working any cases right now?"

"No, not presently."

"What about the last few he was on? What did they involve?"

Chief Slacks turned in his seat and faced his laptop. He used the mouse, then began punching the keys. "Last three cases. Oldest was a theft of some jewelry left at a bar up the road. A watch, a bracelet, and some diamond earrings. College kid from Pace claimed two men accosted her in the back of the bar and took those items off her person. He interviewed witnesses, but no one was able to identify the men. Case remains open and unsolved." He clicked to the next screen. "Second case was a DWI. Driver left a bar in Eastchester and ended up crashing into a house on Summit. Injured one of the owners who was on the road getting his mail." Click to the next screen. "Most recent case was a string of vandalisms he was investigating. Graffiti and general destruction of property in our downtown area. He caught the perps. Three kids from the middle school here. Trying to be gangsters and not realizing they're only upper-class privileged assholes who don't know right from wrong. They were charged, but I'm sure Mommy or Daddy got them off."

"Nothing else?"

"Nope. That's it." The chief leaned back in his seat. "We're a sleepy town. I'm surprised he got that much action. You were thinking he got wrapped up in a revenge thing? Somebody coming for him and went after his family?"

"Maybe," Roman replied. He scratched at his beard, his mind turning. "You ever hear the name Clare Hamms?"

"Nope."

"Laura's been filling prescriptions for her at Harper's. Some dementia drug. Scripts were written from an urgent care in Fordham. I called over there and they wouldn't release any information, so we're working on a warrant."

"Never heard the name. Did you ask Kurt?"

"I will." Roman stood up and gently closed the door to the chief's office for privacy. "You mind if I ask you something off the record?"

"Not at all."

"Were you aware that Laura might have a drinking problem? Drugs? Anything like that?"

The chief quickly shook his head. "I can't imagine."

"We found a hidden stash of booze in Laura's closet. Kurt seemed surprised by it, too."

"What're you getting at?"

Roman shrugged. "Everyone she knows thinks she's this perfect wife and mother, yet she's able to hide an addiction from the people she's closest with, including the man she's been married to for the last twenty years? Makes you wonder what else she could hide."

The chief was quiet. He looked up at the ceiling as he processed the information Roman had shared with him.

"You think either Laura or Detective Anderson could be capable of hurting Nelle?" Roman asked. "The girl's missing, which means someone could've taken her, but, again, everyone I talk to keeps telling me the family was loved in the community. If they had no enemies, that leaves me with the possibility that she's with her mother, and we know Nelle and Laura had some kind of altercation last night. Is it possible Laura killed her daughter and is running? Maybe she was drunk and hurt Nelle without knowing what she was doing?"

The chief dropped his head and looked down at the top of his desk. He took a long, deep breath. "I know you have to go down that road, but truth be told, I can't see it even with the most vivid imagination. Alcohol problem or not, those two love that child more than anything else on the planet. You can't fake something like what I've seen. I'm talking real, unconditional love. Nelle is their world. I think it makes more sense that she's alive and with Laura or that she's missing because someone took her. I don't think she ran away. No reason to. Maybe Laura knows who has her and she's fighting to get her back."

"Then why not get her husband involved? Why not tell the one person who has the connections to get their kid back safely?"

"Maybe that's one of the rules: no outside help. Don't call the police. If you tell anyone, the girl gets it. I have no idea. But Kurt and Laura love that kid. No way either of them would ever hurt Nelle. No way."

"You're sure?"

The chief looked up at him and smiled. "They didn't hurt Nelle. You can't convince me otherwise."

CHAPTER SEVENTEEN

You're not going to make it. Nelle's going to die.

The Volkswagen's tires drummed across the Newburgh Beacon Bridge. Laura was halfway over the expanse, the raging Hudson River 135 feet below. She could see whitecaps in the water, driven by a wind that tried to push her car from side to side. Traffic was heavy, but moving. Rush hour was in full swing.

Laura studied the horizon in front of her. Interstate 87 North was another ten minutes away. She checked the clock on the dashboard and saw that she had less than an hour remaining on the deadline to get up to Caroga Lake, but according to the GPS, the destination was still two hours away.

"I'm not going to make it on time," she said. Her head throbbed to the point where she could feel her heartbeat in her temples. Neither the Xanax nor the Zoloft were working. Her stomach flashed with sharp pains that caused her to double over as she drove. It was almost impossible to drive. Her body needed a drink. "I'm too far away. I can't get there in less than an hour no matter how fast I go."

"Then we have a problem."

"Please. There has to be another way. I wasn't expecting the thing with the cop and having to use so many side streets and backroads. I couldn't go too far over the speed limit and I couldn't take any highways. I'm coming. I'm on my way. I need more time."

"That's not how this works."

"Please!" She looked at the phone's black screen perched up on the dashboard, her pleading face in the corner, covered in cracked glass. "I'll get there."

"No."

The bridge ended and Laura coasted into the right lane. She could feel a fury boiling inside of her that made her want to scream and stop the car and call the police, but she knew she couldn't do any of that. Her stomachache was relentless, her focus drifting from the pain she felt to the determination to get to Nelle.

"What's the point of killing my daughter if I don't get there in time?" she asked through gritted teeth. "You want me, right? You went through all this trouble to make sure I'd get up there, so why mess that all up with some arbitrary deadline? You murdered Nelle's best friend and put her in my trunk to make sure I'd know how serious you were and that I'd follow your instructions. Well, I am. I'm doing what you're telling me. You've done so much to get me where you want me, and I'm on my way. Why not give me more time?" She started to cry, angry with herself for not being able to stop it. "If you hurt Nelle before I get there, I'll call the police and won't come at all, so what's the point? I've done everything you said. Everything. All I'm asking for is a little more time, which is what you know you need to give me anyway. Please."

The voice was quiet, the static the only indication that the line was still open. Laura kept staring at the phone, waiting for the voice to say something. Why wasn't he responding?

"Hello?"

No reply. She rounded a curve and more brake lights came on. She slowed, but traffic kept moving. As the curve straightened, she saw a young girl up ahead on the shoulder, walking backward, thumb in the air. She looked like she was straight out of an LL Bean catalog. Tan khaki pants, navy blue parka, sneaker-boots, oversized backpack. Car after car passed her without slowing down. She kept her thumb up and steady, undeterred by the lack of driver interest.

Laura passed her and pulled onto the shoulder. She turned her hazards on and watched through the sideview mirror as the girl did the best she could to jog toward her.

"What are you doing?" the voice asked.

"I'm picking this girl up."

"You can't possibly be that stupid. Don't make me kill Nelle right now. I promise you, you'll hear every scream."

"I know I will," Laura barked. "You have to trust me. I'm almost out of gas and I need money. There's no way I'll make it to Caroga without filling up. I can't use my cards because they're probably shut down by now or they're being tracked by the police. If I use them, they'll find me. I need cash. The hardware store took most of what I had when I bought the stuff for the back window." She quickly wiped her eyes to try and make herself look as unimposing as possible. "I was going to rob someone at a rest stop when I got on 87, but this'll do."

Laura rolled down the passenger's side window as the girl bent down.

"Hey, thanks for stopping. I'm kind of out in the middle of nowhere around here. No Uber or Lyfts until I'm further into Newburgh."

"No problem."

She was young. College-aged. Smooth skin, blond hair, blue eyes. No makeup needed. She was naturally beautiful.

"Where you headed?" the girl asked.

"I'm on my way to see my sister in Roscoe," Laura lied. "I

can take you as far as there or I can drop you at an exit once you're at a place to get a ride service."

"Great! You mind if I put my bag in the back?"

The lock popped open. "Put it in the backseat. The trunk's full."

Laura reached down into the small compartment in the driver's side door and grabbed the scissors she'd bought for the back window. She tucked them under her left leg as the girl climbed in next to her.

"I didn't think anyone would stop," the girl said. "People don't hitch too much anymore."

Laura smiled, trying to be bright and cheery, swallowing the pain in her head and stomach while trying to quell her shaking from the adrenaline that pumped through her. "I used to do it all the time when I was your age. I know what it's like when the sun's going down and there's no ride in sight. Couldn't pass you up."

"Well, I really do appreciate that."

"Where to?"

The girl pointed in front of them. "West is good enough for now."

"West it is, then." Laura pulled back onto the interstate. "I'm Laura, by the way." As soon as her name slipped out of her mouth, she knew she should've used an alias.

"I'm Gina. It's nice to meet you."

"Where you from, Gina?"

The girl shrugged. "Around."

They slipped into a quick silence, each of them quietly sizing up the other, wondering how much they should talk and what they should talk about. Laura pretended she was looking past Gina out the sideview mirror and noticed an army-green fanny pack hanging over the seatbelt that stretched across her lap. Undoubtedly, her wallet, and more importantly, her cash, was inside.

"What happened to your back window?" Gina asked.

"Tree fell on it during a storm. Shattered it. Haven't gotten it fixed yet."

"And you're going to visit your sister in Roscoe?"

"Yup. I haven't seen her in a while, so I promised I'd pay her a visit after work today."

"What do you do?"

"Nothing really. Odd jobs. A little bit of this. A little bit of that." She wasn't good at lying on the fly. She cringed at her ridiculous reply. "What about you? What do you do?"

Gina sat sideways, knees tucked to her chest, facing Laura. "I'm kind of in the middle of things right now, so while I'm figuring out my next steps, I have this vlog and I hike around and take pictures for it. Post them on Insta with little stories to go with each one. It's got a pretty decent following. I'll never get rich, but I make enough to get by."

"Sounds interesting."

"What I really want to do is write, but it's so hard to get noticed."

"What do you write?"

"Contemporary fiction. I had this great story about a white kid who was born and raised in the Middle East. No worries. No problems. Then his parents move back to the States and when he's in America as a Muslim, he sees the lines drawn in society and the boxes people put other people in. When he finally realizes he doesn't fit in a particular box, the shit hits the fan."

"Interesting."

"You think?"

"Yeah. Totally."

"I sent it out all over the place, but after, like, a thousand agents and publishers passed on it, I moved on. The vlog thing is working for now, but when I can't get a ride service, the hitching sucks. Most of the time, guys pick me up and they think they'll get a blowjob or a quickie as a thank you. So lame."

Something crashed over the speakers and both women jumped.

"What was that?" Gina asked.

"Nothing," Laura replied quickly. Her mind fumbled to come up with an excuse for the noise. "My phone line is open, is all. I have to keep it open for my daughter. It's FaceTime."

"But the screen is dark."

"I don't like to be distracted when I'm driving. I just listen."

"Is she with a sitter? Is this like a version of the nanny cam?"

"Sort of."

Gina reached for the knobs on the radio. "You mind if we have a little music? Can never resist some traveling tunes."

Laura gently took the girl's wrist and placed it down. "No music," she said. "I need to listen."

"Oh, right. Okay. Sorry."

It was hard to smile and act unassuming. Laura knew her body was trembling and she felt like she was falling apart from the inside out, but she wasn't sure if it was noticeable. The headache was dulled by her newfound adrenaline, and she felt like she might actually be able to get to Nelle if she could pull this off. Different scenarios floated through her mind as she drove. She pictured herself reaching over and grabbing the fanny pack as she pushed the girl out of the car. She contemplated simply leveling with her and telling her the truth. Perhaps Gina would feel pity and hand her the money, but she knew the voice would hear her confession, and that would get Nelle killed. She thought about knocking Gina's head into the side window and stealing the money while she was unconscious, but she didn't know how hard you had to hit someone to knock them out. The steel blades of the scissors were also under her thigh. So many choices, none of them good.

"What's your sister's name?"

"Mary." It was the first name that popped into her head.

"Older or younger?"

"Older. Five years."

"Where you from?"

Laura laughed nervously. "You ask a lot of questions. I feel like I'm on a job interview. You want to know my blood type?" She laughed again.

Gina laughed, too. It sounded just as phony. "Trying to make a little small talk with the savior who picked up a helpless girl on the side of the highway." She reached into her fanny pack and took out a cigarette, popping it between her lips. "You mind if I smoke?"

"I'd prefer you didn't."

"No music. No smoking. Really?"

"But you did call me your savior."

"True."

Laura glanced over at Gina and found the girl staring back. She could see a darkness in the girl that hadn't been there before. She wondered if Gina could see a darkness in her as well.

"I have asthma and the smoke gets to me quickly."

"Okay, but what if I lit up, took one puff, and threw the butt out the window?"

"Then I might have to drop you off here and you can wait for another ride where the driver doesn't care if you light one up. He might expect a blowjob or a quickie, though."

Gina held her gaze for a few more seconds, then laughed as she put the cigarette back in the pack. "I like you. You got spunk, and we girls need a little spunk if we're going to survive out here. You win."

"Thank you."

"But I know you're lying. Just so you and I are on the same page."

CHAPTER EIGHTEEN

Laura held for breath for a moment. "What?"

"About seeing your sister. You're lying."

"No, I'm not."

"Then you're lying about her being in Roscoe. Your GPS says Caroga Lake. You got a man up there or something? Sneaking around?" Gina giggled.

"It's a long story."

"I bet it is."

It was time. Laura pulled off the first exit she came upon and stopped halfway down the ramp. It was a suburban area with trees shading most of the roadway, making it darker now that the sun had almost completely set.

"Oh, hey," Gina said, her voice softening. "I didn't mean to piss you off. I'm sorry. I don't care where you're heading. It's none of my business. I'm grateful for the ride."

Laura pulled over onto the exit ramp's shoulder. "It's not that."

"Well, then I'm sorry about the cigarette. Don't kick me out. I'll sit still and shut up, I promise."

"I'm going to need a few bucks from you," Laura said. Her

voice shook as she spoke. "For gas. I'm almost out and still have a ways to go."

Gina looked at Laura and immediately nodded. "Yeah, sure. That's cool. I guess I could give you ten bucks to thank you for picking me up. It's yours as long as you don't kick me out now. I'll be quiet. Seriously."

"I'm going to need more than that."

"Don't you have a credit card?"

"Yeah, but the police are tracing those."

The sentence hung in the air between them. Gina's eyes grew a little wider. She slowly unbuckled her seatbelt.

"I don't want to hurt you," Laura said. Her voice was still shaking. "I need that fanny pack. I need your money. All of it. And you're right, I'm not going to visit my sister in Roscoe. I'm on my way to save my daughter, and I need gas and food. Give me what you have, and then you can get out and wait for your next ride. No one gets hurt."

Gina held up her hands. "It's fine. I'll get out and you can go save your daughter or whatever, and we can forget all this. I didn't see anything. I don't know anything. Okay?"

"I need your money."

"I said I can give you ten bucks."

"I need it all."

"Yeah, well, so do I."

Laura reached under her leg and came away with the scissors. "Please don't make this any harder than it has to be. Give me your money."

Gina pushed herself back against the passenger's side door when she saw the scissors. "Stop playing. That's not funny."

"I'm not joking."

Gina looked to the phone mounted on the dashboard. "Hey, if anyone can hear me, call the police! This woman is robbing me and threatening to hurt me!"

Laura didn't take her eyes off the girl. The scissors were

shaking in her hand. Suddenly, there was no headache or stomach pain. There was only the two of them and the situation that was playing out. "I'm sorry I stopped to pick you up. I'm sorry you have to go through this, but I don't have another choice. Give me your money and you won't get hurt. I swear. I need the money, and you can get out of the car and hitch your next ride. This'll be a great story for your vlog."

Gina blindly reached behind her, searching for the door handle.

"I like to tell myself that I'm a good person, and most of the time I believe it, but the truth is, I'm not always good. You should know that. I can pretend to be good and I love doing nice things for people, but deep down in my soul, I know there's this darkness. I've hurt people. I've done things that you can't undo. I hate myself for it, but there's no fixing things, right? And right now, I got the cops chasing me, a dead body in my trunk, and the nanny on the open line is no nanny. It's the person who kidnapped my daughter. That's where I'm heading. I'm being honest here. No more lies. I need that money to get to my daughter who is the only good and pure thing in my life. I don't want to hurt you, but I can't let you stand between her and me."

The speakers crackled and thumped, and both women looked toward the phone on the dashboard.

"Betty."

The voice was loud and irritated.

"Who's that?" Gina asked, her beautiful blue eyes filling with tears. "And who's Betty? I thought you were Laura."

"That's him. The person who has my little girl. I'm not sure how many others there are."

"Enough of this, Betty. You've told her too much. She has to die."

Gina's hands still fumbled with the door handle. "Leave me alone!"

"Give me the money."

"Don't hurt me."

"I won't. Give me the money."

"Kill her, Betty."

"No."

"You have no choice. She knows too much. Kill her or I'll hurt Nelle again. Is that what you want? Do you want to hear her screams again?"

"Don't touch her!"

"Leave me alone!" Gina's voice was growing hysterical. She began banging on the window. "Help! Somebody help me!"

"Give me the money, Gina. I have to get to my daughter."

"Kill her."

"Too many people have been hurt already."

"Do it!"

"Help me!"

"Do it or you'll hear Nelle scream again!"

"No!"

"Kill her!"

Gina's fingers found the door handle and the girl quickly turned around, flipping the lock up with her thump and opening the door. Before she could get one leg out, Laura screamed in panic and lunged for her.

"Kill her! Now!"

CHAPTER NINETEEN

Laura pulled the girl back into the car with such force, Gina ended up on her lap. Arms and legs flailed, scratching and punching and kicking with abandon. Gina was yelling in the small car, trying to fight her way to freedom. Laura couldn't contain the thrashing. One of Gina's punches landed under her chin and stunned her for a moment. The girl quickly sat up and flew toward the door, opening it again and falling halfway out of the car.

"No!"

Laura threw herself toward the girl to try and pull her back inside. Without thinking, she brought the scissors down and plunged the blades into Gina's gut, just under her ribcage on her left side.

The girl let out a squeal of surprise, and Laura yanked her back into the car, shutting the door behind her.

"Oh my god," Gina panted, more to herself than anyone else. She cowered in the passenger's seat, taking quick breaths as the pain hit. "Oh my god. Oh my god. Oh my god." She instinctively clutched the handles of the scissors protruding from her body as she stared up at her captor, an expression of shock and fear overtaking the panic that had been there only moments before. Blood spilled out from between her fingers and pooled onto her lap.

Laura immediately leapt out of the driver's seat and ran around to the passenger's side. She opened the door, grabbed Gina under both arms, and dragged her off the ramp toward the edge of the tree line where she would be hidden. The woods around them were dark and quiet.

"Where's your phone?" Laura asked as she laid the girl on the ground.

"In... my pack," Gina mumbled.

Laura ran to the car. She opened the backdoor, slid out the hiking pack, and returned to the girl. Her fumbling hands ripped through the pack until her fingers wrapped themselves around something familiar. As soon as she felt them, she let out an exhale that brought her to the verge of tears. A joy she hadn't expected welled up from within. She pulled out the three miniature bottles of Fireball and stared at them in her hand, transfixed, mesmerized.

The girl's moans brought Laura back to focus and she continued tearing through the pack, finally coming away with the phone. She placed it in Gina's hand. "Take this and call 911. Or, if you can, flag down the next car that comes down the ramp. Don't take the scissors out. I know what I'm talking about, and I'm telling you not to take them out. I might've hit an artery or an organ, and you could bleed to death."

"I was going to give you the money."

The girl's voice sounded weak, but Laura tried to ignore it as she bent down and unclipped the fanny pack.

"I wish you did. I wish you listened when I was trying to tell you what was happening and what I needed. This could've gone a different way. I never wanted to hurt you. You have to believe that."

Laura twisted the tops off the three Fireball bottles and

poured the whiskey down her throat all at once. The sweet cinnamon was like acid on her tongue, but she forced it down, so thankful to have found them. The familiar warmth swept over her, her body instantly craving more.

"Don't leave me."

Laura tossed the bottles onto the ground and bent down toward the girl one last time. "I have to go. When the police find you, tell them what happened. Tell them the truth."

The girl was too weak to stay conscious. Laura took the phone and dialed 911 herself. She placed it back on Gina's chest as the operator connected the call, then ran back to the car.

Everything was quiet. No radio. No voice on the phone. No roar of traffic around her. Laura sat in the driver's seat, dazed and stunned, the Fireball settling her stomach a bit and dulling her headache. She absently traced her fingers over the scratches on her arm that Nelle had given her and suddenly remembered why they'd been fighting. Nelle had been trying to sneak out to a party with a new group of kids she'd started hanging around with. The word on the street had been the kids were into coke and there was a rumor that one sold meth. Of course, no one had any proof of this, but as a parent, proof was not a necessary ingredient to concoct fact. Rumor was all she needed, and there was no way she would let Nelle get involved with kids like that and end up on the same road she'd been down herself. When she put her foot down, Nelle had tried sneaking out, and Laura had happened to catch her. One thing led to another, and suddenly Laura was falling into the vanity and smashing the mirror, shattering it as she watched Nelle run back into her room and lock the door behind her. All that seemed so silly now. So long ago.

Laura let go of her arm and leaned forward, certain she was either going to puke or pass out. Instead, a scream bellowed from deep within the darkest reaches of her soul. It surfaced quickly, exploding outward until she felt the strain and pressure in her throat and behind her eyes. The shock of what she'd done, and what she'd been doing since that goddamned phone starting ringing in her glovebox, had lit a fire that she feared could not be put out again. She did it all for Nelle, but that didn't make things any better. She was caught in a horror movie. The scariest one she'd ever seen.

Laura finally sat back and put the car in gear, driving down the remainder of the off-ramp, crossing the road, and getting back on the interstate. As she drove, she unzipped the fanny pack and dug through it. Cigarettes, lighter, ID, two credit cards, and a small roll of bills. She took the rubber band off the roll and spread the money out. It looked like it could be a couple of hundred dollars in twenties, tens, and fives. Enough for gas and something to eat.

"Is she dead?" the voice asked.

"She's dead," Laura lied. She looked over at the blood that filled the center console and passenger seat. Some of it had gotten on her blouse and hands. "I must've caught an artery. She's gone."

"You see that? You are a killer. It's part of you. Always has been."

"I guess I am." Laura could feel more tears coming, but she choked them down and stared straight ahead. She knew if she started crying, she would lose all of the control she'd been trying to maintain since the phone rang in the glove compartment earlier that afternoon. She knew if she lost control, the world would swallow her whole. The anguish in her heart had to be contained for now. She couldn't think about the girl bleeding to death by the side of the road or the cop she'd killed earlier. She couldn't think about the fact that despite trying to convince herself and others that she was a good person, she was not. She was evil. She robbed and hurt innocent girls not much older than her own daughter. She killed men who were only trying to be good Samaritans. She'd taken two lives to save one. How was that fair? How could she justify that? She promised herself that when everything was done and Nelle was safe, she'd turn herself in and take whatever consequences were ahead. It would be the last lesson she'd teach her daughter: actions had consequences. There was no other way. She wondered if she'd even be alive to offer this lesson, then quickly dismissed the thought. She had to focus on getting to the house. No more tears. No more breakdowns. She couldn't afford to fall apart.

"You're not going to make it," the voice said, cutting into her thoughts.

Laura shook her head. "No, I'm not. But you'll wait. I know you will. You want me, not Nelle. You're waiting for me, and I'm coming. Let me get gas and get back on the road, and I'll be there." She took a breath. "And I'll give you this in the meantime. I'm Betty. I'm Betty and I'm coming for my daughter."

The voice was silent for a moment. "Where are the scissors?"

"In the girl."

"Are you lying to me?"

"No. I promise."

"Show me your hands and your lap."

Laura lifted her hands in front of the camera, then took the phone from the mount and showed him her lap and the passenger's side seat.

"Good. Consider your time extended. Betty."

JANUARY 21, 1993

Everyone kept telling them how handsome Donny looked and how pretty the flowers were and how he was an angel now, looking after them all from heaven. Betty played with the white fringe on the edge of the black dress her mother had made her wear and watched as her father thanked each person for coming to pay their respects. The line of people didn't seem to end. Everyone from town and police officers from all over the surrounding departments came to offer their condolences. Mike Schuccle came, too. He shook her father's hand and offered his condolences to her mother, but when he came to talk to Betty, she turned away, unable to face him. He left without another word. She wasn't sure if she could ever talk to him again.

Her father tried so hard to stay upright and smile as he greeted each person, but she could see he was aging before her eyes. His skin looked pale. His hair was a bit askew, and his suit was a little big on him. He kept smiling and shaking hands, and she knew he was dying inside.

The service was nice and awful at the same time. While her father greeted people at the entrance to the viewing room, her mother sat next to her in the front row of chairs, facing her brother's casket, unmoving and silent. She didn't acknowledge anyone who came. She didn't move or smile or cry or wipe her nose with the tissue she clutched. She was a statue sitting where the funeral director had placed her at the beginning of the wake, and she'd stayed put ever since. Betty could smell the fruity perfume her mother always wore, but she dared not look at her. The absolute devastation she saw behind her gray eyes earlier at the house scared Betty, making her mother seem more specter than human. Danny's death had aged her ten years in ten days.

An older woman approached and stood over Betty. She had saggy skin that drooped off of her checks and chin. Faded blue eyes stared at her, red around the edges. She smelled of dampness and cigarettes. Betty smiled to be polite.

"My name is June," the old woman said. "I was Donny's teacher."

"Hi."

"I'm so sorry for your loss. I don't know what else to say. Your brother was a wonderful young man. This is such a tragedy."

"Thank you."

"I'm going to miss him very much."

"Thank you."

Betty wished she could say something else, but what else was there to say? You thank the people for coming and move on. That was the drill, but the old woman lingered, as if she wanted to keep talking.

"I'll keep your family in my prayers."

"Thank you."

Betty closed her eyes for a moment, fighting off a new set of tears. She hoped by the time she opened them, the woman would be gone. Scenes of that day flashed in her mind's eye.

The yelling. The screeching of tires. The metallic thump when the car hit her brother. The sirens and adults yelling and crying. She felt the seed of a headache starting to take root. That would be her fifth one since Donny's accident. The last one actually made her throw up.

Betty opened her eyes and the woman was gone, replaced by a police officer dressed in his uniform. He was bent over saying something to her.

"Thank you."

When he left, she focused on a set of bright orange marigolds in the corner of the room. She'd never seen a flower color like that before and was surprised at how big they were. More people came to stand in front of her.

"Thank you."

From where she sat, Betty could see the profile of her brother's face peeking out from the top of the casket. He looked like he was sleeping. So peaceful and calm. Smooth skin. His brown hair was parted and combed to the side like their mother did it each day before school. He was dressed in a blue suit that looked like it fit perfectly. A yellow tie was snug under his chin. He was handsome. Her little brother would've been a catch one day. If only.

The casket was centered in front of the room, alone except for the wall of multicolored flowers behind it. Red, white, yellow, pink, and that magical orange. It was light blue with silver on it that shined in the light. Blue was Donny's favorite color, and as soon as her mother saw it in the funeral director's catalog, she picked it.

Betty stood up before the next person could come tell her how sorry they were for their loss. She wanted to see her brother and take a closer look at the flowers. Anything to take a break from the sad faces and teary eyes that kept coming, one after the other, in their endless parade of condolences and sadness. As soon as she moved, a hand gripped her wrist and squeezed.

"Where do you think you're going?"

Her mother's voice was nothing more than a whisper, but the vitriol behind it was unmistakable. She continued staring straight ahead, still frozen but for her hand that held onto Betty's wrist and her lips that hardly moved.

"I want to see Donny."

"Sit down."

"But I want to see him."

Her mother turned her head to face her. The look behind those gray eyes was pure hatred. It could be mistaken for nothing else. "You sit and you thank every person who comes through that door because you're the reason we're here." Her voice began to grow louder. "You should've been watching him. You were supposed to make sure he was safe."

"Mom, stop."

The whispers and soft talking ceased and the room grew quiet besides the piano music that played through hidden speakers. Betty could feel everyone staring at her. She could feel their eyes judging her. Hating her.

Spit flew from her mother's mouth as she spoke, landing on Betty's face. "Meeting some boy when you should've been watching your brother. You're the reason we're here. You're the reason my son is dead. You killed my Donny!"

Betty knew the others would agree with her mother. She should've been watching Donny. She shouldn't have done what she did. Her mother was right. They were there because of her.

"You killed my boy!"

Betty's father ran to the front of the room and grabbed her mother's arm, pulling her grip from Betty's wrist. "That's enough, Clare."

He guided her mother out of her chair, and as her mother

reached her feet, she collapsed into her husband, wailing uncontrollably until several officers helped them out of the viewing room. Betty sat alone, crying and knowing everything her mother said was true. She had killed her brother. It was all her fault. It was...

A police officer came and sat next to her. He was dressed in his formal blues with his hat tucked respectfully under his arm. Betty looked up at him and he smiled. He looked much older than she was, but younger than her dad. Pink skin, bright red hair, matching red mustache. He leaned in next to her and whispered, "Don't pay any attention to your mom. She's really sad and doesn't know what she's saying."

Betty wiped her eyes and nodded.

The officer reached into his pocket and came away with a small metal container. "How old are you now?" he asked.

"Sixteen," Betty replied.

"Old enough." The officer quickly unscrewed the top and pushed it into her chest. "Have a treat. It'll make you feel better. Help you get through the day."

Betty hesitated for a moment, but when he pushed it against her again, she did as she was told. As soon as she tasted what was inside the container, she coughed and almost spat it out. The officer chuckled and rubbed her back until the coughing ended.

"That tastes awful."

"Most medicine does. But you'll feel better. I promise. Have another sip. You need it."

Betty held the container up to her lips and tensed as the liquor hit her lips. She felt the burn in her chest and stomach and focused on the giant orange marigolds that had first caught her eye to keep from coughing and gagging again. The flowers were so beautiful. So unique. Like her brother had once been. She focused on the marigolds and felt her head grow woozy. She liked the feeling. It was something she'd never experienced before, and suddenly she felt a bit removed from the pain and anguish everyone else around her was feeling. The medicine wasn't a bad thing. It helped her. In fact, it wasn't medicine at all.

It was a treat.

And she wanted more.

CHAPTER TWENTY

Nelle was on the second floor now, cowered against her bed, hugging one of the posts, hiding her face behind the thin, wrought iron column. Handcuffs held her in place, one end fastened to her tiny wrist, the other around the spindles in the headboard. He could see her in the light now. Round face, pudgy cheeks, freckles so perfect they looked like they were painted on. Her hair was dark and curly, falling in front of her face. Her eyes were green and wide. Her bottom lip trembled. So fragile. It broke his heart to see her cowering like that.

"How you holding up?"

The girl didn't answer.

"Your grandma's sleeping. Before you let your imagination start running away, I didn't do anything bad. I gave her something to keep her calm, that's all. She's resting now."

"Please don't hurt me," Nelle whispered. Her voice was an octave higher in her terror.

"I won't. That part's done. You're safe." He stepped further into the room. "But it does look like things are going off the rails a bit. I think we're going to have to move. Your mom's made a mess of things and put you in danger."

"My mom would never put me in danger. She'd never hurt me."

"I know that's what you like to think, but trust me, there's things you don't know about your mom. You saw the bag from her pharmacy, right?"

The girl nodded.

"Your grandma's got pills from the same place. That's how I know she's the lady we've been looking for." He stopped at the edge of her bed and bent down. "I know it hurts to hear the truth about the woman you looked up to all your life, but the fact is, she lies. She lied about your grandma, and she's lied about who she was in a past life. She lies about being this great mom and loving wife and all that. She lied to your dad when she married him and became Laura Anderson. Lied about growing up in Florida. If you stop and think about it, I'm the only one who's been telling you the truth. Your mom has her demons. Always has. Hell, I just watched her stab a girl only a few years older than you. Stabbed her in the stomach with a pair of scissors, then stole her money."

Nelle shook her head, tears falling from her pretty, round eyes. "No way. Not my mom."

He held up his right hand. "I swear to God. She picked up this girl who was hitchhiking, drove her off an exit ramp, demanded her money, and when the girl tried to get out of the car, your mother stabbed her with a pair of scissors. She dragged her out of her car, took her money, then drove away and left her there to die. I saw the whole thing."

Again, Nelle shook her head, and this time, her hair flew away from her face and he could clearly see the fear. He straightened up and eased himself down on the edge of her bed.

"You don't have to be scared of me. I ain't gonna hurt you, and I'll never lie to you. I don't *want* to hurt you. Your mom's making me."

"Where's my dad?"

"This isn't about your dad. From what I can tell, he's a good man, so I have no beef with him. This is only about your mom."

"Why are you doing this?" Nelle asked. Her voice was soft, exasperated. "We don't have money for a ransom. We're not rich."

He looked past the girl and out the window. It was getting properly dark now. The sun was almost gone. "This has nothing to do with money."

"Then what is it about? What did my mom do to you?"

A sigh.

"You love your mom, right?"

"Yes."

"More than anything else in the world?"

"Yes."

"When you're sick or scared or feeling like you need a hug or something special from some*one* special, you get it from your mom, right?"

"Yes."

He smiled. "That's because moms are the best. Yours may be a liar, but she's the one you go to for comfort. I told you before that my mom died. I was only seven. My sister never even knew her. She was only one."

Nelle said nothing.

"Did you know your mother used to live in Texas?"

A slight shake of the head. "No."

"Did you know she was a nurse there in a hospital?"

"No."

"Then I'm guessing she never told you that she left her job at the hospital in Texas and moved all the way to New York and became Laura Trotz. She left your grandparents and the rest of her family back in Texas and ran. Never went back. Not one time. Even when she married your dad, they had the wedding in New York and she never told her parents about it until years after. Do you know why?"

Nelle shook her head.

He gazed back at the girl. "She ran away from Texas because she killed my mother. And that, little lady, is what all this has to do with. Your mom killed my mom."

"That's not true."

"It is." His smile reappeared. "I told you I don't lie. I'm telling you the truth. Your grandpa never even got a chance to meet you, and your grandma doesn't know who you are. It's sad, really." He leaned in a bit further. "Would you like to meet your grandma? Properly, I mean, when she wakes up? She can tell you what happened. Prove I'm not lying."

Nelle looked away as confusion turned to questioning. She shook her head, but at the same time, he could tell she was thinking about it.

"I'm going to tell you everything," he whispered. "You'll see that I'm not the bad guy. It's your mom. It was always your mom."

CHAPTER TWENTY-ONE

Kurt hurried down the stairs, his feet moving faster than the rest of his body could keep up with. "Have you seen my watch?"

Laura watched him scurry across the living room, his uniform shirt unbuttoned and open, his toned chest and olive skin peeking through as he made his way over to the coffee. His hair was still damp, his ass looked as good as it did the day they'd first met. The man didn't seem to age except for the few strains of gray she could see poking through the darkness on the sides of his head. He still looked like the high school graduation photo his mother had hanging in her family room.

"I'm guessing you checked by your wallet and keys?"

"Yeah, I took it upstairs last night to fix the date and I thought I left it in the bathroom, but now I can't find it."

"No idea, hon. Sorry."

They'd been married for three years and still living in Kurt's apartment on North Avenue in New Rochelle. It had been a whirlwind courtship straight out of a romance novel. They'd met after she and her friend were robbed at gunpoint on Arthur Avenue in the Bronx. He'd been the responding officer and took her statement. There were immediate sparks, but under the circumstances, it seemed inappropriate for either of them to make a first move. After a few days passed, Kurt called under the guise of his required follow-up, and that turned into a half-hour conversation which concluded with her agreeing to meet him for a drink. One drink turned into one date that turned into one marriage proposal and one New York wedding. It had been the first time in a long time that she'd felt truly happy, and she worked hard to make things seem as fresh and new and full of wonder as ever.

"I'm going to be late." Kurt crossed back into the kitchen, opening cabinets and sliding out drawers. "The sarge said 95 was a mess. I need to leave now or I won't make my shift."

"Go," Laura said. "I'll look for your watch while you're gone. You can go one day without it."

"I guess I'll have to." He stood in front of the mirror in the hall and began buttoning his shirt.

"I know this is out of the blue," Laura said as she yanked the pot of coffee from the percolator and poured them each a cup. "But do you think we're outgrowing this apartment?"

A shrug. "I haven't really thought about it. Figured it's a pretty easy commute for me into Manhattan and it's just as easy for you with the medical billing office in White Plains."

"I'm not talking about the location. I mean the size of the place. The square footage. You think it's getting tight in here? One bedroom. One bath. I feel cooped up sometimes, like I need some room to stretch out."

Kurt tucked his shirt into his pants. "Let's talk about it tonight when I don't have to run out the door. I guess we could start poking around to look at different places. Makes sense to buy something and build a little equity instead of throwing our money away each month renting."

"I think it's time."

They met in the middle of the kitchen and he took his travel mug while planting a gentle kiss on the lips. He pulled her into him, and that was what she loved so much. Even after three years being married, there was never a quick peck on the top of the head and the promise to call later as he ran out the door. He always took a moment and kissed her like she deserved to be kissed. Like she was worthy of his love. Every day. "I love you," he said.

Laura smiled and tapped the cleft on his chin with her finger. "Not as much as I love you. Have a good day and be careful."

"I will."

She waited until he got to the door, trying so hard to suppress her smile as she opened the stove, took out his watch, and placed it on the small table next to the window. "Hey, your watch!"

"You found it?" Footsteps coming back into the apartment. "How the hell did I miss it? I was—"

She watched him stop, stare, and slowly approach it as if it might jump up and bite him. His Adam's apple bobbed once as he swallowed, reaching ever so slowly toward the watch and the yellow pacifier attached to the watchband. He took it off the table and examined it, turning it over in his hand, looking up at her with a smile that was made of pure joy.

"You're going to be a daddy," Laura whispered as she slipped her arms around her husband and leaned her head on his shoulder. "The best one ever."

Kurt began to laugh. "I can't believe it!"

"Believe it. I'm already two months in. I found out yesterday."

He spun around in place, yelping and pumping his fist. They'd been trying, but not intently. They figured if it happened, it happened. Now, it had happened.

Kurt stopped. "This place is small, isn't it?"

"Too small for a family."

"We need a house."

"Yes, we do."

"A house with a yard and a tire swing, and maybe we can get a pool and a barbecue area."

Laura laughed. "One thing at a time, sir. Let's start with where we want to live and go from there."

Kurt kissed her again, deep and long. "I love you so much."

"I love you, too."

"I'm sorry to mess this moment up, but I really have to go to work."

"No, you don't," Laura replied, giggling like a little girl. "I already cleared it with McKeary. You have the day off. Today, you're all mine."

Kurt nodded knowingly. "Wow, you're really sneaky. Like, really sneaky. Should I be concerned?"

"Never. Not with us."

"You're better than advertised. You know that?"

"Exceeding expectations isn't really my thing, but I'll take the win this time."

"Yes, take the win," Kurt said. "This one is all yours."

The sun was gone now, the interstate dark with only headlights dotting the north and southbound lanes. Laura found herself dozing in and out of the present, her mind wandering for stretches of time before waking up to realize she'd driven for miles on autopilot. The adrenaline that had surged with the hitchhiker had worn off, replaced by thoughts of what'd she'd done to that poor girl and what else she'd be willing to do to get her daughter back. Her brain tried to compartmentalize what had happened, but she was in a fog that she could not find her way out of. She thought more about that day she'd told Kurt they were having a baby. They'd both been so full of hope for the future. She felt normal than. Not an addict. Not a woman with a past that left scars. Just a simple, soon-to-be mom with hopes and fears and excitement and anxiety. She'd give anything to go back to that time and hang onto it a bit longer. She liked herself back then, even with her flaws.

A blue road sign indicating gas and a rest stop appeared in her headlights. One mile ahead. Laura adjusted herself in her seat and cleared her burning throat.

"I think we're far enough away from the girl," she said. "I need to stop and get gas. I'm going to get something to eat, too."

There were a few moments of silence before the voice replied. "You can get gas, but you're not going into the store."

"I have to eat, and I have to go to the bathroom."

"There are too many cameras. Go to the bathroom behind the building. I don't care if you're hungry. Get the gas and go."

She pulled off the ramp and followed the road into the rest stop.

"Pull around somewhere in the back where you're hidden."

"I'm serious," she said. "This isn't a ploy. I haven't eaten anything since this morning. I didn't have lunch because I had to run to my church event, and I never ate there. I feel faint. I need to eat."

"I don't want you on camera."

"No one's looking for me all the way up here, and no one knows where I'm going. I don't even know where I'm going. I'll rush in and out. Please."

The speakers crackled for what seemed like forever. "Get the food first and then the gas. Make it quick."

"I will."

She drove past the small structure and parked in the rear of the building, near the dumpsters. Her car was the only one in that section of the lot, hidden in the darkness where the overhead lights from the main area didn't reach. She took a moment to check herself in the mirror and fix her hair as best she could.

"In and out. We're watching."

"I know."

Laura got out of the car and walked toward the building with the phone in her hand. She kept her head down, and from her periphery, she could see two cars at the gas pumps and a parking lot that only held about half a dozen cars.

She slipped inside to find a set of restrooms and a deli that reminded her of a gift shop in an airport. There were books, magazines, candy, chips, a wall of refrigerated units holding water, sodas, and dairy products, with a smaller case filled with premade sandwiches. She searched for beer or some hard seltzer, but there was none. Two people were in the store and a small cluster of folks were hanging outside the restrooms, most likely waiting for someone to come out. In the overhead fluorescents, the blood from the hitchhiker, staining her hands and blouse, was way too visible. She crossed her arms in front of her chest to cover as much of it as she could.

The small group of people parted as she eased herself through the bodies, head down, phone clutched in her hand. She entered the women's room and immediately took the first stall. She sat on the toilet and fought a sudden wave of fear and sadness. She wanted her daughter back. She wanted to be home bingeing Netflix with Kurt, holding the heavily buttered and salted bowl of popcorn he was famous for making. She wanted to call out for Nelle to join them and smile when Nelle replied with something obnoxious about never watching movies with her parents. God, she missed them and that wonderfully boring life. Even if the foundation of her world was built on more lies than truth, her life with Kurt and Nelle always felt real. The love, and the unambiguous knowledge that she would do anything for either of them, was like a shield protecting her from becoming inhuman, no matter how far she fell. She needed them more than they could ever need her. Even the simple times were precious. In fact, maybe those were the most precious of all.

Laura finished up and walked out of the stall. She looked at her reflection in the mirror as she scrubbed the blood off of her. She took note of her swollen eyes and running nose and knotted hair and dirty skin, and realized this was the woman that had to save her daughter. This wasn't the time for dainty soccer moms and well-mannered women. The woman she was looking at was hardened, and would do anything to get to Nelle. It was time for her to step up.

A young girl came into the restroom, snapping Laura from her thoughts. She finished washing and left quickly as the girl approached the sinks. When she was back out in the main area, she made her way to the deli and grabbed a tuna sandwich, a water, and a bag of potato chips. There was still some blood on her blouse under her chest, so as she approached the cashier, she kept her hands in front of her to cover it up as best she could.

Cameras were mounted in each corner of the store. Laura tilted the phone slightly away from her and lifted her head up, staring at every camera for as long as she could, ensuring they caught a clear image. The cashier was utterly disinterested. She was a small woman who was too busy talking into the Bluetooth in her ear to notice Laura or any distinguishing features about her or her bloody clothes, should the police ever ask. They'd see her on the camera footage, though, if they ever found out about the house at Caroga Lake or somehow traced her car. It was a long shot, but it was all she had. Between the police chief and the hitchhiker, she hoped she was sending a clear message: *Come find me. Bring backup.*

The woman took each item, scanned it, and placed it in a plastic bag. "That's $11.64."

Laura handed her some of Gina's cash, got the change, and left without any further exchanges.

By the time she was back outside, one of the two cars at the gas pumps were gone. In the distance, traffic on the interstate was light, which gave her hope that she could fill the tank and get on the road without being noticed. She wanted the police to find her, but not until she made it to the house. Being stopped before that would undoubtedly get Nelle killed. Leaving breadcrumbs was a risk unto itself.

As Laura walked to the end of the small pathway and stepped down to turn the corner, she saw a skinny man leaning against the building. He looked old. Thin white hair blew in a cold breeze that swept across the rest stop, an overgrown beard and mustache hiding most of his face.

"Good evening," he said as she passed, his voice thick with phlegm. "Can you spare some change?"

Laura stopped and looked at the man as he pushed himself off the wall and stood straight, a smile buried beneath the beard in an attempt to disarm her. She smiled in return and approached him. Maybe a trade was in order. A good deed for a good deed. She could get her head straight and he could make a little money. Win, win. She knew the voice was watching, but she couldn't pass up the opportunity.

"You got something I can drink?" she asked. "I'll pay you for it."

The man shook his head. "Nah, I ain't got nothing."

"Sure you do."

"I don't. I'm dry as a bone. Just want some cash to buy me some food in there."

Laura nodded slowly. "Let me see what you have," she said. "You might eat like a king tonight."

The man studied her for a moment, then reached into his coat and came away with a half-empty bottle with no label. "It's some shitty tequila. Nothing special. Nothing you'd want."

"I'll give you twenty bucks for it."

"You serious?"

"I'm serious."

The man paused, thinking. "If you're serious, it'll cost you forty."

"Done."

Laura handed over two of Gina's twenties and took the bottle before the man could change his mind. She walked toward the car, cradling it in her arm as she went. She climbed inside the Passat and shut the door, dropping the sandwich and the water on the passenger's seat and holding the tequila in front of her, examining it. She plugged the phone back in the charger and slid it into the mount on the dashboard.

The bottle was so filthy she could barely make out the contents inside of it. The aroma of wet earth began to fill the car's interior and she thought about throwing it out and driving away. But that would be foolish. She needed the drink to get her to the end of whatever this hellish journey was. She needed to reenergize herself so she could focus. For Nelle. This was all for Nelle.

Laura placed her arm on the armrest and was about to twist the bottle open when her elbow slipped and she caught herself from falling forward. She looked down to see what was so slippery, and despite the shadows, she knew exactly what it was. Gina's blood.

Movement behind her.

Laura glanced up at the rearview mirror and couldn't believe what she was seeing.

The backseat had been folded down and Steph from the trunk, still stained with blood, her hair still matted and sticking to the side of her face, sat up behind her.

Only it wasn't Steph. She didn't know who this woman was, but it wasn't Steph.

A flash of absolute happiness and relief washed over her as she realized her daughter's best friend hadn't been in the trunk after all, but that relief was quickly gone as she focused on the woman's white eyes, alive, bulging, wide in the darkness around them.

The woman lunged toward her, and before Laura could

react, a hand covered her mouth. She tried to scream and call for help, but her voice was little more than a mumble.

Laura dropped the bottle of tequila and clawed at the woman while she pressed down on the horn. Her hands were quickly yanked away from the steering wheel as her hair was pulled back to keep her from moving forward.

Laura reached behind her and grabbed a handful of the woman's wet hair in response, pulling it forward and scratching the woman's face as guttural cries of struggle filled the car. Her nails dug into skin and pulled away flesh as the woman squealed and pushed. A clenched fist slammed into the side of Laura's face, stunning her, and then another blow landed in her throat.

Steam began to cloud the windows. Laura tried to turn in her seat to get a better grip, but the woman was slippery from the blood and sweat coating her skin and clothes. Laura grasped another handful of hair and yanked forward, but before she could gain any kind of upper hand, pain exploded in the side of her thigh and her muscles seized. Somewhere in the background, she could swear she heard an electric current, but her body was convulsing from the shock and she had no control over her own movements anymore.

Another shock came and she let go of the woman's hair. This time it was in the side of her neck, near her collarbone. The pain was intense and ferocious, and as quickly as it came, a blackness encroached. She made a final attempt to reach for the woman, but a third shock was delivered and consciousness began to fade. Her body failed her and she fell against her door as a fourth shock hit her in the chest. This time, the pain was muted as she slipped away.

CHAPTER TWENTY-TWO

There was still no sign of Nelle, and no one knew if she was with Laura or not, but the one fact that Roman and his team kept hearing when interviewing those who knew the family was that Nelle's best friend was Stephanie Parson.

The young girl answered the door, and Roman smiled as he held up his shield.

"Stephanie?"

"Yes."

"My name is Detective Estrada. I'm here about Nelle Anderson. Do you mind if we talk for a second?

"Um, sure. I guess."

"Are your parents home?"

"My mom is."

Steph pulled the door all the way open and called for her mother as she ushered Roman inside. He followed her and waited in the foyer, quickly taking in his surroundings. The house was nice. Quaint. Bedrooms upstairs. Living room, dining room, kitchen downstairs. Basic in a bright and sophisticated way. Upscale country. Like Chip and Joanna.

A woman appeared at the top of the stairs. Attractive.

Middle-aged. Dark hair cut short. A bit too much makeup. She looked comfortable in sweatpants and a hoodie. "Can I help you?"

"Mrs. Parson?"

"Yes. I'm Elma Parson."

Again, Roman smiled and held up his shield. "I'm Detective Estrada. I need to talk to your daughter about Nelle if that's okay. I understand the two of them are close."

Upon hearing Nelle's name, Elma barreled down the stairs and stood in front of him in a matter of seconds.

"It's all over the Facebook group I'm a part of with the school," she blurted. "What's going on? Nelle is missing and Laura has the police looking for her?"

"I can't really discuss anything as this is an open investigation," Roman replied. "If I could talk to Stephanie for a few minutes, I would be grateful."

Elma nodded emphatically. "Of course! Come in the kitchen. We can talk there."

Roman followed Elma and Stephanie into the kitchen. Stephanie and her mother were on one side of a small island while Roman stood on the other. He figured they'd know something about what was going on. Word tended to travel fast in small communities, and with the amount of police personnel around the neighborhood and at the Anderson house, it wouldn't be far-fetched to think that the neighbors had already begun to gossip. No one would know the actual truth, of course, but that wouldn't stop them from their theories and innuendos.

"We keep hearing you and Nelle are best friends," Roman began. "Is that right?"

"Yup," Stephanie replied. "Since we were little."

"So you've known the family for a while."

"The kids literally grew up together," Elma interjected. "We've known the Andersons for over ten years."

Roman nodded and turned his attention back to the girl,

hoping her mother would get the hint. "Have Nelle or her parents been acting strange lately?"

"No, not even a little. Totally regular Nelle. I was at her house two days ago and had dinner with Laura. Kurt was working. Everything was cool, like always."

"Any secrets or worries or anything that Nelle shared with you in confidence?"

"Nope. Totally normal."

Roman took out a notepad from his pocket and began jotting notes. "What about this morning? I understand you guys meet and take the bus together each day?"

Stephanie nodded again. She played with a napkin ring on the island, turning it over in her hands as she spoke. "I texted her last night like I always do and told her I'd meet her at the bus stop, and she said she'd be there. She never showed, so I figured she was sick or something. I texted her later on to see what was up, but she never texted back. I didn't really think about it. I figured she was sleeping and then the day kinda took off after that."

"Do you know if anyone else talked to her last night or today?"

"I can ask."

"That'd be great."

Roman thought about mentioning Nelle's schoolbag in the grass on the shoulder of the road that Kurt found next to his mailbox, but he figured that was something his team should have in their back pocket. He knew the moment he disclosed it, Elma would be all over her Facebook group spreading the gossip. He could already tell she couldn't wait for him to leave so she could post about his visit. Social media was a son of a bitch when it came to clean investigations.

The house was quiet before Stephanie spoke.

"What do you think happened?" she asked. "Like, I know you can't share secrets, but this is so crazy."

"I don't know at this point," Roman replied. "We're trying to get as much information as we can. We don't know if anyone's hurt, or if Laura is with Nelle. We're reaching out to whoever might be able to help."

Stephanie began flipping through screens on her phone. Roman couldn't see what she was scrolling through, only that her little thumb was moving faster than his eyes could keep up with. "She posted on TikTok this morning, so at least we know she was okay then."

"Let me see."

She stopped scrolling and held the phone out for him. Roman walked around the kitchen island and took the phone, studying the screen. It was a short video, seventeen seconds, of Nelle. She was walking up the driveway wishing "everyone out there" a wonderful day. Her infectious smile and positive attitude were on full display, something her principal had talked about when he called the school earlier. He watched Nelle spin around, and as the video was ending, something caught his eye.

"Can we replay this?"

"Sure. Hit the button on the bottom."

He did and watched it again, closer this time. "Can we zoom in on anything?"

"Not on the video. You can take a screenshot and zoom that."

"But I can pause it?"

"Yeah, tap the screen when you want to stop."

He played the video again and waited. At the sixteen-second mark, he hit the screen and paused the video. His eyes hadn't betrayed him. He knew he saw something. "I need you to take a screenshot of this and text it to me. I'll give you my number."

Elma walked over and stood next to him, looking at the screen. "You find something?"

"Maybe."

Just over Nelle's shoulder, she'd captured a red SUV coming toward her. Roman enlarged the picture and zoomed in on the license plate. It was hard to make out the details, but he was sure the tech team from the county police would be able to do something with it.

Texas plates in a New York suburb on the same day a girl goes missing and a revered suburban wife starts acting erratically. That simply didn't sit right.

CHAPTER TWENTY-THREE

"Hey, I sent in some plates to get traced," Roman said to Baros as he pulled away from the Parson house. "I think we finally may have something to work off of."

"Yeah, we're running them now," Baros replied. "I'm glad you called. I got a strange one for you."

"Talk to me."

"We got the chief's weapon from the Yorktown officer who seized it at the abandoned shopping plaza after Laura Anderson chucked it."

"Yeah, I remember."

"We ran it for prints. Luckily, Laura wasn't thinking like a criminal and she never wiped the gun before she dropped it."

Roman stopped at a red light. "We already know who we're looking for. I don't need an ID."

"But you do," Baros said. "We got a hit, only it's not Laura Anderson's prints on the gun. Prints belong to a Betty Hamms from Bastrop, Texas. The only reason she was in the system was because she was a nurse. Prints came in clean as a whistle, too. Hardly any partials. Got 'em full and clear."

"Betty Hamms?" Roman asked aloud. "You're sure?"

"Yeah. You ever hear the name?"

"Not Betty, but when I was at Harper's Pharmacy, the old man told me Laura fills prescriptions for a Clare Hamms. Who's Betty?"

Baros sighed on the other end of the phone. "You're asking the wrong question. I think the real question you should be asking is, who's Laura Anderson?"

CHAPTER TWENTY-FOUR

MARCH 27, 2000

Dr. Decker nodded and bent closer. "Sofia, my name is Dr. Decker. I'm going to help you get through this. Can you squeeze my hand? Good. Hang in there."

Betty pushed the cart to the opposite side of the room and placed it next to where the IV station had been set up. Her father's voice echoed in her mind. He needed help. He'd helped her after the accident, and he'd never stopped loving her. Now she needed to return the favor. Her mother wouldn't rest until Sofia Bennett was no longer part of their lives. Without Sofia, there would be no hearing.

The speed with which everyone in the trauma room moved was like choreographed madness. Each instruction was immediately met with a reply and confirmation. Each movement, whether by doctor or nurse, was done without interfering with the other. This wasn't the first emergency Betty had been part of, but she felt as if she was floating above it instead of being a vital member of the team. She tried to block out the images and the memories, but they came, one after the other, convincing her that saving her family was the only option. It was the only way.

"Get the light over here. Good."

Sofia Bennett was bleeding from a wound on the side of her face as well as from her mouth. Her dark hair was moist with sweat and Betty noticed tiny pieces of glass stuck in her curls, shining in the overhead light.

"Pupils are responsive to light," Dr. Decker said aloud. "That's good. Give me a head-to-toe and look for deformations and blatant trauma. The paramedics said she had multiple fractures. If they saw them, we can, too."

Tricia and Pat moved in and began feeling around on the woman's body, searching with both their hands and eyes.

Betty's thoughts wandered. The accident. Donny's funeral. Her mother's hatred of her for not keeping a better eye on him. Her lies. Her father always on her side and never really knowing the truth. It could all go away if Sofia went away. She was the key to all of their suffering.

"I need a CT scan of her head and chest, a C Spine, and a CBC. Let's also get a CMP, type and cross for blood, and a PT/PTT. Let's also check the urine. We have bleeding from the mouth. Might've punctured a lung when the airbag deployed." Dr Decker looked up at Betty. "You with us?"

"Yes."

"Good. Give her two more milligrams of Dilaudid IV stat. We need to stabilize her, and I want her as comfortable as we can get her for now."

There were more calls of instruction from both the doctor and the two senior nurses, but Betty knew they weren't talking to her. She focused on Sofia. There was only one option.

"Hurry up with that painkiller!" someone cried.

PART TWO

OCTOBER 13, 1999

The hinges on the front door creaked in the otherwise silent house as Betty eased her way inside, trying to stay as quiet as possible. It was a little after one in the morning and although her parents were most likely sound asleep, she didn't want to risk waking them. Everyone was still getting used to her new job as an ER nurse as well as the inhuman shifts that came with it. Her current rotation had been four in the afternoon to midnight. Not as crazy as the midnight shift, but prime time for the busiest an emergency room could get. This night had been no exception. Broken bones, stitched-up lacerations from three separate bar fights, an electrocution, and two car accidents passed the time in the most stress-inducing of ways, but she made it through and was beginning to conclude that no shift in the ER would ever be routine, and for that, she'd end up a better nurse.

Betty kicked off her shoes and hung her jacket and pocketbook on the coatrack next to the door. Her head swam a bit from the Smirnoff she'd had in the car before coming in. Enough to take the edge off from a busy shift, like it used to be enough to wind her down after a brutal exam or study sessions for boards.

She sock-stepped her way down the hall toward the kitchen to make herself a cup of tea and maybe toast a frozen waffle. If she could doze off by two, she'd consider that a win. If not, there were sleeping pills in the nightstand that always did the trick.

The light above the stove had been left on, offering a kind of nightlight for Betty to see her way. She walked into the kitchen and flipped on the main light all in one motion as she carried herself toward the cupboard next to the refrigerator, not noticing her mother sitting at the kitchen table, silent and unmoving, until she was already halfway across the room.

"Jesus!" Betty cried as she jumped and stumbled backward.

Her mother looked at her with swollen, red eyes. She was upright in the chair, both hands on the table, a crumpled tissue in one. It immediately reminded Betty of what her mother looked like at her brother's wake, and she shook the thought away. Her mother's robe was on over her nightgown, but it hadn't been tied, so it hung to her sides and bunched on the floor. Her hair was pulled back from her face with a brown plastic headband, but it hadn't been brushed or fixed, so thin strands reached up and out in all directions.

"What're you doing up?" Betty asked. "Are you sick?"

Her mother remained still. "Couldn't sleep."

"Are you okay? You want me to check you out?"

Her mother huffed a condescending laugh. "No, thank you." Tears welled in her eyes and rolled down her cheeks. She brought her hands up to her face and suddenly collapsed into them, sobbing as quietly as she could.

Betty rushed toward the table and sat next to her mother, gently touching her shoulder, always unsure of what to do when she had these fits. The depression ebbed and flowed as the years passed. It was crippling some weeks, almost non-existent some others. She never knew where her mother was when it came to her mental well-being, only that she could never let go of what happened to her only son and never forgive the child who remained. Even after all these years, she blamed Betty for Donny's death. Sometimes she was spared with innuendos and suppositions. Other times, the accusations were forthright and blatant.

"Mom, talk to me."

"I can't," her mother managed, choking on each word. "It's too much."

"What is? Tell me."

More sobbing, her mother's thin shoulders rocking up and down as the sorrow seemed to explode outward.

"Mom," Betty continued. She slid her chair closer and pulled her mother's hands away from her face so she could look at her. The pain she saw was unmistakable. "Tell me what happened."

Her mother shook her head and fell back in her seat. "I can't say the words. I can't listen to myself say the *actual* words."

"Try. I'm right here."

"They let her out."

"Who?"

"Sofia Bennett got paroled today. She killed my boy, and all she served was seven years. How is that even possible?"

Her mother broke away from Betty and leapt up from her chair, scurrying toward the hallway up to her bedroom. When she got to the edge of the kitchen, she spun back around, an expression of fury replacing the sorrow. Her face contorted in the shadows.

"This is your fault," she spat.

"It's not. I'm not going through this again."

"You weren't watching him and she killed my boy and now they're letting her out. How is that fair? The two people responsible get to walk free while my boy is in the ground."

Betty tried to be strong, but the words dug into her flesh.

"She got pregnant in prison after she was allowed conjugal visits with her husband. They said since she was about to give birth and had a young boy at home and she'd been a model prisoner, they let her out early to tend to her family."

"I'm sorry."

Her mother stopped and took a deep, ragged breath. A thin line of drool hung from her bottom lip. "You should be. But don't worry, I won't let that bitch have one peaceful second of the life she thinks she's going to have. If the courts can't deliver justice, I will. If I use my last breath avenging my boy's death, so be it. She will not live in our society without her neighbors knowing exactly who she is and what she did. I'll make sure of it. This isn't over."

"Mom, listen—"

"I want you out of this house." Her mother was calm now. Terse, but even. "I honestly can't stand to look at you anymore, and after today's news, I don't want to be around you."

Betty held her hands up in both surprise and surrender. "I didn't *do* anything. That's all I keep telling you day after day, year after year. What happened to Donny was an accident. That's it. Now I've dedicated my life to helping as many people as I can because I couldn't help Donny. Can't you see that?"

Her mother shook her head. "You can't serve penance when the sin is unforgiveable. Find somewhere else to live. I don't want you here anymore."

Betty watched her mother disappear into the darkness. Her tiny footsteps climbed the stairs to the second floor, and when Betty heard the bedroom door shut, she climbed from her seat, walked into the dining room, and opened the liquor cabinet. She would not leave the dining room until the sun breached the horizon, all the while reliving that day near the schoolyard as her mother's hatred echoed in the quiet of the night.

CHAPTER TWENTY-FIVE

The remnants of her dream—her mother sobbing, the hatred spewed from her lips, the crushing guilt—floated out of reach as Laura woke up. She had no idea where she was, only that her hands were pulled behind her and she was sitting on the floor. As her vision came into focus, she realized her back was up against a radiator. She could feel the warm iron against her blouse, and when she tried to pull her hands back in front of her, she found they were fastened to the base of the radiator itself. Her head throbbed. Her entire body ached. The room was cold.

The fogginess began to dissipate and the disorientation started to clear. Thoughts and memories came back, meandering through her mind. The phone in the glovebox. The hitchhiker. The police chief. The highways. The deadline.

Laura tried to wrestle her wrists free and heard the jingling of chains behind her. More images, like still frames of a horrible nightmare, came into focus. The rest stop. The homeless man she'd paid for his tequila. The woman in the trunk, not dead and not Steph. Very much alive and in the backseat of her car. The struggle. Then the blackness.

The room was dark except for a single nightlight plugged into an outlet by the door. She recognized the bedroom instantly. The two windows flanking an old antique dresser. The botanical pattern of the curtains. The twin bed to her right. The cheap bedframe she'd picked up at a yard sale a year earlier. Without actually being able to see it, she knew there was a wooden TV tray they used as a nightstand on the other side of the bed. On that nightstand, there was a single lamp, the digital clock she'd used in college, and a Bible, King James version.

The coils of the mattress squealed and it was then that Laura smelled the familiar fruity perfume wafting through the air. She looked toward the bed and saw the covers were moving. It wasn't long before the old woman's face appeared, staring down at Laura, her eyes that familiar gray in the shadowy light.

"You're here," Laura said as she felt her body tense. "I thought maybe—"

"I'm fine," the woman replied. "What about you?"

Laura let her head fall back on the radiator. "I'm okay."

"We're trapped in here. This is my room."

"I know."

"You're chained to the radiator and I'm cuffed to this bed. Bastards had me in the basement for a bit, but they brought me up when they carried you in."

Silence came over them, thick in the dimly lit space. Laura looked around, trying to see if there was a way out. The bedroom door was shut. The windows were closed. Options were limited.

"Do you know who these people are?"

Laura nodded and took notice of how heavy her head felt. Not a good sign. "I have an idea."

"The man walked onto my property a couple days ago. Little small talk. Next thing I know, he's pushing me into my own house and has me locked in my room. He takes me to the bathroom and lets me shower, but most of the time I'm in here or in the basement. Has a woman with him, too. She's the mean one. That cat ain't messin' around. He cuffs me to the bed, leaves for hours, and I thought I was going to die right here on this bed. But he came back with the girl. That my granddaughter?"

"It is."

"I wasn't sure if I should believe him when he told me."

"Did they hurt you?"

"No, they been okay. My wrist hurts from the handcuffs, but I'll live. Fact is, the man let me meet Nelle, which was nice. Fine young lady. I think they're treating her good, far as I can tell. Quiet, though. She's very quiet. Except when they make her scream."

Footsteps approached.

Laura stared at the door. "I'm sorry I got you into this, Mom."

The old woman nodded. "Not the first time. Probably not the last. This is what you do, right? Get your family into messes they can't get out of."

Laura hung her head. There was nothing else to say.

"Here they come."

CHAPTER TWENTY-SIX

Kurt Anderson opened the front door and Roman stepped back when he saw the state of the man. He looked wired and jumpy. His eyes were wide and his hair was messy. The suit he'd been wearing the previous day hung off of him, his dress shirt half unbuttoned and untucked from his pants, his ID still hanging from his neck.

"Can we talk a sec?" Roman asked.

"Yeah, of course," Kurt replied, waving him inside. "You got news?"

"A little."

Kurt closed the door behind them and led the way up onto the main floor. "Can I get you some coffee? I made a fresh pot."

"No, thanks."

The two men made their way into the kitchen. Roman sat down across from Kurt, his back facing the sliding doors that opened out to the deck. He noticed a photo album lying open on the table. He could see pictures of Kurt's family when Nelle was much younger. The little girl was grinning from ear to ear, her pigtails in mid-flight when the picture was taken. Kurt was laughing in the background as he spun his daughter. Laura must've been behind the camera. It looked like fun. Better times, indeed.

"You get any sleep last night?"

"How can I sleep?" Kurt asked. He rubbed his hand through his hair and rubbed his eyes.

"You look like you could use a few hours. I could send an officer over to keep tabs on the phones while you take a nap, if you want."

"Nah, I'm good. Even if I knew the phones were covered, I wouldn't be able to close my eyes."

"Yeah, I get it."

Kurt leaned onto the table. "So, what's the news?"

"I spoke with Stephanie Parson and she showed me a TikTok video Nelle posted this morning on her way to the bus."

"Nelle doesn't have TikTok," Kurt replied. "We don't allow too many social media accounts."

Roman took out his phone and played the video Stephanie had texted him.

"I had no idea," Kurt whispered more to himself than to Roman. He clicked back to the profile page and began playing other videos. "We always check social media, but we search for her name. She's made up an entirely bogus profile. I never knew her to be deceptive like that."

"Sounds like a normal teen to me. Pushing back on their parents' rules. Sneaking around a bit."

"I didn't think that was Nelle."

"She's gotta fight with her mom about something, right?"

Kurt didn't answer.

Roman took back his phone, pulled up his recorder, and hit the red button. "I need to record this."

"Okay."

He handed back the phone and replayed the TikTok video, stopping it right before the end. "You see that red SUV in the background?"

"Yeah. Is that who took her?"

"Not sure. But you see those Texas plates? They mean anything to you? Does Texas in general mean anything?"

Kurt shook his head and, again, ran his hand through his messy hair, making it even worse. "No. Texas means nothing."

"Bastrop?"

"What is that? What's Bastrop?"

Roman took a folded piece of paper from his jacket pocket. He studied Kurt, looking him up and down, searching for a tell. He seemed legitimately worried about his wife and kid, and he appeared to be telling the truth. At least, Roman hoped so.

"What's going on?" Kurt asked. "Talk to me. Please."

Roman took a breath. "Tell me about Clare Hamms."

"I have no idea who that is."

"Laura gets prescriptions filled for her and uses your home address for the file. Doc at an urgent care in the Bronx writes the script. Laura fills them when she's at work. Told Mr. Harper they're for a family friend staying with you guys."

Kurt huffed a laugh. "No one's staying with us. Jesus, what the hell is going on? Why is my wife keeping all these secrets from me?"

Roman remained silent.

"What prescription was she getting filled?"

"Rivastigmine. Brand name is Exelon. Used to treat dementia."

Kurt threw up his hands and shook his head. "I really don't know what to tell you. I'm at a loss. A complete loss."

"The plates are registered to a Barry Sicmour from Wyldwood, Texas. They were stolen from his F150 a few days ago. Now we know where they ended up."

"What does Texas have to do with us?"

"We did some preliminary searches for Clare Hamms online. Came up with over a hundred thousand results. Nothing cross referenced with your family, so I was in the dark, too. We thought we'd be digging for a needle in a haystack until we found Betty Hamms. Then it all made sense."

"Who's Betty Hamms?" Kurt asked. Roman could hear his voice getting louder. "I don't know who these people are."

"I'm not sure if I believe you."

"I don't care what you believe! I've never heard of these people!"

There were a few seconds of silence between the two men. Kurt was waiting for Roman to elaborate, but Roman refused to give him the satisfaction of showing all of his cards. He continued searching for a tell until he was finally satisfied the man really was confused. He unfolded the paper and pushed it across the table.

"Your wife took my chief's gun after she ran him down," he explained. "She tossed it a few exits later at an old strip mall in Yorktown. Never bothered to wipe the weapon, so we pulled her prints off of it along with my chief's."

"Okay."

"The prints belong to a Betty Hamms. She was a registered nurse in Austin, Texas, which is why she was in the system. That's a copy of her ID badge from Dell Seton Medical Center in Austin. The picture on it is Laura."

"That's impossible," Kurt muttered. He took the paper from the table and studied it. As he did, his face turned pale, his voice weak. "Laura's from Florida. St. Petersburg."

"These are Laura's prints," Roman said. "Betty's prints. When we dug a little deeper, we found that Betty Hamms graduated from University of Texas in May of 1999. She was employed as an ER nurse at Dell Seton for eight months, from September 1999 to May 2000. On May third, she didn't show up for work, and no one has seen or heard from her since. But Laura shows up in your life a few months later. Isn't that right?"

Kurt stared at him in disbelief.

"I did some back-tracing from her employment records and

found an address. She lived with her parents, Eugene and Clare Hamms. Eugene died in 2020, and according to property tax filings, Clare stayed for a couple of years more, then the house was sold and she disappeared. I'm thinking she came to live near you guys. If she's not living with you, she's close enough that Laura is using your address for her mother's pills. So why don't you save me the hassle and tell me where Clare is?"

Roman waited, but Kurt said nothing. He knew there was nothing that could be said. If he knew about Laura's real identity and the whereabouts of her mother, he'd be implicating himself. And if he didn't, then he'd just found out the woman he'd spent twenty years with wasn't the person he thought she was.

"First we find the hidden liquor bottles. Now we find out your wife is actually an entirely different person. And today, on the day when she goes nuts and Nelle goes missing, we see an SUV with plates from her home state. I think it's safe to assume you don't know your wife like you think you do, and something happened today that Laura's either in on or a victim of. Or maybe you always knew and today's the day it all came to a head. Whatever it is, we need to find what happened, and we need to find out ASAP."

Kurt rhythmically thumped the table as he spoke. "She told me her mother died years ago."

Roman sat back in his seat and pointed to the paper. "Our guys are still digging into how Betty Hamms became Laura Trotz, so if you know anything—and I mean anything—now's the time to come clean."

More thumping. Harder. "I swear to God. I swear on my kid. I don't know anything. This is the first time I'm hearing any of these names. Hook me up to a polygraph. I don't care."

"This isn't the time for bullshit. Cop to cop. Man to man. Do you know what's going on?"

Kurt took a breath to calm himself. He leaned forward and

stared into Roman's eyes. "I swear on anything and everything you need me to. I don't know who any of these people are and never heard the names before just now. All I want to do is find Nelle and Laura."

Roman stopped his recording and stood up from his seat. "Not more than I do," he replied. "Not by a long shot."

CHAPTER TWENTY-SEVEN

Laura couldn't stop shaking. The headache had come back with a ferocity that threatened to crush her skull. She reached up and felt for something that might be covering her face, but there was no blindfold. Her fingers trembled against her cheeks as her consciousness returned little by little. She touched the side of her neck and winced when the pain, sharp and burning, flashed through her body. First, the woman in the trunk had shocked her into unconsciousness, and then the man came into her mother's room and did the same. The wound on her neck was raw and fresh, mixing with the rest of the pain flowing through her.

The darkness she was in wasn't like a starless sky or a bedroom at midnight, dim enough to trip you on the leg of a vanity or the base of a dresser. This wasn't a kind of darkness that eyes could get used to. This was a void, in its purest and most unadulterated form, a blanket of nothingness that stretched forever. She imagined this was the kind of darkness that the depths of the ocean might hold or what the inside of a locked vault might look like. It was so dark, she questioned whether she was still alive or not.

"Hello?" Her voice cracked and she licked her dry lips with a tongue that felt like sandpaper. Even in the dark, she sounded weak when her voice should've been amplified. "Is anyone there? Can anyone hear me? Mom? Nelle?"

There was no answer. Whether anyone had heard her or not remained a mystery. She had no idea where she was, but she knew she was no longer in her mother's bedroom. She looked around again, trying desperately to adjust to the dark, but it was impossible. Was she entombed? Was she buried alive? Would she suffocate as the air in the space ran out? She'd watched the man cross her mother's bedroom, and even though she had tried to fight him off, he'd been able to grab a handful of her hair and whip her head up. That was all he'd needed to shock her. Then she woke in this place.

"Hello!"

Nothing. She was alone.

Laura placed her hands beside her and realized she was sitting on a mattress. She pushed herself up and stood on shaky legs, arms out in front of her, reaching for anything that might help her figure out her surroundings. She stopped when she felt herself press against a wall. She could feel the raw wood, splintered and chipped. She felt around, searching for a seam or doorway, and stopped when she reached the corner of what must've been a window. She blindly felt for the glass, but there was none. Only the roughness of what were probably bricks. It had been a window once, but someone had bricked it up.

I'm in a house. My mother's house.

Laura tried to recall if there had been any bricked-up windows at her mother's lake house, but couldn't remember. Truth be told, she could still be at her mother's as easily as she could be at another house, a school, a warehouse, an industrial building, or an abandoned apartment complex. She could be six floors below ground or twelve floors above it. She could be five feet from a front door or six inches from the abyss. It was too dark to see her hands in front of her face. How could she know where she was?

She heard the chain before she felt its pull. It tugged on her left ankle and she fell hard to her knees. The handcuffs again. This time, one cuff fastened around her ankle instead of her wrists and the other end fastened around a chain. She crawled on the floor as she followed the chain to an old steel pipe sticking out of the floor. The chain had been fed around the pipe like it had fed through one of the radiator's legs in her mother's room. It seemed the slack would allow her to walk about a foot from the mattress, but that was it. She was not only trapped in the room, but also confined to the mattress she'd woken up on.

A phone began to ring loudly, booming through the quiet space. At first, Laura screamed, frightened by the sudden noise as she scurried backwards and hit the wall. By the second ring, she could see the white screen illuminating the space around it. She tried to take in as much of her surroundings as she could, yet even with the aid from the phone screen, she could only see an empty space: walls, a floor, a brick column that could've been a chimney in the middle of the room, then blackness beyond.

The phone was at the head of the mattress. Laura dove to grab it before it stopped ringing. It looked to be the same iPhone from her glove compartment. The tiny spider cracks in the corner of the screen were right where they should have been. But this wasn't a FaceTime call. This was a regular voice call coming in. Laura fumbled, pressing the green button over and over until the call was accepted. "Hello! Hello! I need help! Hello!"

"Mom?"

It was Nelle. She was hearing her daughter's sweet voice for the first time in what felt like forever. It was her little girl. Alive.

"Honey, I'm here! I'm here!"

"Mom."

"I'm here. Are you okay? Where are you? Are you hurt?"

"Is it true?"

Her daughter's voice sounded like it had when she called the first time. She was scared, but focused. There was no time for screwing around.

"I'm here, honey. Are you okay?"

"Mom, listen. Is it true?"

"What? Is what true?"

"That your real name is Betty Hamms and that you grew up in Texas and you were a nurse and you killed a lady named Sofia Bennett?"

The questions were spat from her daughter's lips more like accusations than inquiries. Key words stabbed at Laura's heart. Betty. Texas. Sofia Bennett. Nurse. Laura sat up and tucked her knees to her chest. "Honey—"

"Is it true?"

"Whatever they're telling you—"

"Just say it. Yes or no. You like to sit in my room and ask me question after question about my day, and my grades, and what boys I might like, and what kind of friends I have and what kind of people I can and can't hang out with. You constantly worry about me drinking and doing drugs. You won't let me have a TikTok or Instagram account, and you monitor my Twitter. You say it's because you're trying to make sure I grow up to be a good person, and you always say it's better for me to tell the truth, even if it's something I know you don't want to hear. That's what I'm saying this time. It's my turn. Tell me the truth. Are you Betty Hamms? Did you grow up in Texas? Did you kill Sofia Bennett?"

Nelle sounded so much stronger and more defiant than Laura had at that same age. She had never been as sure of herself or as confident as Nelle was. Laura admired that about her, and it was that admiration that made her lie in the hope that her daughter wouldn't see her as she saw herself.

"It's not true."

A pause. Dead air.

Laura gripped the phone. "Nelle?"

"He said you'd say that. He said you can't face the person you were and that you've spent so much time as Laura Anderson, Betty Hamms is like a stranger to you. Someone you threw away and thought you'd never have to be again. He said that you didn't think you were lying when you said you didn't kill his mother. He said you can't face the responsibility for killing someone when you were Betty."

Laura began crying hard, uncontrolled. She wasn't expecting that. "Honey, you know me. I would never hurt someone like that."

"I thought I knew you, but now I'm not sure. All those stupid arguments we have about growing up to be a good person. A respectful woman. Jesus, Mom. Your name isn't even Laura. And you're a killer. You *killed* someone. How can you lecture me about being good? How can you be such a hypocrite?"

Laura rocked back and forth, the phone pressed to her ear, sobbing as the weight of the secret she'd kept from her family for over twenty years crushed her. She didn't want them to know the person she'd worked so hard to keep hidden. She didn't want her daughter to know her mother was a monster. She wanted her little girl to grow up thinking that she could provide the safety and serenity every child craved. It took so much work to hide the feelings of failure and guilt. It was so exhausting being someone her daughter could be proud of while trying to quell the loser she really felt like. Now it was all out in the open. Exposed like a raw nerve. And it hurt. It hurt bad.

"Sofia had a family," Nelle continued. Her voice was quiet now. "She had a son and a baby daughter and a husband. They had a house and a life and they loved each other and you lied and sent her to jail and then you killed her."

"No. He's the one telling lies."

"He said you were the one who killed Donny and you blamed Sofia. Then you killed her, too."

Laura froze. "Who told you about Donny? How do they know about Donny?"

"They know everything. They have proof of what you did. He said you'd keep denying it because you didn't want me to know the truth, but it's too late for that. I know what happened, and I know you're evil. You're a murderer, Betty. And a liar."

The line disconnected.

"No!" Laura scrambled to her feet, punching the phone to get it to come back to life again, but someone had installed a passcode and she couldn't get in.

Then the phone rang. A new call.

"Nelle! Honey, listen to me."

"This ain't Nelle."

It was the voice.

Laura collapsed back onto the mattress. "Let me talk to my daughter."

"She don't want to talk to you. Not after all the things she found out. Not after all the lies. I'd reckon shame is the one word I would use to describe how she feels about you. Or maybe disgust. That girl's been alive for fifteen years and is only now finding out who her mother is. Not the gentle, caring woman who packs lunches and gets involved with the church and the PTA. Not the fantastic mom who comes to all of her little girl's sporting gigs and works a meaningless cashier job at a family pharmacy to pass the time and bring home a little spending money. No, her mother is a murdering psychopath who kills the innocent, kills her own blood, and then, before she could get caught, disappears, takes on a new identity, and starts a brand-new life. Poor Nelle never would've imagined that could even be possible, but here we are."

"I'm not that woman. I'm not Betty. Not anymore."

"You're always that woman. You know it. I don't have to remind you. Maybe you can hide her from time to time, but Betty's always there. She's a stain on your soul. She's more authentic than this Laura person you made up. Betty is the real deal."

"I hate you."

"I know. If I'm being honest, I kinda hate me right now too. But this is something that's gotta be done. There's no way around it."

"Who are you? What's your name?"

"You know who I am. I'm Sofia's son. Orton."

Laura said nothing.

"We know about Donny. We have an old security tape from the railyard across the street from where the accident happened. You were so cowardly. How could you do that to someone?"

"Your mother killed my brother."

"But you had a hand, Betty. Now we know the entire truth."

"Then kill me. You brought me up here to kill me. Do it and get it over with. But let Nelle go first."

"Maybe," Orton replied. "First, I got a few more things I need to share with Nelle. I want her to learn everything there is to know about the woman you were and how that woman is still in you. I'll show her the tape and tell her how I was watching the whole time you made your way up here. I saw Betty more than I saw Laura. I saw the fear turn to determination, then to focus and rage. I saw the desperation to get your hands on some booze. I saw the way your body starts to fall apart when you can't have any. The craving. The obsession. I've been there. I knew what I was looking at. I'm going to show Nelle the real you, and then we'll decide what we're gonna do."

DECEMBER 8, 1999

The mood inside the car was tense. Betty drove in silence, stealing glances every few miles to find an opportunity to say something that might spark a conversation, but her mother continued to look out the side window without a word. The only noises between them were the song playing softly on the radio, the drumming of the tires, and the intermittent squeaking of the windshield wipers as they drove through a cold, misty rain.

Betty had been rooming with a friend she went to nursing school with for two months now. The two-bedroom apartment in Austin wasn't much, but it was enough to get out of her mother's house and get started on her own. She still called home and mostly talked with her dad, and on the few occasions he forced her to get on the line, her mom too. Just a quick greeting and an assurance that she was okay, and then her mother usually handed the phone right back. That was fine. No sense pushing things. Today had been different. After her mother had exhausted all options, she had called Betty and asked for a ride to the local Walmart so she could pick up her new pair of eyeglasses and her prescription for her arthritis meds. Betty quickly agreed in the hope of mending things, and she picked her up right after her shift had ended. They'd been in the car, silent, ever since.

"Stop the car!"

Betty slammed on the brakes in the middle of the busy parking lot. They were between the main entrance and the garden department of the Walmart Supercenter, an endless sea of people flowing in and out of the store.

"What is it?" Betty asked, craning her neck to see what her mother was staring at.

"It can't be."

"What?"

Her mother was out of the car before Betty had time to react. She watched as her mother hurried toward the main entrance, her arms waving, her pocketbook sliding up and down her skinny arm. Betty pulled over to the curb and hopped out, still trying to figure out what was happening.

"You can't be here," her mother cried, her eyes locked on a woman who stood in front of the sliding glass doors with a baby carriage. A boy waited next to the baby carriage, looking up at the scary lady approaching with wrath. The woman was average height, with thick, dark hair that looked permed. She stared at Betty's mother, her expression changing from shock to recognition and then horror.

Betty finally realized what was happening and ran toward her mother and Sofia Bennett.

"You can't be here," her mother continued, her voice rising. Others were beginning to stop and stare. "Not where I shop. Not where my friends and family shop. We don't want you here."

"Please," Sofia replied. Her face was turning red. She pulled the boy closer to her and pushed her hair out of her face. "I don't want any trouble. I need to get some things and I'll be gone."

"I don't care what *you* want. What *I* want is for you to get back in your car and go somewhere else. Got to Sayerville or Kirtly or Clearview or Austin. Just get out of here. You can't be here. This is my store."

Sofia tried to push past her mother. "I'm sorry for what happened. You should know that. But it's over now. I served my time and I want to live what's left of my life in peace. Please."

"Peace? You're not going to have any peace in your life. Not as long as I'm around. You don't deserve peace. You killed my son. You ran him over like a piece of trash, and you didn't even serve half your sentence. That's what I know. How dare you show your face around here."

Betty made it over to her mother and pulled on her sleeve. "Let's go." She looked at Sofia and swallowed the chill that ran through her. Sofia looked so different from the last time she'd seen her. She wasn't the hulking monster Betty remembered as a kid. This woman was average in every way. Normal. Maybe even kind. A face she remembered as being hardened and gritty was now soft and almost delicate. Her children were adorable. "I'm sorry. My mother's not herself lately."

Her mother pulled away. "Do not apologize for me. Don't make excuses for me when she's the one who doesn't belong here! I want her to leave. I don't want to ever see her face again, and I don't want her shopping where we shop!"

Sofia was calm, a soothing hand placed across her little boy's chest the entire time. "For what it's worth, I'm clean now and I paid my price. I'm sorry for what happened, I really am. You need to know that. But I can shop where I want."

Betty put her arm around her mother's shoulder and tried to turn her away. "Mom, let's go."

"You can't shop here. I won't allow it."

"My kids are here. I don't want any trouble. I think you should listen to your daughter and leave."

Her mother's voice grew even louder. More people gathered

around. "You're telling me to leave? How dare you! You're in my town and you killed my son!"

"It was an accident."

"You drove up on the sidewalk and ran him down like an animal."

"That's not true."

"How do you know? You were too drunk to keep your eyes open behind the wheel! My daughter was there! She told us what happened!"

Sofia looked at Betty as Betty kept tugging at her mother. "It's a tough time right now," she said to Sofia. "Go shop and I'll get her to the car."

Betty lost the grip on her mother's jacket, and as her mother pulled away and twisted free, she fell forward, falling into Sofia and knocking down the little boy. He immediately began to cry as Sofia caught her mother and pushed her away. The onlookers quickly formed a tighter circle as two men stepped in and separated everyone.

"Someone call the police! Please!"

Betty yanked her mother back outside the circle and pushed her toward the car. In her periphery, she could see Sofia helping her son to his feet, cradling him against her chest as they both cried together.

"Jesus, Mom," Betty yelled. "What the hell was that?"

"She killed my baby and now she's here?" Her mother sobbed, leaning against her daughter as they walked toward the car. "How can she be out? How can she be allowed to breathe the same air as us?"

"She made parole. That's the law. You have to deal with it."

"I can't! I won't." Her mother wiped the tears away and pushed away from Betty. "And where were you? Watching? Looking on like the rest of them? I knew calling you was a mistake. You're as much to blame for this as she is. Why weren't you next to me? Fighting with me?"

"Mom, please."

The slap came quick and unexpectedly. Betty stood stunned, looking at her mother and really seeing the hate in her eyes for the first time. It wasn't her imagination. It was unmistakable, and the realization finally came. Her mother loathed her.

She was about to say something when a Bastrop police cruiser stopped in front of them, lights rotating on the roof, headlights strobing. The officer climbed out of the driver's seat and pointed.

"Both of you hold on right there," he said. "Don't take another step."

* * *

"For God's sake, Clare. What the hell is going on with you?"

Betty's father stood over her mother, his hands on his hips, looking the part of a cop interrogating a suspect. Her mother sat at the kitchen table, her hands on her lap. She stared down at the floor.

"You can't go around harassing people."

"She's not people. She's the woman who killed my son."

"That doesn't make it okay."

"It does in my book."

Betty leaned against the doorway that separated the kitchen and the dining room. She tasted the bitter sting of the Xanax dissolving under her tongue, fighting the urge to chase it with a shot of vodka from the liquor cabinet. She had to work later and didn't want to drink, but she knew how satisfying a quick treat would be then. Something to take the edge off. She hoped the Xanax would be enough.

Her mother's anger and intensity had grown since the day she'd driven herself to Lockhart Correctional Facility and parked across the street where prisoners were released. She'd watched Sofia Bennett walk out a free woman and looked on as Sofia's husband and son greeted her. The only reason Betty and her father knew her mother had made the trip to Lockhart was the courtesy call the warden had made to her father. That had ended in a scene in their living room, similar to the one Betty watched now in the kitchen, and a trip to their doctor. Their physician gave her a prescription for Paxil and a referral to a local therapist who specialized in family loss and grief, but her father said not a single pill was taken and the referral went straight into the garbage when her mother got home. What had begun as a grieving mother who was devastated with sadness had morphed into a mother full of anger and rage. Her moods were always on the verge of turning dark. The situation was getting dangerous.

Betty's father walked in front of her mother and bent down so they were facing one another. "You need to stay away from that woman."

"She needs to leave town."

"Yeah, well, she can't. Some folks can't up and move, regardless of what you want them to do. You need to come to terms with the fact that you might see her around from time to time, and you can't go flying off the handle every time you do. I can't bury incidents with the department every time you feel the need to cause a ruckus."

Betty's mother slammed her hands down on the kitchen table, causing Betty to jump and her father to recoil.

"Are you listening to yourself?" she asked. "Are you hearing the words coming out of your mouth? You're lecturing *me* about causing ruckuses and needing to back down and let this woman live? Are you serious? She killed our child, Eugene. She ran over our little boy. It wasn't an accident. She was drunk behind the wheel."

"But she did her time."

"Not enough of it."

"That's not for you to decide. You need to leave her alone."

Betty's mother stood up from the table and leaned forward, speaking through clenched teeth. "You're such a coward. Like your daughter. You should be takin' matters into your own hands, but you're hiding behind that fancy badge on your chest. You ain't the man I thought I married. Not even close."

CHAPTER TWENTY-EIGHT

Time became an unending loop of nothingness in the dark. It was impossible to determine morning or night, hours or minutes, seconds or days. Laura napped on the mattress, disoriented and confused, only to be woken by a fear that someone might be standing over her or that there had been a call on the phone and she'd missed it. It was hard to tell how long she'd been in the windowless, black room.

Movement in front of her. She sat up on the mattress as best she could, and before her mind could register the sound of a doorknob turning, the brightest light she'd ever encountered flooded the space, blinding her. She quickly covered her eyes and fell back as if she'd actually been struck by an object. There was no way to see what was happening. The light had stolen her vision.

"Stay where you are," a female voice. "Don't move."

Laura did as she was told, hugging her knees to her chest as she rocked onto her side. She buried her face in the mattress and inhaled the rot from deep within its coils. Someone was above her now, and she held her breath in anticipation of a next move.

"Please," she said. "I need my pills."

"Shut up."

An object hit the floor.

The light went out.

Blackness again.

The person remained. Laura could feel their presence.

"There's a bucket by the back wall in case you need to use the toilet. No shower or anything, but you won't be here that long. I'm guessing you found the chain and the cuffs, so I reckon we don't need to talk about that."

The woman's voice had that same Texan accent as Orton. Laura opened her eyes, but she was still blind from the intensity of the light. Multicolored circles danced in front of her.

"Are you Sofia's other child? Orton's sister?"

"Stop talking."

"You were in the trunk." Laura's voice was hoarse. "I recognize you. Where am I? Where's Nelle?"

"Nelle's right outside that door," the woman replied. "You want to see her?"

Laura tried to scramble to her feet, but the chain on her ankle made movement difficult. "Nelle! Nelle, are you there?"

"Mom?"

Her voice came from somewhere in the blackness, but her daughter was present. Not on the other end of a phone or FaceTime call. She was only a few feet away.

"Honey! I'm here! Come to me!"

"She can't," the woman said. "You need to make a choice first."

"What? What choice?"

"Your girl, or the thing you really love."

The beam of a flashlight came to life, illuminating the one thing Laura needed to survive. She recognized it immediately. It was the filthy bottle of tequila she'd bought off the homeless guy at the rest stop. It sat only inches from her grasp, waiting to be consumed, silently urging her to take it and rid herself of the pain she was feeling. No more headache. No more stomachache. A few gulps and things could be set straight again. A little treat to get things back on track.

"Your booze or your daughter," the woman said. "You can't have both."

Laura couldn't speak. She wanted to choose Nelle without a second thought. She knew she should choose her. How was this even a choice? But she couldn't form the words she knew she needed to say. They wouldn't come.

"No," Laura choked. "Don't do that. Don't make me choose."

"Come on now. This shouldn't be a hard choice. Your kid got kidnapped and you been doing everything you can to get to her. She's here now. Right behind that door. Just choose her over that there drink and you can be reunited. You can see that she's okay and you can be together. That's what you want, right?"

"Of course."

"Then choose her."

Laura looked back and forth between the bottle of tequila shining in the beam of the flashlight and the door she knew was there, but couldn't see in the darkness. For the brief time she'd been in the darkness, she hadn't thought about drinking, but now that it was in front of her, it was all she could see. Plus, what if she chose Nelle and the woman was lying? What if she chose Nelle and got nothing anyway? The tequila was right there. All she had to do was reach over and grab it. She could get to it before the woman from the trunk could. She was sure of it. A bird in the hand...

Tears, silent and unending, slipped down Laura's cheeks. "Please," she muttered. "I can't."

"You can't choose between your own daughter and some

tequila?" The woman's voice held such condemnation in it. "Wow."

"How do I know you'll let me see Nelle if I choose her?"

"Why would I lie?"

"Why wouldn't you?"

"Choose."

Laura knew if she took the alcohol, she could rid herself of her headache and the pain in her stomach. She knew that would make things clearer for her and she would be able to function again, to come up with a plan to save her and Nelle and get them both out of wherever they were. What would be the benefit of seeing Nelle? She'd get to touch her and hug her, of course, but where would that leave them once the woman took Nelle away again? Laura's ailments would only get worse, and there would be no plan to hatch because her body would shut down. She wanted so badly to see Nelle, to feel her, but she wasn't sure if it would be worth it.

More tears. "I'm a good person."

The woman nodded. "Then show me. Make the right choice."

The pain in Laura's head intensified. She held her stomach and tasted vomit in the back of her throat. She couldn't stop crying, knowing the inevitability of her choice despite trying to convince herself that she actually had one. She rocked on the mattress as she tucked her knees against her chest. The room was so raw and cold. She was shaking and sweating and freezing all at the same time. The pain in her stomach was getting worse.

"Mom?"

Laura sobbed as she let herself fall forward and grab the bottle. She watched her shaking hand reaching for the tequila while a voice screamed in her mind, berating her for being so weak and pathetic.

"I need this," she whimpered. "To get things back in line."

She pulled the dirty bottle closer and twisted the top off, her sobs becoming screams, echoing in the darkness, her inner voice shrieking every obscenity and insult she could think of.

"I'm sorry! I'm sorry!"

The tequila hit her lips, then her tongue, then slid down her throat, burning and caressing every taste bud as it went. She tilted the bottle back, higher and higher, gulping the liquor, swallow after swallow until she was almost drowning in it.

The flashlight went out and footsteps retreated in the darkness. A door opened, then closed again. As Laura finally pulled the bottle away from her lips, she looked into the void of nothingness and found herself alone.

"Nelle?"

No answer.

She was gone.

Laura rocked the bottle in her hand and could tell that half of it was already gone. The smell of dirt and the taste in her mouth made everything seem so vile. She threw the bottle as hard as she could and listened as it shattered somewhere in the blackness. How could she have ever let herself get to this point?

"I'm a good person!" she screamed as loud as she could. Her throat burned with the words she knew weren't convincing as she collapsed on the mattress and a new set of sobs burst forth.

"I'm a good person! I am! I love my family. I'm a good person!"

Even as she screamed it, she wasn't quite sure.

CHAPTER TWENTY-NINE

MARCH 27, 2000

"Hurry up with that painkiller!" someone cried.

"Coming!"

Betty's fumbling hands unscrewed the first syringe of saline and screwed it into the IV that the paramedics had already prepped. She repeated the instructions she'd first learned in nursing school to calm herself: Flush first, drug second, flush third. Flush first, drug second, flush third. Flush first, drug second, flush third.

"Let's go, Betty. We need that Dilaudid pushed."

"On it!"

Betty unscrewed the empty syringe that held the saline and grabbed the syringe full of the painkiller. She quickly screwed the syringe into the IV line and pushed the Dilaudid as fast as she could without overwhelming the patient's system. "Dilaudid is in!"

More personnel came rushing into the room, taking scans and X-rays as they continued to examine, evaluate, and stabilize. Alarms began to go off, one after the other. Everyone stopped and looked at the monitors.

"We have an arrhythmia on the monitor," Pat said.

Another voice from the back of the room. "She's going into V-fib!"

Dr. Decker ran over and stared at the heart monitor. Betty could see the lines of the patient's heartrate jumping up and down rapidly. Alarms continued to ring out.

"Heartrate is erratic!"

"She's going into cardiac arrest!"

"Starting CPR!"

Dr. Decker leaned over the woman and began administering CPR while the other nurses ran around the gurney, calling in the code. Betty watched all of it, half-frozen, the syringe still in the IV, her thumb still on the plunger.

Pat rushed over to the crash cart and snatched the vial Betty had used. She examined it, her eyes widening. "Oh my god," she muttered. "This is potassium. You pushed the wrong med."

CHAPTER THIRTY

Gina Toads lay in her hospital bed at St. Luke's Cornwall in Newburgh, clutching the bandage around her stomach where the surgeons had removed the damaged edge of her liver. She'd lost a lot of blood and was still weak. The painkillers, combined with the trauma her body had endured, made her semi-conscious at best. Roman had been in the room for the last fifteen minutes and had already watched her doze off three times.

The night before, Gina had dialed 911 from the side of an off ramp past the Newburgh Beacon Bridge, but had been unable to speak by the time the operator engaged the call. Another driver had stopped and taken the phone out of her hand to direct the ambulance. The scissors Laura Anderson had plunged into the hitchhiker's stomach were still protruding from her abdomen when she was brought to the ER. She'd been saved, but had a long road to recovery in front of her.

"Gina, can you wake up?" Roman said, his voice loud as it cut through the room. "Can you hear me?"

The young woman slowly opened her eyes and turned toward the direction of his voice. She couldn't sit upright, so

Roman walked to the edge of her bed. "Gina, do you know where you are?"

"The hospital."

"Do you remember what happened to you?"

"That lady stabbed me."

Roman nodded. "Good. My name is Detective Estrada. I'm with the Westchester County Police. We're trying to find the woman who stabbed you. Her name is Laura Anderson."

"Yes... Laura. She told me that."

"Mrs. Anderson is in a lot of trouble and we're considering her dangerous. We've been trying to track her down since yesterday."

Gina's face contorted as she squirmed a little in the bed. "She's not a bad person. She saved me."

"No," Roman replied. "She almost killed you. She left you on the side of the road to die, and she robbed you."

"That's not what happened." The young woman's eyes were two saucers. "She's not bad."

"Okay, then. Tell me what happened."

Gina pressed the red button that activated her painkillers and took a moment as the effects of the drug took hold. "She asked for gas money, and then she wanted all of my money. I told her no, but she said she needed it because she had to get to her sister's to save her."

"She had to get to her sister's?"

"That's what she said. The nanny kidnapped her sister and she had to save her, but the police were after her because of the body in her trunk, so she couldn't use her credit cards. She needed my money."

Roman took his notepad from his pocket and began writing. "Laura said there was a body in the trunk of her car?"

"Yeah, and the babysitter on the radio had her sister and she had to save her."

"Where was her sister?"

"Roscoe," Gina declared triumphantly. Her words started to slur from the painkillers coursing through her veins. "The babysitter had her sister in Roscoe and he was listening on the phone. He was always listening. Except to the person in her trunk. That person was already dead."

"Who was in the trunk?"

"I don't know."

"Was there anyone else in the car besides Laura?"

"Me. I was in the car."

"Anyone else?"

Gina shook her head.

Roman stopped writing. "Was Mrs. Anderson already on the phone with the babysitter when she picked you up?"

"Yes. I said the babysitter was always listening."

"How do you know that?"

"That's what Laura said, and I heard him. He told Laura to kill me, but she didn't want to. She wanted my money. She didn't want to hurt me, but I tried to get out of the car and she had to stop me. I get it, I guess. The voice kept yelling at her to kill me because I knew too much, and she kept arguing with him that she didn't want to. I go for the door, and all of a sudden, she stabs me. Next thing I know, she pulls me out of the car and puts me on the side of the road. She could've done me in right there, but instead she got my phone from my backpack and called 911 for me. Here I am."

"Laura called 911 for you?"

"Yes." Gina lifted her arms and let her hands dangle limply from her wrists. She looked at them for a moment, then sighed and put her hands back at her sides.

Roman leaned in closer. "Gina, I need you to concentrate for a minute."

"Okay."

"Does the name Betty Hamms mean anything to you?"

"No."

"How about Nelle?"

"Nope."

"Do you know who the voice on the radio was? Other than the babysitter? Did you hear a name, or did Laura use a name or nickname or anything that might tell you who this person was?"

"She said it was the babysitter, but how could the babysitter be on the radio and on the phone at the same time?"

"What about the person in the trunk? Did she say who that was?"

Gina's eyes widened and she pointed at Roman. "I forgot to tell you, there was a body in the trunk."

"I know."

"Laura said she had to get to her babysitter and save her sister."

Roman's head dropped. Gina was too doped up to be of any use at the moment. He thanked the young woman and made his way out of the room, walking briskly down the hall toward the elevators. It was obvious he wasn't going to get any pertinent details from her when she was in such a state, but she'd given him enough to go on. It appeared Laura Anderson was being instructed by an outsider to do the irrational things she'd been involved in. He feared the person in the trunk might be her daughter. Who was Laura's sister?

Roman picked up the phone and dialed the department in Valhalla.

"Westchester Police. Sergeant Baros."

"Yeah, it's Roman. I think I got a bit of a lead on Laura Anderson. I need someone to check to see where her sister lives. Not sure if the last name would be Anderson or Trotz or Hamms, but it would be somewhere up near Roscoe. Give some folks up there a heads up to keep a lookout. Send our BOLO to all the state police barracks up there, too."

"Ten-four," Baros replied.

"How's that full background check coming on Betty Hamms?"

"They're working on it. It's federal jurisdiction, so it's gonna take a little time."

"That's the one thing we don't have. Make it happen. Now."

CHAPTER THIRTY-ONE

Laura opened her eyes and felt the hardness of the floor on her face. She tried to move, and the pain in her lower back shot up her spine. Even in the darkness, the familiar sensation of her intoxication was unmistakable. Her head felt like it was floating and heavy at the same time. Her body tingled, somewhat numb. She heard the tin of food drop onto the floor next to her and the door close in the empty space. The sound of the lock engaging was as loud as a shotgun cocking. She pushed herself off the floor and crawled onto the mattress.

"Why didn't you want to see your daughter?"

Orton's voice on the other side of the door cut through the quiet. A wave of guilt washed over her as his question stung.

"I did." It felt like her words were slow and drawn out. She started to cry as quietly as she could. She didn't want Orton to hear her. "I wanted to see her so badly. You have no idea."

"Then why'd you take the booze? You came all the way up here and overcame all these obstacles, and the second I was gonna let you see your daughter, you choose something else. I don't get that."

Laura's heart shattered as she recalled the moment she

reached for the bottle instead of her little girl. She bit her bottom lip to keep from screaming. "I needed a drink to clear my head. I couldn't think and I needed to think."

"Okay. What'd you come up with?"

Laura shook her head in the darkness.

"You needed to think and the booze helped you think. Cool. What's the plan?"

"No."

Orton chuckled. "Whatever."

"I'm going to fix this."

"I reckon this ain't fixable. You're going to die here, Betty. I don't know if you're gonna get another chance to see your girl again. To be honest, I don't know if she'd even want to."

"Don't say that!"

Orton tapped on the door as he spoke. "Yeah, I reckon Nelle don't have much to say to you anymore. You betrayed her trust, and that's one of the worst things a parent can do to their kid. You took away her sense of security."

"Shut up!"

"She can never feel safe again. You showed her that you can't protect her and, when given a choice, you chose something other than her."

"I said shut up!"

"To me, that's the ultimate betrayal between a parent and a child. It doesn't get much worse than that. I'd know."

Laura screamed and tossed the tin tray toward Orton's voice. She fell back on the mattress, crying, exhausted and defeated.

"She's a good kid, too. I like her. She's tough. Has some spunk. You should be proud."

Laura listened to Orton's footsteps dissipate as he climbed down the stairs. She sat up and wiped her eyes, then felt around the floor. She came across a sandwich and she held it up to smell it. Peanut butter on white bread. She opened her mouth to take a bite, then stopped when she heard it.

There was no way to know with any certainty. It could've been the way the wind was blowing just right or it might've been the complete silence that enveloped the space or it could've been the fact that her mind had begun to relax a bit. Whatever the cause, it didn't matter. What mattered was the fact that Laura could hear water rushing outside. It was faint but unmistakable. If she could hear it, that meant under the right conditions, someone outside might be able to hear her, too.

She climbed to her feet and felt her way over to the wall, hitting the rough wooden planks before sliding over and touching the bricks that she knew were the window. The room was so cold. She pressed her ear against the cool surface, fighting to concentrate through the fog that had settled in her head.

She knew where she was. Not exactly, but she knew that sound of the water rushing. It was from the rocky falls at the end of a stream that came down from the peak of the mountain and snaked alongside her mother's house. The falls then spilled into Caroga Lake. She could see it in her mind, as clear as if the window she was pressed up against was made of glass instead of brick. Sometimes when she'd come up to visit her mother after moving her from Texas, Laura would walk the property and wander near the stream. Only this time, the sound was coming from a different direction, which told her she was still near her mother's place—just not in it. She recalled an abandoned house across the stream with a crane parked next to it and other heavy machinery strewn about the property. Could that be where she was? The dilapidated house across from her mother's lot? It made sense. The house was deeper in the mountains than her mother's and hidden better from neighbors who could only be on one side. The other three sides were taken up by the base of a mountain the house sat up against. She was in the middle of nowhere.

Laura kept moving further along the wall, pressing her ear against the wooden planks as she went, hearing the rush of water grow faint when she moved to the left and a little bit louder when she moved to her right. It was hard to tell exactly where she was in relation to the falls because of the limited amount of movement the chain on her ankle offered, but she figured the room she was in faced the stream, which meant she was somewhere on the southern side of it. Her mother's lake house was on the northern side.

The tips of her fingers caressed the edges of the window frame and her nail caught on a cracked piece of wood. She gently pulled at the crack, forcing her nails inside the thin crevice to gain more leverage. She added pressure, pulling slowly instead of yanking at it, wincing at the pain in her fingers and knuckles.

"I have to stop kidding myself," she said aloud. "They're not going to let us go. I can't hide from that truth any longer."

Her fingers kept pushing into the window frame, her nails digging deeper.

"They want me to suffer, and they know hurting Nelle is the way. I can't let that happen anymore. I can't let them win. I have to find a way out."

The chain on her leg pulled as she started to work faster.

"I need to get to Mom's house and save my family."

Just as she thought her nails would shatter, the wood gave way and a large piece of the window frame broke off in her hand. She couldn't see the piece of wood, but she touched every part of it as she examined it with her fingers. It appeared to be about six inches long, maybe even eight. The edges were coarse but sharp. It reminded her of old barn wood and how easily she could get a splinter from the roughness of it. One end of the wood was straight and dull, most likely part of the flat end of the frame, but the other side had broken into a sharp point. She pushed the pad of her index finger down on it, and it felt like she was pushing the tip of a steak knife into her flesh. It was thick and strong, not bending or cracking. It was more than she could ask for. It was more than she ever expected.

Laura Anderson had a weapon.

And maybe a way to escape.

CHAPTER THIRTY-TWO

Laura pressed her ear against the bricks, listening for the rushing water while playing with the jagged space in the window frame. Her fingers pushed deeper into the hole, her nails scratching and digging, pulling more of the frame away. The blackness was still too thick for her eyes to adjust to, so it was hard to see if she was making any kind of progress. She was blind, digging into the wood, dropping pieces onto the floor, listening to the chain around her ankle jingle with each movement, the hum of quiet in her ears. There was nothing else but that faint rush of water somewhere beyond.

Light exploded in the room again, powerful and unexpected. Laura dropped the piece of wood and crashed onto the floor below the bricked window. The door slammed open, followed by rapidly approaching footsteps.

A shadow stepped in front of the light, but there was no way Laura could see anything other than a shape standing above her. To focus for even three seconds was too painful, and she squeezed her eyes shut. She didn't see the taser pointing at her or the figure shuffling closer to ensure they wouldn't miss.

The same intense pain ripped through her body, jolting her

like at the rest stop and in her mother's room. Her muscles seized. Somewhere in the background, there was a metallic buzzing sound, but Laura was too focused on the epicenter of the pain in her chest. Everything else emanated out from there. She wanted to scream, but the current coursing through her body stole her ability to move or speak or breathe. All she could do was wait for the pain to stop as seconds stretched into hours.

They're here to kill you. Now. This is how they do it. No fanfare or grand plan. They walk in and end you. They're going to kill you, then Nelle, then Mom, and then they'll leave and let your bodies rot in this place.

The pain ceased and Laura's muscles went limp from fatigue. Before she had a chance to take a proper breath, she was shocked again and the agony began anew. It felt like forever before the pain stopped, and this time, there was no reaction from her, involuntary or otherwise. The room, aflame in white light, spun above her as she teetered on the brink of consciousness. Warm urine spread across her legs. She was too weak to move.

"Go on," the woman said. "She's down."

A second set of footsteps stomped into the room and Laura tensed, waiting to be shocked again or beaten or stabbed or choked. The inevitability of her death hung in the air. She could smell it, taste it on the tip of her tongue.

The jingling of the chain around her ankle was the only sound. A set of large hands pulled her to her feet and pushed her forward. She stumbled, trying to catch herself and rebalance, but her legs hadn't started working yet and her feet were nothing but a snarl of pins and needles.

"Please," she mumbled, unable to speak properly. She felt like she'd been hit by a truck. "What are you doing?"

"Shut up and keep walking," the woman said from behind her.

They made it out of the room and the light dimmed. Laura

opened her eyes a bit and saw a set of stairs in front of her, narrow, walls closing in on either side.

I'm in an attic. These are attic stairs.

She couldn't see anyone else. Someone pushed her forward and she could hear two sets of footsteps. The woman and Orton, no doubt. They were both behind her.

A hard left brought her down another hall, past two bedrooms. One bedroom door was open, the other closed. They walked to the end of the hall and down a wider set of stairs.

Going down to the main floor. This is the second floor.

There was no furniture in the house. No artwork on the walls. No rugs laid across the warped hardwood floors and no mirror above the crumbling fireplace. She was right. They were in the half-built house across the river. From the inside, it looked as if it had been abandoned for decades. The new owners were tearing it down and starting all over. There was no fixing these years of neglect.

Laura was pushed through what was supposed to have been the living room, through a kitchen that held only pipes protruding from the walls, and out a back door that had no door on it. As soon as she was outside, she could see the sky was dark with rain clouds that covered the entire area. The wind off the lake was cold and biting, causing her to shiver. The area at the base of the mountains was secluded and desolate. She knew her mother's house was beyond the small forest in front, but she couldn't see anything from where she was.

"Mom!"

Nelle's voice pulled Laura from her thoughts, and she spun around to find her daughter tied to a white plastic Adirondack chair. Her thin wrists and tiny ankles were bound with thick layers of duct tape. Her beautiful green eyes were wide with horror and sweat stuck her curly hair to her forehead. Mascara had run down her face and turned to dirt and grime on her freckled cheeks. She looked terrified, but seeing her brought

Laura both relief and regret. How could she have chosen a treat over her daughter? How could she be such a failure as a mother? She'd change if they got out of this. She'd change and make everything better again. She'd be the woman and the wife and the mother her family deserved. And Nelle was alive. That was what mattered.

Laura's mother was next to Nelle, separated by about five feet, tied to another Adirondack chair in the same fashion, the almost identical look of fear on her wrinkled face. They both watched as Laura was pushed forward. Her legs were regaining their strength and she picked up her pace, trying to separate from Orton's grip. She spun around without warning, but as soon as she squared her shoulders, the woman shocked her to her knees.

Everything stopped.

The pain was quick this time, over before it had a chance to begin.

The woman from the trunk stood over her. No more blood or matted hair or stained plastic coverings. She was clean and young and beautiful and strong, her eyes wild with an unhinged fury.

"You're Orton's sister," Laura said quietly. "You look like your mother. You have her eyes and nose."

"Annie," the woman replied. "Annie Bennett. And I wouldn't know if I looked like my mom or not. I had to grow up without her."

"I'm sorry."

"Shut up." Annie held up her taser. It looked like a yellow plastic gun. "This ain't the regular taser I've been using. This is the kind the cops use. I can get you at a distance, and trust me, those barbs aren't coming out anytime soon. I have control. You do what I say or you get shocked. Got it?"

"Okay."

"Get up."

Orton pulled Laura to her feet and pushed her forward again. The grounds around the abandoned lake house were overgrown and unkempt. The brown grass was knee-high and bushes grew wild. The landscape was untamed. She would've given anything to have a clear sightline to someone who could help. Alas, there was nothing.

As they approached the edge of the property that bordered the woods, Orton grabbed Laura by her shoulder and spun her around. She looked at him. "Orton."

The man nodded, then walked behind her, yanking her arms behind her back and fastening them with the same duct tape he'd used on the others. When he was done, he took her by the shoulders and pushed her down until she was kneeling in the tall grass, her eyes fixed on her daughter and her mother.

"I'm sorry," Laura cried across the yard. "For everything. You shouldn't have to be part of this."

"Tell him what he wants to know and we can go home," Nelle shouted back.

"He's not going to let us go, honey. He's lying to you."

Laura looked up at Orton, but she said nothing. There was nothing more to say. She knew why they were there and she knew they were trapped.

Orton took a shotgun that was leaning against the house and made his way over toward Nelle and Laura's mother.

"What are you doing?" Laura asked as panic began to bubble up. "This is about you and me. Come back."

Orton nodded. "Yes, it is. And this is the part when you feel the hurt and the loss that me and Annie felt when you took our mother away from us. No crazy antics or comic book villain ways to kill someone. Just a shotgun to the head for you to watch. Your daughter can die like my dad did. I have other plans for your mom."

Laura struggled to get to her feet, pulling at the tape on her wrists. "Get away from her!"

Orton grabbed a fistful of Nelle's hair. Nelle screamed as he pushed her head down and placed the large barrel of the gun against the back of her skull. "This is it, Betty. This is the moment we've been wanting for twenty years. This is our revenge. You got until the count of five to say goodbye."

"Nelle!"

"Make her pay!" Annie cried.

"Leave her alone!" Laura screamed, frantic.

"Mom!"

"Get away from her!" Laura's mother yelled.

Laura made it to her feet and ran toward Orton, her arms still tied behind her, her sight fixed on her daughter. She could feel the barbs in her skin pulling as the taser was yanked from Annie's grip and fell to the ground. All she could think about was protecting Nelle. There was no plan. Only instinct. "No!"

"Five!"

Laura was halfway across the overgrown yard, the taser dragging behind her like a dog leash without an owner. Her breath was heavy as her adrenaline raged. "Leave her alone!"

"Four!"

Almost there. Laura leaned forward to allow her momentum to carry her into both Orton and Nelle. She aimed herself at the center of them, knowing he'd probably shoot her before she reached them, but she focused on trying anything to protect her little girl.

"Three!"

"You can't do this!"

Movement came from Laura's periphery, and before she could react, Annie tackled her to the ground.

"Nelle!"

"Mom!"

"Two!"

"Don't do it! Please!"

"Mom!"

The shotgun cocked. Orton's hand went white around its stock. He pressed the barrel hard against the back of Nelle's head. She was in hysterics, helpless and bound to the chair, Laura's mother shrieking and crying next to her granddaughter.

"I don't want to die!"

"Leave her alone!"

Laura turned herself onto her back in time to see Orton look over at her. His face was a mixture of anger and agitation, but there was a clear undertone of sadness as well.

"This is on you, Betty," he said calmly. "Has to be this way."

"I love you, honey!" Laura screamed.

"Mom!"

"One!"

"No!"

Laura sat up the best she could, taking in every detail of her daughter's last moments. She felt like she was outside herself—just like when she'd run down the chief on the side of the parkway—as if she was watching something on television. She could hear herself crying, straining, her lungs ripped apart as she used every last breath. She could see Annie grinning like a mad fool. She could see herself trying to get to her feet in a last-ditch effort to take the bullet instead of Nelle, but she was too far away.

And then everything stopped.

The trigger was pulled.

The hammer released.

Click.

Orton pulled the gun away from Nelle's head and stood straight. He looked at everyone as his chest rose and fell with deep, ragged breaths exploding from his nose.

"What're you doing?" Annie asked.

"A bullet to the head would be too easy," Orton panted, looking at his sister, who stared back with shock on her face. "Not yet."

"Kill her."

"Soon."

"You people are animals," Laura's mother said through gritted teeth. "Your dirtbag drunk of a mother killed my little boy and now you're trying to take the rest of my family away? You're all worthless, nothing, pieces of shit. Your family name is a disgrace."

"Shut up," Annie spat.

"I will not shut up. Your mother was a loser drunk who killed innocent people. I'm glad she's dead, and if Betty actually did kill her, then that's the best news I heard all day."

"I said shut up!"

"Get away from my family and go to hell."

Annie paused and looked up at the darkening sky. Before anyone could react, she rushed toward Laura's mother.

"Hey!" Orton cried.

Annie didn't respond. Working fast before anyone else could react, she ran behind Clare and placed one hand under her chin and one hand on the old woman's forehead.

"No!" Laura screamed. "Please!"

Annie looked at Laura as she applied pressure and twisted as hard as she could.

"Mom!"

The snapping of Clare's neck was loud in the otherwise quiet outdoors. The old woman let out a single squeal, then went limp, her head falling forward. Nelle began to scream and fell over in her chair. Orton placed a hand over the girl's mouth to quiet her.

Annie glared at her brother. "We either do this or we don't. You might be playing games, but I'm not."

A fury bubbled up from within. Fixed on her target, Laura tried to scramble to her feet to rush the woman who was still standing over her mother. All she could think about was jumping on top of her and ripping her nose off with her teeth so she could eat her alive until her screams eventually died to nothing. She got to her knees and started to move, but her body seized again as Annie reengaged the taser. The pain was long and torturous. Time stretched forever.

A distant voice. "You can't win this. Stop trying."

Then everything went away.

FEBRUARY 12, 2000

Betty parked in the driveway and saw her father sitting on the top step of the front porch, his back leaning against one of the support posts, a beer in hand. He didn't notice her get out of the car and walk around to the front of the house until she stood in front of him. He stared up into the sky, his eyes glassy.

"Hey, Dad."

He tried on a smile. "Hey, hon. Didn't expect to see you."

"Wasn't expecting to stop over, but I saw you on the porch when I was passing by. I was coming from the mall."

"How'd you do?"

"Good. Got most of what I needed. They didn't have too much for the kitchen, though. I'll try the plaza next week. You don't think about things like a cutting board and pizza stones and all that weird stuff Sam already had when you're buying things for your own place. It's crazy."

"Can't rely on the roommates anymore. You'll be fine. Let us know if we can help. We might have some things lying around that you can have."

Betty walked up the stone path and climbed the five steps

up to the porch. "Why are you home so early?" she asked. "I thought your shift didn't end until six."

Her father pointed a thumb toward the house behind him. "I got a call from Bastrop PD. They arrested your mom after she went to Sofia Bennett's son's school and approached him when he was out playing at lunch."

"She went to his school?"

"She's not in her right mind, Betty. I don't know what to do."

"What happened?"

"Witnesses say she approached him on the playground and started telling him all the bad things Sofia had done and how she was a drunk who killed Donny. Made the kid cry, and even when he was crying, she kept going."

Betty shook her head. "He's just a kid."

"Apparently, your mother kept getting louder and the teachers came over to get her away from him. The principal called the police. They picked her up and brought her to the station. Sofia and her husband are pressing charges, so this ain't something I can make go away. I got her out on a quick bail, but now we gotta get a lawyer and go to a hearing and all that nonsense."

"Has she been taking her meds?"

"She tells me yes, but her behavior says otherwise."

"Where is she now?"

"Upstairs sleeping. I don't think she feels any remorse for what she did. I think she sees this as some kind of win."

"Jesus."

Betty sat next to her father as he dropped his head and cried into his hands. Aside from Donny's funeral, she had never seen her father cry. It made her uncomfortable.

"Mom needs help," he said.

"I know."

"She needs to talk to someone, but won't do it. And I can't

trust that she's taking her pills. All she wants is for Sofia Bennett to go back to jail, and I keep trying to get her to understand that ain't gonna happen. But she won't stop. She's so angry."

Betty closed her eyes and felt the breeze hit her face. "This is my fault," she said.

"It's not," her father replied. "You have to stop blaming yourself. It was a tragic accident. There's nothing you could've done."

"What if I told you the statement I gave isn't one hundred percent accurate?"

Her father shook his head and looked up at her. "Then I'd tell you to forget whatever it is you think you want to tell me right now."

"But Dad—"

"Your statement was evidence, and the case is closed. Remembering something new at this point doesn't do anyone any good. We know what happened. She came up on the curb, hit your brother, end of story."

"Yeah, but—"

"That's what happened, Betty."

Betty focused on two kids playing hopscotch down the street. "I was sixteen, Dad. I was scared. My brother was killed in front of me and I didn't know what was going to happen next. Everything was over before I realized what was happening. Next thing I know, I'm writing statements and giving testimony and you're there telling me what to say. It kept snowballing, one thing after the other. Got to the point where I knew if I went back on anything, I'd be in serious trouble too. But I want you to know the truth."

"I already know the truth."

"You don't."

"Enough!" Her father's voice exploded in the serenity of the neighborhood. "What happened is what happened. End it. I need to concentrate on your mother right now. She needs help and I'm gonna get her some. That's where we are with this. Anything else is an unwanted distraction. Do you understand?"

"Yes, sir."

"Good."

Her father got up from the top step and went inside without another word. Betty stayed where she was until the sun began to slide down the sky and the streetlights popped on, one at a time.

CHAPTER THIRTY-THREE

Orton carried Nelle into one of the bedrooms on the second floor and eased her onto the mattress. The worn springs moaned in the quiet house, the only sound other than the young girl sniffling. He took one end of a set of handcuffs and gently took Nelle's hand, closing the other cuff around her tiny wrist.

"Shhhh," he said as he sat down beside her. "It'll be over soon. I'm sorry you have to go through this."

Nelle looked at him, her eyes wide and wet, her bottom lip quivering. "She killed her."

"It had to be done."

"She was my grandma. You let me meet her and then she killed her right in front of me. How could you let that happen?"

Orton tried to stay calm so as not to frighten the girl any more than she already was. "I'm sorry. That's all I can say."

"Now I know you'll never let me and my mom go. You're going to kill us, too. It doesn't matter how nice you are to me. You can say all the things you want to try and make me feel better, but you still hurt me whenever you feel like you have to get my mom to do something. You're not sorry, and you're not letting us go."

"You don't know that."

"I do. And I don't want to die." She cowered from him, absolutely terrified, as a new set of tears burst forth.

"I'm sorry you have to go through this."

"Go away. Please."

Orton nodded and climbed to his feet. "I'll bring you something to eat soon. Try and get some rest."

She turned away from him and buried her head in the mattress. "I don't want to die."

"Don't think about that."

"I want my mom and dad."

The bedroom door swung wide and slammed into the wall. Both Orton and Nelle jumped from the abrupt crash of wood and drywall. Annie stood in the threshold, one hand still pushing on the door, the other grasping a large hunting knife.

"Get out of here," Orton said. He tried so hard to remain calm, but the mere sight of her was enough to make him want to rage.

Annie sneered at him. "This is ridiculous. All these games and all this bullshit. I'm done with it."

"Get out."

"No." Annie spoke through clenched teeth. Her eyes were distant yet focused, wide and dilated. She pointed the knife at Nelle but looked at him. "We're going to kill them. That's the plan. That's been the plan all along. What are we waiting for? Let's do it and get it over with."

Orton grabbed his sister by the arm and led her out of Nelle's bedroom. When they were in the hall, he shut the door behind them and lowered his voice.

"You need to relax."

"I can't relax. This needs to be done, and we need to get back on the road before anyone puts two and two together and figures out where we are. There's no reason to keep pushing this along. We know Laura's Betty, which means she killed Mom.

Now we can kill her and finally end all of it. Why are we waiting?"

Orton sighed and leaned against the wall. "I need time," he said.

"Why? This is happening."

He brought his hands up to his face. "This isn't normal, Annie. What we're doing here is far from normal. I was a goddamned meat delivery worker a few weeks ago. I was living my shitty life, minding my own business, and existing in anonymity. Now, all of a sudden, I'm a kidnapper and a killer and accomplice and all this other shit I'm not supposed to be. And you're asking me to keep killing. Do you know what it felt like to hold that gun against that kid's head? I didn't feel power or vengeance or anything other than dread. I'm not this person I keep pretending to be. I can't do it. I'm sorry."

He felt relief as the truth finally poured out of him, but as he kept talking, he could see Annie's eyes glaze over.

"This has to end. I want to go back to my life in Bastrop and move on. All this anger and need to set things straight. That's you. That was never me. I didn't even know Betty existed until a few weeks ago. I don't think I really cared, to be honest. I can't do this."

Annie stared at him, her eyes burrowing into his soul. He could see her skinny chest rising and falling as her grip on the knife whitened her entire hand.

"This is what we've wanted since we were kids," she growled.

"No, this is what *you* wanted."

"Bullshit! This was our dream. And it's come true. Now we can make the one person pay for giving us the childhood she gave us. All the whoopings and the beatings, and the touching and us having to endure it because we were kids and we were too small and insignificant to fight back. And those times when we did try and fight back, the beatings were worse. All the scars, physical and mental. The trips to the ER and the lies we had to tell those doctors. All the nightmares and shit we were forced to experience growing up. This is our chance to take it out on that bitch and set things right. That's always been the plan."

"Your plan," Orton replied. "It's always been your plan. Not mine."

Annie backed up a few steps and crossed her arms. He could see her mind was racing. Her eyes grew wider. "All that time crunched up in the trunk of that car, practically suffocating from the plastic and choking on the stench of the pig's blood and my own sweat. I should've hid in the backseat and held a gun up to her head until we got her up here like I wanted to. If it was all my plan and all my idea, why couldn't we do that? Why all the goddamned theatrics?"

"I told you if you did that, she could crash the car on purpose to take you out or she could get the gun away from you. It wasn't worth the risk."

"No!" Annie screamed. "It wasn't worth the risk! Not after all this. I bring her up here like you told me to, the *way* you told me to, and all of a sudden, it's not your plan. It's my plan and you're too scared to avenge your own mother. I should've had her drive to an abandoned parking lot or the woods and just shot her in the head. I brought her up for us."

Orton shook his head. "I don't want any of it. I thought I did, but I was wrong. Let's just leave them tied up, pack our things, and get on the road. We could be back home in a couple of days and we can go on with our lives. They can yell for help until someone finds them. People are going to start coming up here for the spring. Someone will find them, and by the time they do, we'll be back home and things will be normal again."

Annie laughed as she studied Orton, looking him up and down. "You think things can go back to normal after they've seen our faces?" she asked. "They know who we are. How do you fix that?"

"I don't know," Orton replied. He let his hands drop to his sides.

"This only ends one way."

"There has to be another way."

Annie stepped toward Orton and reached up to his face, fixing a tuft of hair that had come loose, tucking it behind his ear. "You're just like Dad always said," she whispered. "A loser. A coward."

"Shut up."

"I'll take care of everything. You sit back and pretend this never happened."

Annie pushed past Orton and opened the door to Nelle's room. Nelle was lying on the bed, staring up at her, tears creating fresh streaks within the mascara and mud. Annie raised her knife and held that same blank but focused expression she had when she'd snapped Clare's neck. She locked in on Nelle and ran toward her.

Orton burst into the room when the screaming began. He had no time to take in the scene and simply tackled Annie to the ground before she reached Nelle's bed. He scrambled to his feet and placed his boot on his sister's throat. He'd knocked the wind out of Annie and watched as she gasped for breath, wheezing, a frantic look in her eyes.

"She's off limits," he said calmly. "You know that. If you lay a finger on this girl, I'll end you. Do you understand?"

"I'm changing the rules," Annie choked.

"No. You're not."

Annie dropped the knife and Orton took his boot away. He stood at the foot of Nelle's bed until Annie left the room. When she did, he followed her out without looking behind him to see if Nelle was okay. It really didn't matter at this point. Annie was right. They'd seen their faces and knew who they were. If he was being truthful with himself, he'd agree that there was no way they could ever let them go and only one realistic solution to end what they'd started. But he couldn't let his sister kill the girl yet. Perhaps there was another way that he hadn't thought of. Probably not, but maybe. He needed time to map things out. Time to figure out a next move.

Things were quickly getting out of control.

CHAPTER THIRTY-FOUR

Roman was on his way back from visiting Chief Derry when he got the call from Tarrytown PD. The chief was still in the intensive care unit. They'd taken him off the ventilator after his surgery and he was breathing on his own, but the damage caused to his legs was extensive and there were some slight complications the doctors were keeping an eye on. Everyone was hoping and praying for the best. The next few days would be critical.

Roman pulled off to the side of Route 9 when he saw the police cruiser and tow truck idling on the shoulder of the road. The sun was beginning to set behind rain clouds that were moving in, casting shadows that would grow deeper as the storm took hold and evening moved on. He wanted to get to the scene before they'd need flashlights or spotlights. It was just over twenty-four hours since Laura Anderson had tried to kill his chief and more than thirty-two hours since anyone had seen Nelle Anderson. Time kept slipping from his grasp and there was nothing he could do to stop it. The questions kept piling up, but so far, no answers.

"Thanks for calling me," Roman said as he approached the

two men. "I appreciate you not touching the evidence. As you know, this is a fluid investigation."

The officer was from the village of Tarrytown. A local guy. He put his hands up. "You're good. Nothing was compromised, as far as I can tell. Gus here called it in, so I'll let him explain."

The cars along Route 9 slowed as they went by, the rubberneckers something Roman had never gotten used to in all his years of law enforcement. The cruiser had its bar lights on as did the tow truck, so people were expecting to see some kind of an accident. They had their phones ready to take a picture or shoot a video, but as they passed, they found only the three men huddled together on the side of the road. No wreck. Nothing to post about.

Gus, the tow truck driver, crossed his arms in front of his barrel chest as he spoke. "Yesterday I was coming back from a call in Croton. Engine seized on this guy and he lived here in town, so he wanted a local garage to do the fix. Anyway, I loaded the car up on the flatbed and was driving back when I saw a Passat on the side of the road. No hazards or anything, but I could see there was a driver, so I pulled behind it, threw on my lights to caution the drivers coming up on us, and I hopped out to see if I could help."

"And it was Laura Anderson."

"Yes, sir. Obviously, I didn't know who she was when we were talking, but later on when I saw the story on the news and then went online, her picture was all over the place. I recognized her from when I stopped. It was her. No doubt."

"How was she when you were talking with her?" Roman asked. "Attitude? Mannerisms? Anything catch you funny?"

Gun nodded. "Yes, sir. She was crying. I asked her if I could help with the car and she told me the car was fine. Said she just got word that someone had died and she pulled over because she was upset. Sounded reasonable enough. I got back in my truck and let her be."

"Other than crying, did she seem nervous or agitated or angry? Anything like that?"

"A little jumpy, but you gotta put yourself in her shoes. You're sitting on the side of the road minding your own business and a burly guy like me walks up. You might be a little jumpy, too. That's why I left her alone. Didn't want to freak her out."

The officer pointed to Gus. "Tell him about the phone."

"Yeah, right." Gus pointed to the ground and took a few steps closer. "After I realized who I'd been talking to, I drove by this spot on another run today and noticed something shiny on the shoulder. I heard Laura Anderson took that chief's gun, so I thought maybe she tossed it when she saw me coming, and I didn't want any kids to get it. I turned around and got out to see what it was."

"Her cell phone," Roman said.

"Yes, sir. I called 911, and they sent help and called you. Here we are."

"Here we are." Roman put on a pair of latex gloves from his pocket. He bent down and retrieved the iPhone from the ground, turning it over to examine it. He wasn't a tech guy and had no idea what model it was, but it looked fairly new. Expensive. The screen was smashed and the back was cracked. He pressed it and swiped up and down, but there was too much damage to bring the phone to life.

Roman placed the phone in an evidence bag. "Explains why the husband couldn't locate the phone on his app. I'll get this to our technology group to see what we can find."

"Cool," Gus replied. "I hope it helps you find her."

The three men disbanded and Roman walked back to his car. He climbed in, snatched Laura's casefile from the passenger's seat, and opened it. He made a quick note on the folder, stating the name of the tow truck driver, time of the retrieval of the phone, and a few sentences recounting Gus's statement.

When he was done, he closed the file, put it back on the seat, and fished his own phone out of his pocket.

"This is Detective Estrada. I'm bringing in Laura Anderson's phone. Looks pretty damaged. I want to see if we can somehow get it unlocked so we can have a look inside. Might point us to where she's heading. I'll be at HQ in about twenty minutes."

He hung up and put the car in gear, pulling back out onto Route 9, hoping what they'd found would help point them in the right direction. He was beginning to suspect that Laura—or Betty, or whatever her name really was—wanted him to find her as much as he did.

CHAPTER THIRTY-FIVE

There was no confusion this time when Laura opened her eyes in the darkness. She knew exactly where she was and every last detail of what had happened. The blinding lights. Being pushed through the dilapidated house. Nelle tied to the chair. Orton. Annie. Her mother's last gasp of sound before she was killed. Her reality had become a nightmare she couldn't wake up from. It was all too much.

She sat up on the mattress and felt along her body. The barbs from the taser had been removed while she was unconscious. Tiny bits of cut and swollen flesh popped up to meet the tips of her fingers as she examined herself. Everything hurt. She could recall Annie pulling the trigger on the taser and the immense pain of the jolt as every muscle in her body locked up. She could also remember the buzzing sound the taser made every time the electricity hit her, and Orton's voice that still whispered in her ear.

A bullet to the head would be too easy. Not yet. Soon.

Remnants of the screaming and crying filled the chambers of Laura's memory. She replayed the scene with Orton, the gun to Nelle's head and the absolute panic Laura had felt watching helplessly. The gun had been empty. But what about next time? Those scenes were quickly replaced by the picture of Annie standing behind her mother, grabbing her head. They were going to kill her and Nelle. At this point, it was just a matter of when.

There were no more tears. Laura came to terms with the fact that she could no longer hope Orton or Annie would show mercy. It was foolish to ever have thought that in the first place, but what they did to her mother confirmed their true intentions. She had to act to escape and save them. No one was coming to their rescue. It was up to her, and she'd do anything she could to save her little girl. That wasn't hyperbole or something said to convince herself that she was trying her best. She meant it. She'd crossed that line and there was no turning back now. She'd do *anything* to save Nelle. Nothing was off limits anymore.

She crawled off the mattress and felt around the floor. In a house that was falling apart, she knew it wouldn't take long until she came upon a nail that had come loose from the floor. After a few minutes of feeling around and sticking her hands on splinters and rough edges, she found the head of a finish nail protruding from the floor about a quarter of an inch. It was enough for Laura to get her fingernails under it and start pulling. At first, the nail wouldn't budge. She pulled and yanked, wanting to cry out from the pain in her hands and fingers, until the nail finally began to move from side to side. She started making circular motions with it, and for whatever reason, she was reminded of how she used to loosen her teeth when she was a kid using the same method. You can't just pull, she told herself. You have to maneuver it until it becomes loose enough around the edges so the roots can no longer hold it. Laura kept working the nail until it finally came out of the floor, ripping at the skin on her forefinger in the process.

The lack of light made it close to impossible to see, but she pinched the nail between her fingers and felt it from top to bottom. It was thin and about an inch long. It wouldn't be much to work with, but she'd have to make do. She knelt down and carefully pressed the end of the nail against the floor at a slight angle. She added the pressure slowly. The nail dug into the warped and worn hardwood. That wouldn't do.

She got up and went to the bricked window. Placing the tip of the nail against one of the bricks, she applied the same pressure. The head of the nail cut deeper into her fingers, but she kept pushing, swallowing the pain. The nail finally gave way with a sudden collapse and fell from her grip.

"No."

Laura got on her hands and knees, feeling around on the floor at the base of the window until her thumb bumped against it and she picked it up. She traced it with her finger and felt the slight L shape. Good enough. It would work.

When they were dating and Kurt was still with the NYPD, they used to play around with his handcuffs in the bedroom. It was fun and they were young and it never became anything more than that. One night, when they were lying in bed watching TV, Kurt taught her how to pick a lock on his set. It was quite easy, and she learned that it could be done with anything you could bend into an L shape. He taught her, and she practiced, and every once in a while, he'd get her in a certain position, put the cuffs on her, and make her escape. It was like a game, but at the same time, it was a lesson in self-preservation. She'd become fairly proficient. They hadn't played with the cuffs in almost ten years, but the skill he'd taught her was something that stayed with her long after those nights of naughty giggles and playful arrests. She never thought she'd be in a position like the one she found herself in now, but she was grateful for the lesson that had taken place so long ago.

Her slow and steady fingers found the keyhole in the cuff fastened to her ankle. Laura pushed the nail in the hole and pressed down on the top to release the ratchet. As soon as she applied a little pressure, the jaw of the cuff disengaged and she was free. Easy.

She scrambled to her feet and felt around the perimeter of the entire room, finding what she needed, then made her way back. Other than the mattress, the room seemed to be empty. The space was cold, though, and her body shivered. She hugged herself and returned to the mattress, figuring it had been a little while since anyone had come up to check on her, which meant Annie might be visiting soon. That was what she wanted.

Laura would be waiting.

CHAPTER THIRTY-SIX

The lights came on, eviscerating the darkness in a nanosecond and blinding Laura in the process. She ducked down, fighting the urge to drop to the floor. This time, she was ready.

She reached under the edge of the mattress and came away with the sharp piece of wood she'd pulled from the window frame. She rose to her feet and sprinted into the light as fast as she could, unseeing and desperate, a roar bellowing from her throat, adrenaline coursing through her entire body.

The door opened as Laura was running at it, the sharp end of the wood pointed out like a spear as she ran into battle. She focused on the shadow of a figure in front of her, hoping she was giving Annie enough of a surprise to catch her completely off guard. No one would be expecting her to be out of the cuffs. Before Annie would register what was happening, Laura would be there.

She aimed for the center of the shadow and felt the tip of the wood hit the woman's body. She kept pushing through her momentum, the sharp end of the wood holding steady without breaking off. She began to feel something moist on her hands as the wood grew slippery. She stopped as Annie fell backward and almost toppled down the narrow staircase. Laura lost her balance and fell on top of the woman, out of the light that was now behind her. She panted and grunted like an animal, still trying to grip the wood that had found its spot, too frightened to let it go. She looked into her captor's eyes, hoping to see her take her last breaths so Annie would know it was Laura who was taking her life back and saving her daughter.

But it wasn't Annie.

Laura was lying on top of Nelle.

"Nelle!" Laura choked.

She scrambled to her knees and pulled her daughter up into a sitting position. The wood was sticking out of her abdomen, the blood soaking her clothes and running onto the floor. A piece of duct tape had been placed across her mouth so they couldn't communicate. A tray of food fell from her hands, spilling everywhere.

"Nelle!"

Nelle's eyes rolled into the back of her head.

"No!"

Laura ripped the tape from Nelle's mouth and pressed her hands against the wound as best she could without extracting the wood for fear she'd make it worse. It was the scene with the hitchhiker on the exit ramp all over again. "Nelle, talk to me. Stay with me. Honey, can you hear me? Open your eyes. Talk to me!"

Nelle's body had already been through so much stress. The kidnapping, the mental torture, the physical pain. And now this. She placed her hand on her daughter's chest and felt her heart beating rapidly.

Footsteps climbed the stairs toward them.

Laura got to her feet and tried to lift her daughter, but she was too heavy. She slipped her hands under Nelle's arms and began to drag her back inside the room. "Come on, baby. I got you."

Annie appeared at the top of the stairs. "I figured you'd try something like this. Didn't know exactly what it might be, but I knew you were desperate enough to try something. I've had Nelle coming to check on you the last few times. Just in case."

"Get away from us!"

"How did you get out of the cuffs?"

"Get away!"

"*And* you made a weapon. Impressive, although you are a killer. It's in your nature. I shouldn't be surprised."

Laura dragged Nelle across the threshold and shut the door, leaning against it to keep Annie out.

"There's a lot of blood out here," Annie said from behind the door. "I think your little girl might be in trouble."

"Leave us alone!"

"If she dies, that's on you. Wouldn't be your first victim. But my brother and I will make sure it's your last."

A lock from the other side of the door engaged and the lights went out. Rainbows of color burst in front of Laura's eyes as she slid down the door and crawled to her daughter. "Honey, stay with me."

"Mom," Nelle moaned.

"I'm here. I'm sorry. I didn't know it was you. I couldn't see anything." She could tell Nelle's heartbeat was weak. She could barely feel a pulse. Panic began to rise like a fever. All the training she'd had and the natural instinct to stay calm immediately melted away. She was a mother holding her daughter who was dying. There was no rational thought, just terror.

What did you do?

"Stay with me, baby!" She gently slapped Nelle on the cheek. "Stay with me!"

"Mom."

Laura bent down. "What, honey?"

"Help us."

She knew she needed to save them. It was time. Right then and there.

And there was only one way out.

CHAPTER THIRTY-SEVEN

MARCH 27, 2000

"No," Betty replied instinctively. Her head was swimming, her body trembling. "Third drawer. White label with the blue stripe. Dilaudid."

Pat turned the bottle around. "They both have a blue stripe. Dilaudid is dark blue. Potassium is light blue. You just pushed 20 mEq of potassium. You're killing our patient."

"Well... I..."

The senior nurse stepped in front of her and extracted the syringe, quickly flushing it with the second syringe of saline and screwing in something new she couldn't see.

"We got the wrong med pushed," Pat cried out. "The cardiac arrest is from giving potassium IV push."

"We've got no rhythm. Going into asystole!"

"Get the paddles!"

"Blood pressure plunging! Unable to get a BP!"

Betty backed herself into the far corner of the room, out of the way of the others, as she stared at the woman who'd stopped moving. Everything was happening in slow motion. Somewhere in the background, she could hear Dr. Decker's calls for intervention and Tricia crying that the patient's heartrate was failing. It felt like a dream. Like a nightmare she couldn't wake up from. Dr. Decker began shocking the woman while the monitors beeped with alarms until it all became the single tone of a flat-line. In the chaos of trying to save a life, Betty had pushed the wrong med and ended up taking one. She had killed her patient. A woman she'd known and been connected to ever since that fateful day in front of the school, where she'd gone to meet a stupid boy she'd had an adolescent crush on. Their lives kept connecting in the most tragic ways, and now it was Betty's turn. Her mother called Sofia Bennett a murderer. Betty was no better.

She was a murderer, too.

CHAPTER THIRTY-EIGHT

Help us.

The words hung in the air as Laura ran through what she needed to do to make things right.

She tried to lift her daughter, but Nelle was too heavy. Instead, she took Nelle under the arms and dragged her across the floor, hoisting her up onto the mattress the best she could. Her feet slipped in the trail of blood that was left behind.

"Honey, can you hear me?" Laura asked as she knelt beside her daughter. She'd never been more scared in her life, but there were no tears. There was no *time* for tears. Not now.

Nelle's breath seemed ragged and shallow. Laura felt her baby's face, touching her nose and mouth and feeling the stickiness of blood oozing from her lips. Her eyes were closed. She kept swallowing repeatedly. She was fading fast. There was no doubt about it.

"Nelle, I'm going to go for help. You need to hang on for me. I'll be back. Stay conscious and put pressure around the wound."

"I didn't mean those things I said," Nelle muttered, hardly audible. "The man made me say them. I love you."

Laura smiled and kissed Nelle's hand. "It's okay, honey."

Nelle was slipping in and out of consciousness, and Laura knew there was no way her daughter had the strength to keep herself awake if she left, but staying wouldn't do either of them any good. Laura gently touched the piece of wood frame sticking out of Nelle's stomach and tried to examine the wound in the dark. She felt down to the base of where the wood penetrated the skin, then measured where that was in relation to her other organs. The wound appeared low enough to have missed her heart and lungs, but deep enough to cause damage otherwise. It was clear that she'd bleed to death if Laura didn't get out of the attic. The mattress was already beginning to soak through.

"I'll be back. I love you. I'm sorry. For everything."

"I didn't mean what I—"

She kissed Nelle one last time, then jumped up and threw herself against the wall. She walked the perimeter and slid her hand until she bumped into the frame of the bricked-over window, her fingers immediately finding the hole she'd been digging into the wood.

Help us.

A voice in the back of her mind whispered that she'd never get help in time and that her daughter would die because of all the mistakes she continued to make. It wondered why she didn't stop to make sure it was Annie coming up the stairs and not someone else. It wondered why she thought she could save them anyway. It asked for one example of a time when Laura could be counted on when things really mattered. Making a deadline for a fundraiser or finding fabric at the last minute so costumes could be fixed and a school play could go on were not examples of coming through in the clutch. It wanted a real example. An example of when Laura rose to the occasion for herself or her family in a life-or-death situation. An example of when she chose her family over her addiction.

Laura did her best to ignore the voice as she worked. The splintered wood cut into her flesh, ripping at her knuckles and tearing at her tendons. Her nails were bending back and breaking, the sound of them snapping making her bite her bottom lip to keep from screaming. She didn't stop. She kept digging with both hands, working her way toward the bricks, tearing at the wood as quickly and as recklessly as she could, fearing Orton or Annie might come back and stop her. The faster she got through the window and out onto the roof, the faster she could get down and, hopefully, surprise them. Or they could turn on the lights, storm the room, and tase her into unconsciousness again. It truly was fifty-fifty and she tried not to think about it. She had to get through the wood. For Nelle. That was her focus.

A rumble of thunder broke through the sky outside. Quiet groans turned into animalistic grunts of determination. Laura dug and yanked and punched the wood frame. Her blood flecked onto her chest and neck every time she pulled a piece of wood free. As she dug deeper, the wood cut into her palms and wrists. Thin lines of blood made their way down her forearm. Then she stopped.

She'd made it all the way through the frame to the window.

The first brick loosened.

Laura pushed and dug her fingers around the corner of the brick, working it up and down and back and forth, just like she did her loose tooth when she was a kid, like she'd done with the nail in the floor. She tugged and pulled as she heard the mortar around it beginning to crack.

Help us.

She cried out as she yanked the first brick free, listening as it fell to the floor with a thump. Laura could see outside. It was dark.

Another rumble of thunder as the other bricks came easily after that. Laura pushed and pulled, punching each one with an open palm to get the mortar weak, and then got to work on yanking the brick out and placing it at her feet so no one downstairs would hear. Within minutes, she had a hole large enough to climb through, and she poked her head out to plot her next move.

A roof from the back porch looked to be about ten feet below her, and then there was another ten feet after that to the ground. Two quick jumps and she could run through the woods, cross the stream, and get to her mother's house. It should only take about five minutes once she was on the ground, but if she broke an ankle or twisted a knee on the way down, all bets were off.

Laura swung her legs out of the opening of the window and eased herself down, balancing herself on the window ledge by her waist as a gust of wind almost made her fall. She could feel her heartbeat in her bleeding hands and glanced at what she thought was the shadowy outline of her daughter. She could hear her ragged breathing, which meant Nelle was still alive. For now.

Help us.

That was exactly what she was going to do.

MARCH 16, 2000

Betty opened the front door and peeked her head inside, hearing only quiet.

"Mom? Mom, you in here?"

She let herself in and walked to the bottom of the stairs.

"Mom? I know you don't want me here, but Dad asked me to stop by. He said you're not answering the phone, and he doesn't want to ask the Bastrop PD to do a wellness check on you. I'm coming up. I brought some food."

She climbed the stairs to the second floor, carrying a container of soup and some water she'd bought from the deli. Soup and tea were all her mother could stomach as of late. She'd whittled down to nothing but skin and bones, and between the antidepressants, anti-anxiety, and insomnia meds Laura's father and the doctor were making her take, she was almost in a state of catatonia: unconscious most days, waking to eat a few meals here and there and sometimes to take a shower. She'd sequestered herself in her bedroom since coming home from the Bennett boy's school that day, her own husband treating her like a child, the town treating her like a maniac. Their lawyer had been over a few times to plot the course as they moved toward the hearing, but she'd refused to come down for the meetings, opting instead to let others handle her fate.

Betty couldn't stand being away from her mother while she was sick. Despite her mother's recklessness and the inability to ever let go of Donny, Betty loved her the way a daughter is supposed to. She wanted so desperately for her to get better and see a way out of her grief, and she'd promised herself she would stay with her as long as it took to see things through. When she wasn't at the hospital, Betty was at the house, ignoring her mother's request for her to stay away, and trying to help as best she could. It was hard watching the woman she grew up knowing as strong and smart and full of energy become a shell of a human, sleeping most of the day and deteriorating into nothingness. It was the approaching hearing date that had everyone on edge. The tension in the house was unbearable. Her mother was always sleeping. Her father was always worrying. They were only a month away from the hearing, and now her mother had stopped talking altogether. Betty wondered if it could get any worse.

She knocked on the bedroom door as she opened it. "Mom, you need to answer the phone. It's important."

The room was dark as it usually was. Shades drawn. Door to the bathroom closed. TV off. Betty reached for the light switch on the side wall and flipped it on.

"Wake up. I got you dinner."

At first, she didn't quite understand what she was staring at. Her mother was lying on top of the covers, wearing the nightgown she had on the night before. She was clutching a framed picture of Donny against her chest, and the top half of her was wet. Betty traced the water to an empty glass on the floor. Three empty pill bottles had also been discarded onto the floor, and then she saw a smattering of pills scattered about. She looked back up at her mother and saw her eyes closed, mouth slightly agape, unmoving.

"Mom!"

Betty dropped the soup and heard it crash to the floor as she rushed to her mother's bedside.

"Mom! Wake up!"

She shook her mother by her bony shoulders, but she was limp, no structure to her frame whatsoever. Deadweight. She took her mother's wrist in her hand and checked for a pulse. It was faint, but it was there. Her mother was dying in her arms.

Betty grabbed the phone from the nightstand and dialed 911, then climbed on top of her mother and straddled her as she began administering CPR while, at the same time, explaining to the situation to the 911 operator.

"Come on, Mom. Stay with me. Please don't leave. I'm sorry. Do you hear me? I'm sorry!"

She kept repeating those words as she continued CPR, waiting for the paramedics to arrive and take over. It was the last thing she said to her as they loaded her mother into the ambulance and the first thing she said when they arrived at the hospital.

I'm sorry.

CHAPTER THIRTY-NINE

Roman's eyes were heavy and his joints sore as he walked across the parking lot to where floodlights illuminated Laura Anderson's Passat. A state trooper from the area met him halfway.

They had found the Passat in Malden, NY, on the banks of the Hudson River, beyond the outskirts of George J. Terpening Sr. Memorial Park. The interior had been burned black, but the car itself was largely intact, the unmistakable VW emblem still visible on the grill along with the license plates no one had bothered to remove. It had taken Roman about an hour to make it back up to Malden, and the sky was dark now. He'd gotten the call as he was making his way to the station after dropping off Laura's cell phone with the tech team in Hawthorne. As soon as they told him they'd found the car, he'd raced up the interstate as quickly as possible.

"Good evening," the trooper said, hand extended. "Trooper Kritzer."

"Detective Estrada. Thanks for waiting before you towed it. I wanted to have a look."

"We got the call a few hours ago. Fire and Rescue arrived on scene, but the fire had already burned itself out long before. Fire chief thinks it might've been sitting here most of the day, judging from the way the soot and char dried up. We're thinking gasoline was the ignitor, but it doesn't look like they had much to use. Mainly the interior of the car was burned. Exterior took a little hit. Nothing major."

Roman stopped in front of the car. The smell of burned rubber and charred fabric filled the air. He placed his hands in his pockets as a cool chill came off the river.

"Plates were visible," Kritzer continued. "Registration sticker was burned, though. We ran the plates and your BOLO came up. That's how we knew to call."

"Who reported the fire?"

"Couple of fishermen heading down the river. They saw some smoke, but couldn't see any flames from where they were on the water."

"And when was this?"

"About two o'clock?"

"Were you able to pull any prints?"

Kritzer nodded. "Our guys picked up one by the gas tank in the back and one on the driver's side quarter panel. Looks like a thumb and an index finger by the gas tank. A palm in the front. We'll run them and let you know if anything turns up."

"You get anything from inside the trunk?"

"Trunk was empty. That got lit up pretty good, too. Fire chief says a bunch of plastic melted back there, but that was about it. We searched the interior storage. Found the insurance card and a couple of CDs in the armrest storage along with a sunglass case."

"People still keep CDs in their car?"

"Looks like it. No Apple CarPlay, I guess." Kritzer held up an evidence bag containing a small pendant on a chain. Roman took it and examined it closer. "Found this in the glovebox. It's a St. Christopher's medal and chain."

"Looks dirty."

"And old."

Roman handed it back to the trooper. "Bag it with the other stuff. Might mean something. Might not."

"Ten-four."

Roman walked around the Passat, staring inside. The seats were burned and the dashboard looked charred, but the fire had never been hot enough to truly engulf the vehicle, nor had it been hot enough to melt much of the plastic. "I'm not sure if they kept the fire low on purpose to avoid the car being seen, or if they were in too much of a hurry to get it done right."

Kritzer retrieved a second evidence bag from his patrol car and handed it over. "We also got this out of the passenger's side floor. It was half-melted into the mat."

Roman took it and examined it, spinning the bag around in his hand.

"It's a tuna sandwich still in the plastic container," Kritzer explained. "You can see a part of the sticker they use to keep the lid closed."

Roman looked closer and saw the blue-and-white sticker, stained and burned. Half a word was readable.

"Chuck's," he said. "What's that?"

"Chuck's Gas-N-Go on 87. Right outside Saugerties."

"She stopped to get something to eat."

"I already have men in route to check to see if they have camera footage."

Roman smiled. "Good man," he said. "Let's go join them. Hopefully there's something to see."

CHAPTER FORTY

Roman followed the trooper's cruiser for the ten-minute drive back to the Gas-N-Go rest stop. He felt like they were close, but to what, he wasn't exactly sure.

He parked in the front of the store and followed Trooper Kritzer through the sliding doors. They approached the main counter where the other trooper was already behind the register, hunched over an iPad, fast-forwarding through captured footage.

"See anything?" Kritzer asked.

"Nothing yet," the trooper replied. "Got some outside footage that shows the suspect's car coming into the lot, then she drives around back and we lose her. Time was stamped at 8:37, so I'm catching up on that now with the interior footage."

Roman bent down and watched as the footage stopped at 8:36. The small group of men concentrated on the screen as four different camera angles rotated every ten seconds.

"There," Roman said, pointing at the figure coming in through the sliding doors. "That's our suspect."

"Okay," the trooper replied. "Let's follow her and see where she goes."

They watched as the cameras kept rotating. It was difficult to track exact movements when one second, Laura was walking across the floor toward the deli section and the next, the camera was filming above the counter.

"She's entering the ladies' room," Kritzer said.

They waited and watched until she emerged and made her way into the deli section, quickly perusing what the night's offering was, then taking a sandwich, a bag of chips, and a drink. The camera rotated at the right angle this time and they watched her pay. As she did, she looked up and stared into the camera, her eyes meeting theirs, unmoving until the scene rotated to the front entrance again.

"That's her," Roman said. "Staring right at us. She wanted us to see her. She wanted us to know where she was and at what time."

"That doesn't seem like a woman trying to evade the law," the trooper said.

Kritzer nodded. "Agreed, but we understood she might've been traveling with her daughter. I don't see the girl."

"We don't have a clear idea of who she's traveling with," Roman explained. "We've gotten reports of a body in the trunk. That could be her daughter, and if that's the case, it would explain why we don't see her with our suspect."

The other men grew quiet at the thought of a kid being dead in the trunk of a car.

"She's clearly alone," said the trooper holding the iPad. "Why wouldn't she ask the cashier to call the police?"

Roman pointed at the screen. "I don't think she's alone. Look, you can see she's walking with her phone out. I'm thinking someone's listening to make sure she doesn't try and get help. She can't ask, or the person on the other end of that phone would know."

"What about a note?"

"Maybe her looking up at the cameras was her note. Maybe that's the best she could do."

They watched Laura leave the Gas-N-Go, and the trooper ended the video. He used the thin keyboard connected to the iPad to switch to the outside cameras again and found the time-stamp that coincided with the time she was inside.

"There."

Laura emerged from the double doors, turned right, and disappeared behind the building. Several minutes passed until the Volkswagen with the missing rear window and dented rear bumper drove past the gas pumps and turned left, back onto the road that led to the interstate.

"I can't see if there's anyone else in the car," Kritzer said. "You want to see it again?"

"Yes," Roman replied. "Let's play it a few more times to make sure we didn't miss anything. I'll be right back."

As the trooper rewound the coverage to the beginning of the video, Roman crossed the floor and made his way toward the restrooms.

"Where're you going?" Kritzer asked.

Roman didn't answer. He walked down a small corridor and pushed into the ladies' room, stopping inside. It was a typical public restroom. Sinks on one side. Stalls on the other.

"Police," he called as he stood still. "Anyone in here?"

There was no reply, so Roman walked to the first stall. He pushed the door open and examined the interior. Nothing of note. Toilet. Toiletry stations. The end. He moved to the second stall and poked his head in. Same as the first, except for the very important graffiti on the interior wall.

Roman heard the main door to the women's room open.

"Detective Estrada?"

"Over here."

Kritzer joined him outside the second stall. "Video's ready."

Roman pointed. "I think we found her note," he said. "She can think on her feet, I'll give her that."

The lipstick was still fresh, written on the side wall, next to the toilet.

"Son of a bitch," Kritzer muttered.

"I had a feeling she might've tried something when she used the bathroom. Didn't expect this." He turned toward the trooper. "We got her. Call this address in and get a unit up there right now. Let them know I'm on my way."

Kritzer took out his radio. "On it."

Roman hurried out of the ladies' room, across the rest stop lobby, and out into the parking lot. He jumped in his car and started the engine, punching the address into his GPS, then hitting the gas. Tires squealed as he sped through the gas pumps and turned onto the service road that would connect him to Interstate 87. He looked at the navigation map that told him they would arrive at Caroga Lake in an hour. He figured he'd make it in forty-five minutes if he hit the lights and sirens. A half hour if everyone got out of his way.

She told them exactly where she was. Wrote it down for them to find.

122 North Shore West Caroga Lake Road, Caroga Lake, NY. Hurry!

CHAPTER FORTY-ONE

Laura dropped from the bricked window and, for a moment, thought she'd missed her target. But when she felt the hardness of the asphalt shingles scrape the bottoms of her bare feet, she allowed her body to fall limp onto the porch roof so she wouldn't make such a thud. She laid still for a few seconds, listening for anyone who might be coming to check on the noise she'd made dropping down from the story above. After enough time had passed, she crawled along the roof and peeked over the edge.

A flash of lightning brightened the sky for a moment, and then everything went dark again. Laura could barely make out small whitecaps of the stream that flowed forty yards away. She took a breath, trying to block out the pain in her hands, then eased herself over the edge of the roof and shimmied down a porch post until she was able to jump to the ground and roll flat on the grass.

Thunder grumbled somewhere over the lake, then went quiet. There were other noises, too: the crickets singing their nocturnal song, a gas engine idling, the angry stream up ahead. Except for a few windows that glowed from the broken-down house, there was no light. Laura tried to remember where she was in relation to her mother's house. Crossing the stream too far up or too far down would be a waste of time. She had to get to her mother's house and call for help. There wasn't a second to waste. Nelle was bleeding to death, and time was ticking away her advantage. She had to get moving.

Laura scrambled to her feet and started running toward the stream. She wondered if her mother's body was still lying in the yard, then pushed the thought away and tried to focus. As soon as she crossed into the small, wooded area that hid the dilapidated house from the banks of the lake, the underbrush scratched her ankles and shins. Pine needles stabbed the bottoms of her feet and small rocks stubbed her toes. But the pain was becoming a distant thing, a dulled sensation in the back of her mind that held no real relevance. Her concentration was on the stream. Then the house. Then the phone. If she could find a weapon while she was there, all the better.

As the woods thinned, she reached the streambed. The water flowed with vigor, but the whitecaps weren't too high and the flow looked manageable. The stream itself sounded less intense than what she'd heard through the bricked window, but this would be no easy wade across. The winter melt kept the water rough, and although its width was only about twenty yards, she knew one false step would send her careening down the rapids and into the lake itself. By then, too much time would be lost. She had to be careful.

She exhaled once, then stepped in. As soon as she did, lightning flashed, and she stood still for a moment, knowing how exposed and vulnerable she was. She wondered if anyone could see her from the house, if Orton or Annie were watching. She waited until the sky turned dark again, then moved forward.

The water was pure ice and made her body immediately tense up. The pain from the freezing temperature crept up her chest, even though she was only submerged from the waist down. She no longer felt her scratched feet or cut-up hands. Just the freezing water. She kept walking, her breath coming in short bursts. She picked up each foot purposefully and placed it down, making sure she was steady before taking the next step. Her toes were pins and needles. Her legs were numb, yet at the same time, glass shards of pain from the freezing temperature. The current was much stronger than she thought it'd be, and she fought to stay upright. Her body began to shiver and she wondered if someone could go into shock in waist-deep water. She knew that if Orton or Annie had seen her running from the house, there'd be nothing she could do. If they appeared at the streambank, there was no moving fast or being agile to escape from them. Moving too quickly would knock her off balance and send her toppling over as the current ripped her away. And even if the water was shallow enough to make an evasive move, her frozen legs would be unreliable. If her captors wanted, they could calmly aim their weapons and hit their target. She dared not turn around for fear they'd be standing there, watching her, laughing at her foolishness. Instead, she focused on the opposite side as it drew closer and closer, each step pushing her across the icy water. Almost there.

Laura grabbed onto a set of branches and pulled herself onto solid ground. She crawled through mud and climbed to her feet, shivering from both the cold water and the adrenaline that coursed through her. Only then did she look back across the way, but there was no one there. No one watching. No one aiming a weapon. No one standing with her daughter at knife-point, calmly asking her to come back. She'd made it and paused for a brief moment, wondering how Nelle was faring back at the house. She hadn't been stable when she'd left her and could only hope she was hanging on for a little while longer.

"Almost there, baby."

Her mother's house was another hundred yards away. She'd

picked it because she thought the view of the lake would be calming, and she knew her mother always loved being surrounded by nature. She thought the house would be an opportunity to keep tabs on her mother while, at the same time, keeping her as far enough away from her new life as she could. She had hoped moving her to New York from Texas would give her an opportunity to reconnect with a woman who had hated her for most of her life. Now that was too late. Her mother was gone and her own family's lives hung on whether she could get help or not. She was determined not to disappoint them.

Laura ran as fast as she could, stumbling and slipping more than once as her legs tried to work properly again. More thorns and pine needles and branches sliced and poked and scraped her as she ran, but she hardly felt any of it. Her focus was the house. She wouldn't take her eyes off of it.

Laura ran up the front porch and slid down next to a set of potted annuals she'd planted when she had visited last summer. They were clustered at the corner of the porch where the light was always the most consistent. Of course, they were nothing more than dead stalks and brittle leaves now, having just been through a harsh winter, but none of that mattered. Laura picked up the second pot and grabbed the housekey that she'd hidden underneath.

She stood up and raced for the front door, opening the screen first, then reached down to unlock the deadbolt, only to find the door had already been unlocked. Laura eased herself in, listening for movement or the creak of a floorboard, but it was completely silent. She opened the utility closet next to the half bath and grabbed the flashlight she knew would be on the bottom shelf. She turned it on and searched the main floor, listening for any signs of movement, feeling her heart thumping in her chest.

The main living area was one big room, which made things easy. Laura walked through the kitchen and then around the dining table and in between the couches, swinging the flashlight from side to side, checking to see if anyone was hiding. That tiny voice in the back of her mind reminded her that there was a bottle of Prosecco in the cabinet above the sink should she feel the need to take a moment and recharge. Maybe a couple of sips to calm her nerves. Nelle would be alright. In fact, Laura would be in a better state of mind to take care of her daughter after a treat. It'd be quick. No one would have to know.

"No."

Laura shook the thought from her mind as she climbed the stairs and checked the three empty bedrooms. She had to stay focused. The house appeared to be empty. It was safe to make the call.

She scrambled back down the stairs and grabbed the wireless house phone that was in the kitchen. She picked it up and turned it on, but nothing happened. There was no power. She looked at the stove and saw that the digital clock was on, then glanced in the living room to find the tiny green light lit on the TV. The house had power, but no phone.

Dammit! Please!

She shined her light down next to the jack where the phone service came into the house and could see the wire had been cut. There was no way to call for help. She was truly on her own.

"Well, aren't you Little Miss Tenacity."

CHAPTER FORTY-TWO

The sound of Annie's voice made Laura jump up and scream. The woman was standing inside the front door holding Orton's shotgun, pointing it at her.

"You think we'd go through all this trouble up here and not cut the phone line?" Annie asked. "Come on. Use your head."

Laura slowly got to her feet and leaned against the counter.

Annie's eyes wouldn't leave Laura's. "This was supposed to be over already, but Orton don't have the guts to do the hard things sometimes." She licked her lips and spit on the ground. "Lucky he got me. I got no problem with the hard things."

She cocked the shotgun.

"And here we are," Laura said.

Annie nodded. "Yes, ma'am."

The moonlight cast shadows in the house, sucking the color out of everything and making Laura's world gray. Laura stood motionless, staring at Annie and the shotgun, the barrel aimed at her chest. The house was quiet, the windows overlooking the black lake. Another flash of lightning in the distance. Another rumble of thunder. The moon would be gone soon, swallowed by the storm clouds.

"I've seen the tape," Annie said. "I know what you did to my mother and your brother. You can change your name and volunteer at your church and be the perfect mom, but you and I know better, right? We know."

Laura was careful not to make any sudden moves. She cocked her head to the side and smiled, hoping she was pulling off some kind of confidence, wondering if it would all end there, if she was literally taking her last breaths.

"You think you know what happened, but there's so much more to the story," she said calmly. "Details no one knows except me. I think you and your brother should hear them. Then you can do what you have to do."

The front door crashed open and slammed against the wall. Light flooded the dark living room and the two women froze.

"State police!" a voice shouted from behind the light. "Everybody put your hands up!"

Neither woman complied. They each stared at the other, Laura peering into Annie's eyes as Annie tried to steal a glance behind her.

"I'm a good person," Laura said. "Despite what you think."

"Hands up!"

"Like hell you are," Annie replied, ignoring the trooper. "Look at what you did just to get up here. Look at the lives you changed forever. You ain't good. No way."

"I said get your hands up!"

"Officer, I can't!" Annie screamed, breaking into character. Her voice cracked as her eyes immediately glassed over. She started to cry. "I can't lift my arms. Thank God you're here. This woman is trying to kill me!"

Laura shook her head. "That's not true. She has my daughter at the other house, and she's hurt badly. She needs help."

"I'm so scared."

"She's lying! She has a gun!"

"I had to protect myself! This is the woman the police are looking for downstate. She killed a cop down there! Help me!"

The trooper pushed forward and lowered himself into a shooting stance. "Everyone shut up. Lady, drop the gun and get on the ground! Both of you on the ground!"

Laura watched as Annie started to get down and stopped right before her knees hit the floor. She watched Annie spin around and fire her first round into the light, and then watched the light come off of her and tumble up and back. Laura started moving when everything turned dark again.

Annie's back was to her now, focused on the trooper who'd taken them both by surprise. Laura snatched a knife from the cheap cutlery set she'd bought at a local hardware store last summer, then hit the deck. It was a boning knife. The blade was only about four inches long, but it would have to do.

Scurrying on her hands and knees, she made her way around the kitchen island and out into the hall. A second shot was fired, exploding in the quiet house, the air around her instantly dulled with smoke. Her lungs burned from the gunpowder.

Almost there.

As Laura made her way closer, she could see that Annie was standing over the fallen officer, watching him die. Laura was gaining on her, knife up and ready to strike.

Almost there.

Just as Laura was about to reach up and grab Annie, Annie spun around and brought the barrel of the shotgun down hard across Laura's face. Laura fell, a burst of stars dancing in her field of vision as a tooth dropped from her mouth. The back of her head slammed against the floor in the living room, and all she felt was pain.

Annie was on her in seconds. She stood over Laura, the shotgun aimed, the shell waiting in the chamber. But before she could pull the trigger, Laura kicked up and grabbed Annie's ankle, pulling as hard as she could until she knocked Annie off balance and both women ended up on the ground, the shotgun dislodged as it bounced across the floor.

Laura pulled herself on top, straddling Annie as she stabbed down twice with the knife, not really seeing where the blade was penetrating, but Annie's screams told her she was hitting a mark. Annie's arms were free and she tried to counteract Laura's attack by pushing away the knife and scratching her in the face, clawing her neck and chest, pulling her hair, and punching up, connecting with her jaw.

The shot to the jaw dazed Laura and she dropped the knife. She gathered herself and instinctively took two fistfuls of hair. She began pounding the back of Annie's head onto the floor until Annie finally reached up and poked her in the eye. Laura recoiled and let go. As soon as she did, Annie rolled Laura off of her, and now she was on the bottom.

Annie snatched a large lamp from an end table and smashed it over Laura's head and face. The base was ceramic and heavy, and Laura fought to stay conscious. The wet stickiness of her own blood dripped from what must have been countless cuts and gouges on her face and neck. But she was in survival mode and felt no pain. The adrenaline screaming through her body wouldn't allow it.

Annie's hands slid over Laura's neck. Laura frantically felt around for the knife that had to be near them, but couldn't find it. Annie began to squeeze, and the sudden sensation of her throat being crushed sent her into a panic.

Laura's fingers touched something thin that snaked across the floor. She pulled it closer and, in the depths of her fading consciousness, knew it was the cord from the lamp Annie had hit her with. She gripped it and slipped the cord across Annie's chest, then brought it up quickly. Annie, surprised, let go of her neck for a moment to grab at the cord.

That was all Laura needed. As soon as Annie let go and sat

up, Laura forced herself into a sitting position and kicked Annie off of her lap. As Annie fell away, Laura wrapped the cord around Annie's neck twice and got behind her. Nelle's words whispered in her mind again.

Help us.

Laura placed her knee in the middle of Annie's back and pressed down as she pulled up on the cord as hard as she could. She could see her mangled hands bleeding more as she pulled, but felt nothing. The gargled choking sound filled the room and mixed with Laura's grunts. She kept pulling up on the cord and pushing down with her knee. All of the fear and remorse and rage came out of her at once as she groaned and spat, pulling and pushing, her breath heavy and labored. She cried out as an overwhelming sensation of loss and guilt fell upon her. She sobbed and wailed as she kept pulling on the string.

"I'm sorry!" she screamed over and over again.

Annie's body went limp, and the choked gargling ceased.

Laura waited for a few minutes longer, still pulling on the cord to make sure Annie was dead, still crying and apologizing to Annie for what she'd done, and to her mother for getting her in that situation, and to Nelle, who she'd hurt in so many different ways. When she finally let go, she collapsed next to Annie's body, exhausted and scared. She held Annie's head in her hands until the tears stopped.

The pain revealed itself as Laura slowly climbed to her feet. Her face. Her chest. Her hands. Her knees. She wiped the blood off of her face with her shirt and blinked until the eye she was poked in was able to focus. She could feel it beginning to swell, but it didn't shut, which was a good sign. She winced when she touched her nose. It was undoubtedly broken. Her jaw seemed a little off, too. She had trouble opening her mouth all the way.

Laura picked up the shotgun, checking the chamber. Four more shells. She'd have to use them sparingly. She walked through the kitchen and stopped when she reached the cabinet above the sink. She opened it and pulled out the bottle of Prosecco, studying it, rolling it around in her hand, contemplating. If she ever needed a drink, now was the time. She'd been through so much, and a treat would set her straight. Make things right so she could get back up to the house and end it all with Sofia Bennett and her family. She had to save Nelle. In order to do that, she needed her mind right.

Help us.

"No," Laura said aloud again.

She let the bottle go and listened as it shattered on the tile floor. No more bullshit. It was time to save her little girl.

The trooper was lying on his back, his arms and legs spread out before him. It looked like his vest had saved him from Annie's first shot, but the second had hit him in the head and neck area. Laura stepped over him and bent down to grab his radio, but it had been shattered by the shotgun blasts. She dropped the shotgun and took the Glock from his hand, stumbling out of the house.

The patrol car sat in the gravel driveway, no lights, no siren, engine idling. The trooper had come in quietly and neither she nor Annie had heard him. Laura ran to the car, opened the driver's side door, and slid inside. Her shaking hands took the radio from its cradle. "Hello. Can anyone hear me?" she asked.

No answer, but she could hear the crackle of the radio over the speaker, so she knew it was on.

"If anyone can hear me, there's an officer hurt at 122 North Shore West Caroga Lake Road. My name is Laura Anderson. Orton Bennett and his sister kidnapped my daughter, and he's keeping her at the house across the river in the back of 122. Please hurry. My daughter is injured and needs help. Officer down. Family kidnapped. Help us."

She dropped the radio and climbed out of the car, her hand slipping on the hood as she ran around the front of it. The smudged bloody handprint sat in contrast to the cruiser's clean blue paint. It was the officer's blood. Or maybe it was hers. Or maybe Annie's. She'd been through too much to keep track.

Laura checked the Glock and slid the cartridge out of the gun's grip to see how many rounds she had. It was full. Seventeen rounds. That would be plenty. Having a police officer as a husband had its advantages, especially one who took the family shooting on a semi-regular basis.

"I'm coming, Nelle," she said as she gripped the Glock and started to move toward the house. "This ends tonight. One way or the other."

CHAPTER FORTY-THREE

Laura pushed her way back through the brush and overgrowth of the forest and returned to the icy water. She flung herself into the stream without hesitation this time. No careful steps or quiet movement to keep herself upright and silent. Her adrenaline was too high and she crashed across the stream, splashing and slipping as she went, her legs burning like they did before, quickly turning to pins and needles and then growing numb. She focused on the lights inside the half-built house, a generator churning to keep those lights on.

The streambed on the opposite side came quickly and Laura staggered onto land, lying in the mud for a moment, trying to get feeling in her legs and feet. She didn't know how long Nelle could hang on. She didn't know if her call over the police radio had worked or not. It was up to her to end this. Tonight.

She climbed to her feet and fell forward, leaning against a large oak tree so she could take a second and study the house. It appeared the flood lights were on in the attic, glowing through the hole she'd made in the bricked-out window.

There were a few more lights on throughout the lower

floors, and from her vantage point, she could see that several windows had plywood covering them. The property around the house was still. Nothing moved but the tops of trees from the strengthening wind.

More thunder east of her. Closer now.

Laura ran across the yard fast as she could, hunched over as if she was a soldier storming an enemy's compound. She leapt up onto the porch and pressed her back against the side of the house, sliding ever so carefully toward the front door. She stopped and counted to ten, listening for movement or any other noise that would tell her where Orton might be. It was hard to hear anything with the generator going. She bent down, turned, and carefully opened the screen door.

She would've given anything to hear the sound of police sirens coming up the side road or crossing the bridge onto the property. She didn't want to do this alone, but she had to. She figured someone knew something if they'd sent a state trooper to check the house, but she had no idea if the police would be waiting for the trooper to report back or how long they'd wait for that report before figuring something was wrong. This was the only way forward for now. It was time.

The foyer was new to her. There were no interior walls, just studs and some soiled insulation. Laura walked further inside and saw the living room. The crumbled fireplace stood at the end with a broken mirror that had been built in above the mantle. Laura took notice of herself as she walked by it. Her eyes were slits, one almost swollen shut. She was filthy with mud from the streambed drying on her skin and clothes. Her hair clung to her skull, wet and cold. She couldn't help but giggle a little hysterically as she went by. If only the other soccer moms and church peers from Garrison could see her now.

Laura walked into a hallway and saw the kitchen with only the pipes popping out of the walls. She recognized where they'd taken her out the back door that had no door on it. At that point, she knew where she was.

She retraced her steps and climbed the main stairs to the second floor. She aimed the trooper's Glock in front of her as she glanced back over her shoulder every few steps. The few scattered lights cast shadows and aided her as she went. Like before, she could see the years of neglect that had befallen the place and realized how alone she was. They were in the middle of nowhere, offseason, with only a smattering of residents anywhere near the lake. It would be like that until Memorial Day.

She stopped at the top landing and waited. The house was silent. Lightning strobed the corridor for a moment. There were lights on, one in each room lining the hallway. Laura turned right and started walking, weapon at the ready, safety off, finger gently on the trigger.

The bedrooms were empty. She checked under each bed in all three rooms. Nothing. In the third bedroom, a lone table lamp sat on the floor with no shade, making the bare bulb seem even brighter than it was. The light in this room was intrusive, cold, and sharp. The shadows on the walls had hard edges to them. The bed was empty with one half of a set of handcuffs hanging from a banister. She wondered if that was where they'd been keeping Nelle.

"Orton!" she cried as she stood still, listening for movement. "Come out! Show yourself!"

Nothing.

She walked into the hall. "Orton!"

"Betty," a voice bellowed from above her.

She looked up at the ceiling.

"I think you should come up here and take a look at Nelle. I'm worried about her. It looks like she lost a lot of blood. When Annie told me what happened, I couldn't believe you could do something like that to your own kid. Choosing a bottle of shitty tequila over seeing her was one thing, but this time you really did a number. This is unforgivable."

Laura crept down the hall toward the stairs.

"She's so pale," Orton continued. "I think she needs serious medical attention. She's dying."

Thunder rolled again, louder, closer. A patter of rain began to fall on the roof as Laura stopped at the bottom of the stairs.

"You better get up here. Things are turning critical."

Laura took a breath. "I'm coming."

The storm had finally arrived.

CHAPTER FORTY-FOUR

Roman rocked and bounced as he climbed the hill, wanting to move faster, but not willing to take the risk on such a narrow path with a steep drop on the left side. The darkness was intense at Caroga Lake. Storm clouds blocked the moon, making the blackness even deeper. The car's headlights stretched as far as they could, illuminating the road that was only half paved in spots, and ending at a void where nothing further could be seen.

A rumble of thunder bellowed in the distance, and after a few minutes, raindrops began to patter on the windshield. He hit his wipers once and sat up in his seat so he could see better.

He crested the hill and found the state police cruiser idling in the driveway of Clare Hamms's dark and quiet house. Roman cut his headlights and pulled next to the cruiser, shutting off the engine and rolling down his window. The car was empty. He unholstered his weapon and leaned out of the window to listen.

Something wasn't right.

Roman slowly climbed out of the car and ran around to the cruiser to peek inside. The keys were still in the ignition, the engine grumbling. The radio had been turned down. Remnants of what might've been a bloody handprint was on the hood of the car. The rain had begun to wash it away. The lake house was dark, nothing more than a large silhouette against the backdrop of more darkness. There wasn't a single light on anywhere that he could see.

He crouched down, waiting and listening, hoping to hear something. The last thing he wanted to do was surprise the officer who might've been patrolling the grounds. That's how accidental shootings happened. But at the same time, he didn't want to call out and give away his position should someone else be on the property. He stayed in his crouch for a few minutes longer, and when his knees started to bark, he got up and ran toward the house.

The rain was falling steadier now. He hopped onto the porch and stopped next to the open front door. The air was stale and he could smell gunpowder. He took a breath, gripped his Beretta, and turned into the doorway, weapon aimed out in front of him, ready to fire if need be.

Even in the darkness, Roman could see the trooper's body inside the door. The man's face had been blown off. Pellets from a shotgun were scattered on the hardwood, stuck in pools of blood that surrounded the trooper's body. It was clear he'd been assigned to check the place out after they'd radioed the address from the rest stop, and it was even clearer that he'd found where Laura had been heading. The only questions that remained were who was still left in the house and whether or not he was too late to save whoever might need saving.

Careful steps brought him further inside, and as soon as he cleared a small hallway from the front door, Roman saw the woman's body on the ground. She was lying facedown with a cord wrapped around her neck. The base of a broken lamp was beside her, the brass ring still attached to the power cord. He pulled his penlight from his pocket and walked over to the body, shining the light onto the victim's face. It wasn't Laura Anderson, nor was it her daughter, Nelle. He didn't recognize this woman and had no idea if she was an innocent victim, an abductee herself, or someone involved with everything that had happened downstate. He didn't spend much time on her. She was dead, and he had to keep moving and search the rest of the place.

The house wasn't big, and Roman swept the main floor and the second floor in a matter of minutes. Aside from the two victims, the place was empty. He walked back outside and stood on the porch to check his phone. No service. He ran toward the police cruiser and climbed inside, snatching the radio from the passenger's seat.

"Do you copy?" he asked as he continued to scan the grounds around him. "This is Detective Estrada. Westchester County Police. We have an emergency. I have an officer down. Does anyone read?"

He waited, but there was no answer. He peered at the radio console itself, switching to another channel to try again.

"Does anyone read me? This is Detective Estrada. Westchester County Police. I have an officer down at this location. Over."

Nothing.

He tried a third channel.

"This is Detective Roman Estrada, Westchester County Police. Is anyone there?"

The radio crackled.

"Go ahead, this is Gloversville PD. We copy."

Roman quickly offered his location and explained the situation at hand. The dispatcher confirmed his location and instructed him to stay put as he sent backup and an ambulance. Roman agreed.

The rain was coming heavy now: a steady, soaking rain. He sat in the patrol car, his eyes scanning everything around him, his weapon at the ready, trying to think where Laura could've gone and how much time there was left to put an end to the death and destruction she continued to leave in her wake.

Thunder rolled.

A single gunshot followed.

Roman jumped out of the car and stared in the vicinity of where he thought he heard the shot come from. Back in the woods. Behind the house.

Without hesitation, he took off running as the storm settled in for the long night ahead.

CHAPTER FORTY-FIVE

Laura climbed the narrow stairs slowly, stopping on each one and listening to determine where Orton was. He'd stopped talking, and everything was quiet besides the rain drumming against the slate-tiled roof. The lights were on, illuminating every detail. The worn treads. The chipped and splintered walls. The grime. The blood that had spattered when she'd plunged the wood into her daughter's gut. The puddle pooled on the floor. She could see it all.

She crested the stairs and walked through the open door. Nelle was the first person she saw, lying on the stained mattress. Her daughter gripped the wood protruding from her stomach, her tiny fingers colored crimson, her wrists and forearms stained with her mother's catastrophic mistake.

"Nelle," Laura said. "Honey, can you hear me?"

"I'm pretty sure she can hear you," Orton replied. "But she's too weak to respond."

Laura's eyes widened as she looked around the attic, her Glock aimed and ready. The floodlights were fiercely bright, but they were focused directly at the mattress, which made the shadows beyond them thick. It was hard to see where he might be hiding. The attic space was large, encompassing the length of the entire house below.

"I like Nelle," Orton said, his voice rising over the rain that pounded the roof above them. "She's a good kid. Never gave us trouble. Respectful. She's the kind of kid I'd want one day. She's someone you can depend on. It pained me to have to hurt her. You should know that. I never wanted to do it. That's the truth."

"What did you do to her?" Laura could hear the panic in her voice and tried to choke it down.

"Nothing close to what you did. A few burns on the meaty part of her calves to get her to scream so I could get you to pay attention. I figured that was the spot that I'd do the least amount of damage. I never wanted to hurt no one, Betty. Not even you, if you can believe that. I was a regular guy living a regular life up until a few weeks ago. I wasn't made for all this. It's not in me."

Laura kept the gun pointed in front of her. "Then let us go."

"Maybe. Tell me why you killed my mother first. Tell me why you ruined my family."

"It was an accident," Laura began, crouching down and feeling exposed in the openness of the attic. "I was new, and the ER was so hectic. It was hard for me to keep up. Your mother came in on the brink of death. For whatever it's worth, there was a good chance she wasn't going to survive her injuries anyway, but that's no excuse. I was supposed to give her a drug called Dilaudid, and I grabbed the wrong vial. They looked similar and I was confused. I gave her potassium instead and that caused cardiac arrest. Her body was already too weak to fight. We lost her because of my mistake."

"But you knew her. You knew who she was and what she did to your brother and you never told anyone."

Silence.

"Our families are connected," Orton continued. "She gets hit by a car just like she hit Donny. She was an alcoholic. You're an alcoholic. We had no mom growing up. Now Nelle won't, either. It's like we're all living the same nightmare. Crazy when you think about it."

Laura kept glancing back toward Nelle as she tried to concentrate on where Orton might be hiding. She focused on Nelle's midsection, trying to see if she was still breathing. Her bloody stomach rose and fell ever so slightly. She was alive, but time was running out. Her daughter hadn't moved since she'd come through the attic door.

"I didn't tell anyone I knew your mom because I was young and scared. I didn't have the courage to face what I'd done, and I thought if anyone found out about my history with Sofia, they'd think I made my mistake on purpose. I ran away and tried to forget it, but I never could. Not through all the years and not by making myself someone new. I drank to try and forget, but there wasn't a single day that went by that I didn't think about what I'd done to your mother. Not one."

"And your brother?"

Laura started to cry as she kept the gun pointed up and out. "My brother died because of me. Your mother hit him, but he died because of me."

The rain drumming the roof underscored a long period of silence. Finally, Orton spoke, his voice quiet. "Thank you for telling me the truth."

Movement from the back corner.

"You need to let us go," Laura said. "Nelle's not going to last much longer. I have to get her to a hospital."

"Annie's dead, isn't she?"

"Yes."

"She found you and tried to kill you?"

"Yes."

Shadows moved.

"She was so angry. She wanted this vengeance so much more than I did. She never had a chance to know our mother.

And the things she had to go through growing up in the system was more horrific that you could ever imagine. You have to understand that. In her mind, you put her there. You gave her the life she had to survive through. It was almost sad to see how excited she was to kill you."

Laura took a breath. "Orton, please. You have to let us go."

"I can't do that." Orton's voice cracked as if he'd started to cry himself. "I'd reckon we passed the point of no return a while back. I can't see a way out for either of us."

"You just said you didn't want to hurt me."

"I didn't. I don't. But I simply have no choice. You've seen what I look like. You know who I am. My sister's body is over in your mom's place. The police will have me in cuffs before I hit Ohio. I gotta do what I gotta do and get moving. No other choice."

Laura aimed the gun toward the darkness. "The police are on the way. I called them."

"It doesn't matter. They won't make it in time. We're out in the middle of nowhere. I'm sorry."

Orton emerged from behind the spotlight, but before Laura could fire, he yanked at an orange extension cord and the light went out. The contrast from light to dark was as blinding as it was from dark to light, and it took a moment for Laura to realize what was happening. She fired once, the shot exploding in the confined space, then threw herself toward the mattress so she could protect Nelle. As she was about to leave her feet and dive forward, something hit her from the side, sending her sprawling across the floor. The gun slid from her grasp as she hit the ground hard.

Orton was on her. He was strong, determined. He pulled her onto her back and straddled her, trying to pin her arms under his knees, but she kept her arms moving, scratching at his face with her broken and jagged nails, pulling his hair, and trying to gouge his eyes, like Annie had done to her earlier.

Help us.

Orton punched her, his knuckles connecting with the center of her skull, crushing her nose and splitting her top lip open to match the bottom. Stars exploded in the darkness as Laura's arms went limp. She could taste a steady wave of blood running into her mouth and down her throat, choking her.

Large hands wrapped themselves around Laura's neck and Orton started squeezing as she tried to take a breath. Her legs kicked uselessly under him, weak as the effects of the punch still lingered.

"I'll make sure Nelle doesn't suffer," Orton said. Tears fell from his eyes onto Laura's face. "I promise."

A rainbow of cloudy colors appeared from her periphery. Laura knew it would crawl across her field of vision and that would be the last thing she'd ever see. She thought about what he'd do to Nelle once she was dead and how Kurt would never know what really happened there. But this was it. There was no doubt about it. Orton was going to kill her. The police would come, but it would be over by then. Laura and her daughter would be dead. Their case would be closed.

The lights suddenly turned on and the pressure around her neck immediately disappeared. She lifted her head the best she could to find Orton staring up at Nelle who was kneeling over by the outlet, the orange extension cord plugged back in the outlet. She held the trooper's Glock in her two trembling hands.

"What're you doing?" Orton asked as he got off of Laura and slowly spun toward Nelle.

"Get away from my mother," Nelle whispered. Her voice was so fragile, yet so defiant.

"I thought we were friends. I protected you."

"Get... away."

Orton smiled. "You're too weak to hold that gun for much longer. I'm surprised you made it across the room. I'll wait until you can't hold it no more. I got some time."

Nelle looked down at the piece of wood protruding from her stomach and looked back up at Orton. "I don't."

Before Orton could react, a single shot rang out, piercing Laura's eardrums. The bullet flew clean into Orton's chest and he stumbled back one step before falling to his knees. He tried to regain his balance as he looked at Nelle, his eyes wide and frightened, but his leg gave out and he stumbled out of the room and down the attic stairs.

As soon as the shot was fired, Nelle collapsed, the Glock slipping from her grip and thudding onto the floor. Laura climbed to her feet and staggered over to her daughter, taking her head and cradling it in her lap.

"I got him, Mom."

"Yes, you did," Laura replied. "You saved us."

She checked her daughter's pulse and it was hardly there.

"I'm going to find help. It's almost over. We're almost done. You just have to stay with me a little while longer."

Nelle didn't answer, and Laura knew she didn't have much time. She climbed to her feet and ran down the attic stairs, hoping there would be a working cell phone that would allow her to call the police. She pushed through the door that led to the second floor and stopped. For a moment, she thought she was hallucinating as she stared at the woman who stood before her holding a large carving knife.

"Mom?"

Her mother nodded.

"We ain't done, Betty. Not yet."

CHAPTER FORTY-SIX

"Mom," Laura stammered, shocked to see her mother standing in front of her. "I thought you were dead. I heard your neck break."

Clare was unmoving, planted between Laura and the stairs that led from the second floor to the first. She grasped the knife tight in her hand. "I was hoping you'd be too dumb to know the difference between a bone breaking and a branch snapping. Some nurse you would've been."

"What are you doing?"

A low growl.

"All those years, you let me believe your lie," Clare said. "I knew you were responsible for Donny's death. I could feel it. I knew, like a mother knows."

Laura could see the fury in her mother's gaze. "Mom, please. I have to get help for Nelle. She's bleeding to death."

"All those years, you let me blame Sofia for running up on that curb and taking my boy from me. You let me believe that horrible picture I had in my head of him getting run down by some out-of-control drunk. But the truth eventually comes out, Betty. It finds its way. Always."

"Mom. Put the knife down and let me pass."

Her mother took a step closer.

"You framed this woman. Caused her more pain than she was already feeling? Making her crime into something worse than it already was? I found the security tape from the railyard tucked away in your daddy's things after he died. Why do you think he kept it? Maybe to remind himself of how evil his own flesh and blood was? Maybe to hide that fact from the rest of the world? I never saw what was on the tape when I was in Texas since we didn't have a VCR, but when I got here, I had my nurse get me a cheap one online and I was able to play it. My god, Betty. What did you do?"

Laura looked behind her and wondered how long Nelle would have before she slipped away. She wiped the tears from her eyes and tried to think of a way past her mother as the words spewed from her mouth cut deep.

"I always knew there was something dark inside you. Some people are born bad, and I could feel it the second I laid my eyes on you. But not Donny. He was always a good boy. My favorite. I know a mother's not supposed to have a favorite, but I don't care. He was special. He'd never grow up to be a drunk like you. Like Sofia. You ever think about the irony of all that? A drunk woman kills your brother in front of you and then you become the drunk woman? Funny how that works."

"Get out of my way."

"I never asked you to be in my life. I didn't want to come here. And I don't want your evilness or your weakness anywhere near me. I was fine when it was your daddy and me. I pretended I had no children who were still living and nobody gave me no gruff about it. Then your daddy dies and you come swoopin' in and take me away from my friends and my church and the place I knew for almost my entire life. I can't visit your daddy's grave. I can't visit Donny. You took me away from everything I loved and no matter how many times I begged you to bring me back, you kept me here, alone. You should've let me die that day I tried to kill myself. I wanted to be with my son, and you took that away from me too."

"I brought you here so I could try and reconnect with you. I wanted to rebuild our relationship. I wanted you to stop hating me."

"I don't want to rebuild anything with you!" The knife shook as she screamed. "Not after what I seen. Not after knowing what kind of a person you really are. I found more in your daddy's stuff than just the tape. I found Sofia's death certificates. There were two of them, which was weird. The first one had a handwritten note about a lethal dose of potassium being a contributing factor to her death the night she was brought into your ER. The second certificate didn't have that note. I figured your father had something to do with that."

"Mom—"

"I found Orton and told him everything. I had to make amends on behalf of my family. It was the right thing to do. Then he started looking into who actually gave the lethal dose, but he and I already knew. He hired a private investigator and found the hospital's old sign-in sheets. There you were. Betty Hamms."

Laura stood frozen, the memories of that night flooding her mind.

"Next thing I know, Orton and Annie are at my doorstep, showing me what they found and talkin' about all the ways you ruined their lives. I knew exactly how they felt. But then things got a little crazy. They became angrier and angrier, watching the tape from the railyard over and over. They started talkin' about taking Nelle and killing her so you would know what it's like to lose someone you love. I couldn't have that. I couldn't have another child die. So, I convinced them to leave Nelle alone and kill you instead. That would be the real vengeance, right? Going after the actual person who killed their mom? I told them I could get you up here, but they wanted to use Nelle as bait so they could see you suffer a bit before they killed you. I agreed. I figured I could protect Nelle and have some control that way. They took that girl, and you came running."

"Mom, I—"

"Nelle thought I was a prisoner, too. If I was going to have a relationship with her after all this, it was important for her to think I was a victim, too. That's how we'd bond. Same with Kurt. He'd welcome me as a victim. And in the last few years before this goddamned disease took me, I'd have a family again. Not the one I wanted, but close enough. But even after they got you up here, you couldn't die like you was supposed to. You escaped and mucked things up, thinking you was doing the right thing, and you hurt Nelle so bad. How could you be so careless? She's dying up there, Betty, and you're the one who did it."

Laura fought so hard not to collapse in a heap of guilt and remorse. Everything her mother said was true. Everything she touched got screwed up, and now her own daughter was on the brink of death because of her mistake.

Her mother took another step forward. "You're supposed to die. That's the end of this story. I'm going to kill you, and then I'm going to save Nelle. I'll get her help and make sure she's okay, but you'll be dead. That's how it has to be. Two victims survive, but the third doesn't. I can't have you in my life anymore."

Laura was about to open her mouth to speak when she heard rustling one floor below.

"Police!" a voice shouted. "Show yourself!"

Laura's mother instinctively turned toward the voice, and as she did, Laura rushed her, pushing her with all her might back and away from the attic door. Her mother stumbled and lost her footing, crashing to the ground, the knife skipping from her grip. Laura pulled her mother's arms behind her and knelt on her back to keep her from getting up.

"This is the police!" the voice shouted again. "Call out now!"

"Up here!" Laura cried as the weight of what she'd been through finally crashed upon her shoulders. "We need help! My daughter is injured!"

"That you, Laura?"

"Yes. Hurry!"

"Hang in there," the voice replied. "Help is on the way."

That was the one sentence Laura had been longing to hear since the cell phone with the cracked screen rang in her glove compartment.

Help is on the way.

CHAPTER FORTY-SEVEN

THREE WEEKS LATER

The hospital seemed busier than usual, but considering Albany Medical Center was the largest facility in the region, Laura figured they were always busy. Perhaps the hustle and bustle of the staff rushing around outside in the hall was always happening, and she was finally feeling well enough to take notice. They were on the third floor in a recovery wing, off the ICU. They'd been afforded a private room until Nelle was strong enough to start rehab, and then she'd be transferred to the medical-surgical floor and given a roommate for the remainder of her stay.

Nelle had been touch-and-go for a while. When the ambulance came to the lake, she'd lost consciousness, and Laura was told her daughter's heart had stopped in the helicopter to Albany, but the medical techs had gotten it going again, and she was in surgery ten minutes after landing. The wood Laura had stabbed her with had pierced her intestines, and there was massive internal bleeding. The surgeon was able to completely cut out the damaged part of Nelle's large intestine and reconnect the remaining ends. They'd stopped the bleeding and induced a coma to get her stable. It had taken almost ten days to get her where they wanted, but she made it. Of course, she'd have a long road ahead, one full of physical recovery as well as mental rehabilitation, but Laura knew Nelle would be okay. Her daughter was one of the strongest people she knew.

Kurt had been with them the entire time. Except for quick trips to grab them something to eat or to run down the street to the hotel for a shower, he never left their side. The staff had set up a cot for them to sleep on next to Nelle's bed, and they alternated between the hospital room and the hotel. Most nights, neither of them wanted to leave, so Kurt would sleep in a chair. It was the same chair where Laura sat now, watching her daughter snoring softly as her body recovered. Kurt was dozing on the cot. She couldn't wait until they could all go home.

Detective Estrada, the man who'd appeared at the lake property, knocked on the door and took a single step inside. "Is this a bad time?" he asked.

Laura shook her head and waved him in. "It's fine."

The detective walked to the end of Nelle's bed and placed a small bouquet of flowers onto her food tray as Kurt sat up. Daisies. Perfect.

"Thank you," Laura said. "They're beautiful."

"My pleasure," Detective Estrada replied. "I read that daisies symbolize innocence and purity. I thought that was fitting. Maybe she can recapture some of that when she gets better. Lord knows she's been through a lot." He tapped the edge of her bed with his palm. "I wanted to stop in to see how everyone was doing. I'm glad to see Nelle's out of the ICU."

"Any news on my mom?"

A quick nod. "She's been cooperative with us, and the DA is taking that into consideration going forward. She's been transferred to a county facility for now."

"Can I see her?"

"Sure. I can arrange that."

Laura offered a polite smile. She wasn't entirely sure she wanted to see her mother after everything that had taken place, but there was still something inside her that wanted to reach out. In the meetings she'd started attending, her group often talked about making amends. Perhaps that was why she was feeling like she was. Lord knows cutting bait on a mother who repeatedly tried to exorcise her from her life seemed the logical next step, but Laura was aware of all the harm she'd inflicted on her family. Nothing had been the same since Donny's accident, and it would feel good to reach out one last time to tell her mother how sorry she was. For everything.

"How're you feeling?" Detective Estrada asked, pointing to his mouth and chin.

Laura instinctively touched the bandages and stitches that covered the lower part of her face. The doctors had sewn up her two lips and reset her nose. She still had remnants of two black eyes, but those bruises were fading. She could hear the clicking in her jaw, but there was nothing anyone could do about that. Her tongue filled the space where her tooth had been, a fix for later on when her body was a little stronger.

"I'm feeling better each day. Stitches come out next week, and I'm not having any more concussion symptoms. My hands were just cuts, thankfully. No broken bones."

"That's great news," Detective Estrada said. He spun away from Nelle and faced Laura and Kurt. "And speaking of great news, we got confirmation last night that Chief Derry is up and walking. Just a step or two, but it's a start. The doctors say he's going to be able to keep his legs. His rehab has officially begun."

Laura placed a hand over her heart and closed her eyes. "I'm so happy to hear that."

"He gave his statement, and no charges will be filed. We all understand what you did and why. Of course, we all wish you'd found another way, but truth be told, you probably saved his life by not opening that trunk. Now that we know Annie Bennett was in there, we figure she would've shot him. He's looking forward to meeting you when you get back down to Westchester."

Laura couldn't help but feel a sense of relief. She hadn't killed the chief after all, and he would walk again. Given the circumstances, it was the most she could ask for.

"What about the hitchhiker?" Laura asked.

"Gina Toads," Detective Estrada replied. "She's also recovering and will be okay. We explained what happened, and our information helped fill in the gaps from her information. She said she wants to interview you for her blog."

Laura laughed and wiped her eyes. "Please tell Gina that she's my first interview. No matter who else comes calling, she'll be my first."

"How's it going with the press? Are they hounding you?"

"Thankfully, it's been pretty quiet," Kurt replied. "We'd like to keep it that way, if possible."

"I hope we can." He looked back and forth between Laura and Kurt, then reached into his coat pocket and came away with a small notepad. "I had to come up and file my closing report with the state police and Gloversville PD. I'm also in the process of completing my file for my department, and I'd like to go over a few things. Make sure I have everything in the right order."

"Of course," Laura replied.

The detective opened the notepad. "We got the incident report back from Dell Seton Medical Center. Everything you told us checks out. Back in 2000, you were new to the ER. The vials of Dilaudid and potassium were similar in color, and in the chaos of trying to save Sofia Bennett, you grabbed the wrong vial and administered the potassium. It's tragic, but even the hospital administrators didn't think what you did was grounds for termination. They recommended suspension, a new period of probation, and more training. Why go to the extremes of leaving Texas and assuming a new identity?"

Laura could sense Kurt watching her. He'd tried to talk to her about the same things so many times between Caroga Lake and now, but she'd kept putting him off, explaining that they needed to put all of their energy in getting Nelle better and that she'd answer all of his questions when the time was right. It appeared that time had come.

"This is going to sound too simple to make any real sense," she said. "But it comes down to the guilt I felt. I took an innocent woman's life because I was too inept of a nurse to help her. My calling had been to help people and save lives, and I ended up taking one because I couldn't tell the difference between a dark blue stripe on a bottle and a light blue stripe. I tried to get over it. I tried so hard to move on. I sat through the hospital board's inquiry and gave interview after interview about what happened. I accepted their punishment and acted grateful when they didn't fire me. But really, I wish they had. Every time I stepped into that ER, the incident came back. The memories of what happened, the feeling of panic and helplessness. I could see the way the other nurses stared at me and talked about me behind my back. I knew what they were saying. I could've gone to another hospital, but word of the incident had spread and my name had already become tarnished."

"But even if you left the state," Detective Estrada said, "you didn't have to assume a new identity."

Laura nodded and looked down at the floor. "The new identity wasn't about getting another nursing job or hiding from the incident with Sofia Bennett. The new identity was about shedding the person I was and becoming someone completely different. I didn't want to think about what I'd done anymore. I wanted to start over. I wanted a safe life. A predictable one. No more nursing and ERs. I still wanted to be around medicine in some capacity, but not like that. I didn't even contemplate a new identity until one day, I pulled up to the Bennetts' house. I was planning on knocking on Mr. Bennett's door to apologize and explain what happened, but then I saw Orton. He was all alone, sitting on his walkway drawing pictures on the slate with chalk. I noticed how alone he was, and it hit me. I did that. I caused that poor boy to lose his mother, and I knew right at that point that if I kept being Betty Hamms, I'd never escape what I'd done. I drove away without having had the courage to even get out of my car, let alone knock on Mr. Bennett's door. I had to leave. To me, it was leave and live or stay and eventually kill myself. I couldn't see any other roads to take. Not then."

Kurt reached over and placed a hand on her thigh. He squeezed it once. That was all she needed to know he was there.

"I hooked up with this guy in Dallas who made authentic IDs. A friend from school made the introduction, and it cost me ten thousand dollars to get a driver's license, social security card, and birth certificate and to be hacked into all the government systems. I paid with the signing bonus money the hospital gave me when they recruited me out of college. He came up with Laura Trotz from St. Petersburg, Florida. I have no idea where he got the name or the social security number, but it worked enough to get me on a plane to New York, a job in Midtown, and an apartment with a roommate. Then I met Kurt, and it felt like I *was* Laura. That this was my new life. What I didn't realize at the time was that the guilt would follow me no matter where I went or who I became. My need to quiet that guilt had always come with alcohol and pills and as much volunteer work as I could get. I was trying to pay for my sins, but there's never any ample payback. The guilt never fades. But I'm working on that now. I want to get better."

"What about your parents?" the detective asked. "Did they know where you were?"

"No," Laura replied. "I sent them a Christmas card each year to let them know I was still alive, but I drove to different places to mail it so they couldn't trace the postmarks. Pennsylvania. New Jersey. Ohio. Trips I could turn around in a day. I also called my father from a pay phone once a year in the spring. He didn't know where I was or that I changed names or any of that. One year, I called and it was my mom on the other end. She told me my father had died. Then she told me she'd been diagnosed with early-stage dementia, and I knew I couldn't leave her alone to deal with that herself. I also knew how much she hated me, and I didn't want to suddenly bring her home to Kurt and Nelle and have to explain all my lies, so I picked out her place on Caroga Lake and we went from there. I filled her prescriptions, and she had my number if she needed me. I never imagined she hated me enough to help someone kill me, though. That's a hard thing to wrap my head around."

Laura sat back in her chair as tears fell from her eyes, looking over at Kurt.

"One last question," Detective Estrada said. "If Orton was watching you on the FaceTime app the entire time up to Caroga Lake, how did you get the chance to write your mother's address on the bathroom stall?"

Laura shrugged. "I wouldn't let him see me actually going to the bathroom, so I held the phone camera high and close to my face to make sure it took up the entire screen. He couldn't see what I was doing because my face was in the way. I wrote it without seeing what I was writing. All I could do was hope it was legible and that someone would see me on the rest stop cameras and find the address, which is, thankfully, what happened."

Detective Estrada nodded once, folded his notepad closed, and slipped it back into his jacket pocket. "I'm going to need you to come with me to Albany PD's headquarters on Henry Johnson Boulevard," he said. "It's not far. About a mile from here. I need a fully recorded interview with eyewitnesses in the observation room. If I could do it here, I would, but if we're going to close this case and put it to bed once and for all, I need a final statement done one hundred percent by the book."

"Do you think there'll be charges associated with the second identity?" Laura asked.

The detective shook his head. "I don't know. Let's get this done and go from there."

"Okay," Laura said. "I'd like my attorney on speakerphone during the interview. Can we arrange that?"

"Absolutely."

Laura turned to Kurt and took his hand, placing it on her lap. "I'm sorry," she said. "I know I've apologized a thousand times already, but I don't know what else to say. You thought you were marrying someone you weren't. All these years, and you're just now finding out about me. You don't deserve that. You're too good of a man to have to learn all this now. I don't know what else to say except that I'm sorry."

Kurt smiled and gently rubbed her cheek with his thumb. "I know."

"Take care of her while I'm gone?"

"Of course."

"When I'm done, I'll stop by the hotel to shower, then I'll come back here and switch with you."

"I'll be here."

As Laura got up from her seat, Kurt's cell phone started to ring. He pulled it from his pocket and looked at the Caller ID. "Work," he muttered.

She watched him retreat to the opposite end of the room and place a hand over his ear so he could hear better. She allowed Detective Estrada to escort her from Nelle's room, and as she touched the faded remnants of a scratch on her wrist from a fight she had with her daughter a lifetime ago, she heard Kurt engage the call.

CHAPTER FORTY-EIGHT

Laura walked into the hotel room and dropped her pocketbook onto the floor. She was tired and her body ached, but her final, official statement had been given to Detective Estrada and his team from Westchester County. It was over. All of it. Her attorney would continue his dialogue with the district attorneys in both Westchester County and Travis County in Texas regarding the false identification she'd been using for the last twenty years, but he was confident not much would come from it. So much time had passed, and she hadn't used her new identity for any criminal activity. Laura Anderson had been an upstanding citizen who paid her taxes and followed the rules of law, so other than purely hiding her real identity, there wasn't much meat on the bone. Perhaps a fine and probation, and, of course, it was strongly suggested she return to being Betty, but the jury was still out on that. She liked being Laura. She wasn't sure Betty would ever see the light of day again.

She'd been at the police station for the last two hours and longed for a shower and something to eat. The small hotel room housed two queen beds, a dresser, a television, and a small writing desk. She stopped, startled to see her husband sitting at the desk. His back was turned to her.

"Kurt," she said as her heart leapt in her throat. "You scared me. I thought you were still at the hospital."

"How'd it go?"

"It's done. I gave my statement and everyone's satisfied. No more visits from the police. It's over."

"Not quite."

Kurt stood from his seat and slowly turned around. He leaned on the edge of the desk, his eyes burrowing into hers.

"Why aren't you with Nelle?" she asked.

He didn't answer her.

"Someone needs to be at the hospital when Nelle wakes up." Laura watched her husband watching her and felt uneasy. Something was off. "We need to be with our daughter."

"Nelle's fine," Kurt finally said. His voice was clear, crisp. "She woke up for a few minutes and ate some soup. The doctor gave her more pain meds and she dozed back off. I told them we'd be back soon, and the nurses agreed to keep an eye on her. They have our cells if they need us."

"What's going on?"

"You and I have to talk."

The tension in the room was unmistakable. Laura folded her arms in front of her and shook the hair out of her face. "I'm sorry about all of this. I don't know what else I can say."

"Why didn't you tell Estrada the entire truth?"

"I did. What are you talking about?"

Kurt pulled a VCR tape from behind him and placed it on the desk. He then reached into the breast pocket of his shirt, his eyes never wavering from hers. He came away with something that Laura couldn't quite see until he flicked his wrist and it fell from his fingers like a yoyo. The small clatter of metal sounded off in the absolutely silent room. The St. Christopher pendant from her glovebox swung lazily from side to side.

"Estrada found this in your car after it was abandoned. He bagged it for evidence, but he gave it back to me while you were still laid up. I told him you always kept it in there."

"And the tape?"

"I found it at the lake house. Nelle kept mumbling about it to me. Didn't know exactly what she was talking about until I saw it in your mom's closet."

"Did you look at it?"

Kurt ignored the question and held the pendant higher so he could stare at it. "Estrada missed it when he first found it, and he never sent it to the lab, so no one ever did any analysis on it. But when I got the right look at it, something caught my eye."

Laura remained quiet.

"I was getting ready to take a shower the night after he gave me the medal, and I emptied everything from my pants onto the bathroom sink. It must've been the way the light hit the chain, because I could see the dried material on it, plain as day. I'm sure they all thought it was rust or dirt, but I know what dried blood looks like."

Tears welled in Laura's eyes. "Kurt."

"I FedEx'd the medal to my buddy at the bureau so I didn't raise any red flags locally. He did the analysis. The call I got in Nelle's room was from him. Blood came back Type A. You're Type O, so I know the dried blood wasn't yours. Nelle's also Type O, so it wasn't hers."

"Kurt, please."

"I'd already started doing a little digging on your family once I knew who your family was. I was waiting on the blood analysis to come back to confirm what I suspected. Only two people had Type A in your family. Your father and your little brother, Donny. I got your father's type from the coroner's report after he passed. Then I found your brother's blood type from the public records surrounding his accident. I thought it was interesting that you have a pendant with your brother's blood all over it. I mean, I get that you'd want to keep something of his, but why not wash it off first?"

Laura took a deep and ragged breath. "You've been busy."

"I was an investigator investigating. It's what I do."

"But you don't know what you're talking about. Trust me."

Kurt ignored her. "While I waited on the blood analysis, I started back-tracing records around Donny and his death. That's when everything started to make sense."

"Stop."

He kept staring at her.

"Your brother was wearing this necklace the day Sofia Bennett killed him. This is his blood from the actual accident. I read the reports. All of them. Police report. ER intake forms. Medical examiner's report. I went through everything associated with Donny's death. There were a few articles in the local papers, too. I saw them all. You were there. You witnessed the accident. That's why you kept the pendant with his blood on it. At least, that's what I thought until I found this tape."

Laura stared at her husband, her bottom lip quivering, her sight blurry from tears. She knew she loved the man standing before her with all of her heart, but in that moment, seeing the know-it-all expression on his smug face mixed with the revulsion of him looking at a woman he never really knew, she'd never hated anyone more. The tears she shed weren't made of sorrow and regret. They were constructed of anger and rage. She felt exposed, and now he knew what no one else was ever supposed to know. These were her secrets to keep, and he wasn't supposed to be part of it. Now she had no choice but to tell him the truth, and she hated that he'd backed her into a corner like that.

"You want to know the truth?" Laura asked.

Kurt nodded. "That'd be nice."

"Okay," she whispered more to herself than to Kurt. "The truth is, Sofia Bennett hit my little brother with her car, but I'm the one who killed him."

"Tell me everything."

JANUARY 3, 1993

It was an unusually cold day for Bastrop, Texas. The overnight temperature had dropped to twenty-three degrees, and as the sun came up the next morning, not much had changed. Betty passed the garage and looked at the thermometer her father had hung there. Twenty-nine. As far as she was concerned, it might as well have been zero.

She'd been too far into the planning to let the cold weather change anything, and the fact of the matter was, she'd been looking forward to that afternoon more than she'd been looking forward to Christmas that year. The promise of some time with Mike Schuccle brought the kind of excitement that gave her stomach butterflies and plastered a clownish, ridiculous smile on her face. Mike had been the one to corner her outside the gym on the last day of classes before the holiday break and asked her if she wanted to meet up at the elementary school during vacation. Her friends had always warned her not to seem too anxious when it came to boys, but in that moment, she found herself nodding in agreement before the end of the sentence was even out his mouth. She focused on the adorable freckles that dotted the bridge of his nose, listening to his words as that dumb smile on her face grew wider and more absurd. They'd agreed to meet at eleven on January third, confirming the date through a quick and embarrassing phone call two days prior. He promised to pack a little picnic of snacks for them and they'd hang out. She could hardly contain herself.

Telling her overprotective and always-argumentative mother she was meeting a boy for a picnic lunch wasn't an option. She'd be told she couldn't go, and then the lectures would begin. She was too young for boys. She needed to be a proper woman. She needed to be reminded that the Hamms name was in good standing in the community, and if neighbors and friends from the church learned that she was sneaking around with boys, she would be tarred with a reputation she'd never be able to wash off. Her mother would refuse to stand for such a cruel sentence. Telling anyone in her family the truth was completely off the table, so Betty told her mom that she was meeting her best friend, Tammy, at the swings at the elementary school. Her mother agreed, but only on the condition that she take her little brother with her to get him out of the house for a few hours. An argument ensued, which morphed into an all-out screaming match between mother and daughter, but when Betty sensed her mom was on the verge of sending her to her room for the rest of the day, she relented and agreed to take Donny with her. There wasn't much else she could do. Donny would be her cover, and Mike Schuccle would be waiting.

"This is stupid," Donny whined as he kept pace with Betty, who walked ahead of him at a brisk pace. "I don't want to go to the swings."

"Yeah, well, I don't want you to, either," Betty snapped. "But Mom said I need to get you out of the house, so deal with it."

No one had the proper gear for temperatures under thirty

degrees, but Betty did her best to layer up, and her mother had done the same for Donny. They waddled their way three blocks toward the school.

"I'm cold."

"Tough."

"Let's go back home. Tammy can come with us and we can be warm. Mom can make us cocoa or something. It's too cold to play on the swings."

Betty felt her anger rising. "Look, it's bad enough I have to drag you along. I don't need you whining the whole time. Just shut up and play. We'll go home when I say it's time to go."

Donny wiped the snot running from his red and frozen nose. "Why can't Tammy come to the house?"

"Because we're meeting other friends, too."

"Who?"

"You don't know them."

"Tell me."

"No."

"Tell me!"

Donny stopped. Betty turned around, her patience quickly fraying. "Let's go!"

"Who's coming to the school besides Tammy?"

A sigh. "Mike Schuccle."

Donny's face lit up. "A *boy*?"

They were across from the swings now, and Betty craned her neck to make sure Mike hadn't arrived yet. "Shut up."

"Your boyfriend?"

"Shut up and let's go!"

Donny began jumping up and down, his red cheeks shining in the otherwise gray morning. "I'm telling Mom! You're meeting boys! You have a boyfriend!"

Betty rushed over and grabbed her brother by the collar of his jacket. "You better shut your mouth before I shut it for you!"

More laughing. "I'm telling Mom!"

"You better not!"

"I am!" He broke away and began running in circles, screaming as loud as he could. "Betty loves Mike! Betty loves Mike!"

The world around her seemed to be melting at her feet. A wave of panic and embarrassment washed over her as she saw her brother circling her, screaming and laughing and mocking her. Mike was on his way to their meeting spot, and Donny was being so loud. Mike would definitely hear, and that would be enough to make her want to die of embarrassment. He wasn't her boyfriend. She wasn't sure what he was, and maybe one day she wanted him to be her boyfriend, but none of that would happen as long as her little brother was there to ruin everything.

"Shut up!"

"Boyfriend! Boyfriend!"

Betty latched onto the arm of Donny's jacket and swung him around. The momentum he'd already been caught in caused him to lose his balance and he flew into the road. He landed with a thud and Betty could hear the skin of his forehead scrape against the pavement. She'd silenced her little brother, but she'd also made matters worse. Way worse.

Donny crawled into a sitting position and looked at Betty, his mouth agape, his eyes wide and glassy. The scrape on his forehead was starting to bleed down his face. He was in shock, staring.

"I told you to shut your mouth," Betty said, trying to act defiant and in control, but the panic was starting to rise in her. She wondered if Mike had seen what she'd just done. She was too scared to turn around. Now the day was over, anyway. She'd have to take her brother home to get cleaned up, and he'd tell their mother everything. Betty would be punished for the remainder of break, and all opportunities with Mike would be gone. The thought of it all made her even angrier.

"My head."

"Yeah, well, you should've thought about the consequences before you started acting like an idiot. You need to grow up or bad things happen. Remember that."

"I want to go home."

"Don't be such a baby."

Donny got to his knees and started to stand. He placed a hand on his head and wobbled a bit. "You're in so much trouble," he barked. "I'm telling Mom everything!"

Betty stepped off the curb, furious. "If you're going to be a tattle, then you can stay on the ground and crawl around with the other snakes."

She got to Donny before he could stand all the way up and placed her shoe on his chest, pushing as hard as she could. He stumbled backward, and before either of them could register what was happening, the flash of a car roared through and Donny disappeared.

Screeching brakes filled the otherwise quiet air. Betty stood completely still, not quite understanding what she'd just seen. She turned and saw a white car stopped sideways in the street, pointing toward the curb. Half of Donny's body was under the car, his light gray ski jacket soiled with dirt and blood.

"Donny!"

Betty ran toward her brother, collapsing at his side, wanting to pull him out from under the car, but not sure what she should do. There was blood. So much blood. And she didn't think her brother was moving.

"Donny!"

Her world began to fade as she heard other cars stop and people scream for help. Someone eventually pulled her away and sat her at the curb. She couldn't remember if Mike ever showed up or not, but such silly things as boys and crushes didn't matter anymore. Now there was death and carnage and a heartache that would never end, a crippling guilt that would never relent. The accident would always be her fault. She would always be the person who killed her brother. It would be a chain that she'd be forced to wear around her neck like Scrooge's partner, Jacob Marley. She'd never escape it. The accident, and her role in it, would define her forever. So, she stared at the middle swing on the swing set across the way for as long as she could. That was Donny's favorite swing. She stared until her father came to take her home.

CHAPTER FORTY-NINE

Laura eased herself down on the bed. Her body trembled as she took deep breaths in and exhaled slowly, trying to calm herself. The memory of that day was something she thought about often over the years, but verbalizing it was killing her. She thought she might break down or lash out or scream or vomit, so she kept breathing. For the first time since being rescued at Caroga Lake, she wanted a drink. She knew she needed to call her sponsor, but not until she was done with Kurt. Once and for all.

"The nurse in the ER gave us Donny's belongings, and his St. Christopher necklace was in the bag. I took it to remind myself that I was really the one who killed my brother that day. I pushed him into the street. I was so angry and wanted him away from me. I never saw the car coming. It happened so fast."

Kurt was silent.

"My dad starting coaching me about what to say, and the more I told the lie, the deeper the hole I dug. I was young and scared and thought if the police caught me changing my story, they'd send me to jail. I tried to confess to my dad a few times when I got older, but he didn't want to hear it. I didn't know he already had that tape. He always knew what happened. I figure he must've gotten it from the railyard and hid it. It's crazy, because all those years he knew I was lying, and he never stopped loving me." She placed her hands over her face and started to cry.

Kurt put the necklace on the desk next to the tape and walked closer toward her. His body was rigid, the expression on his face uncompromising. She wasn't talking to her husband. She was confessing to a cop.

"Tell me about the night Sofia Bennett came into the ER," he said. "Tell me what really happened. The truth."

Laura looked up, wiped her eyes, and shook her head. "I don't need to tell you what you already know."

"Was the potassium an accident?"

"I had to save my family," Laura whispered. "I didn't have a choice."

"Talk."

"It was like it was meant to be. How else could Sofia Bennett end up in my ER the night I was on shift? What are the odds of that? It's an impossible coincidence, but one I couldn't ignore. Fate put her on my gurney that night."

Laura stood up from the bed and walked across the tiny room toward her husband. She took both of his hands in hers and pulled him close.

"You know the rest. My mother found the tape and got Orton and Annie involved. She always hated me for not watching Donny that day, but seeing that I was the one who actually pushed him into the path of Sofia's car made the hate something more. She wanted me dead and got Orton and Annie to focus on me instead of Nelle. But I beat them both and saved Nelle. Now we're going to be okay and the past doesn't matter anymore. We can have the life we've had for the last twenty years. We *have* to have it. And it can be real this time. No more secrets. I'll keep my name, and we can put Betty and Donny and Bastrop and the Bennetts behind us forever." Her grip on her husband's hands tightened. Her voice went up an octave. "We can tell our friends that Orton and Annie mistook me for someone else, and that the entire thing was a horrific mistake. We can move on, Kurt. I want to move on. There's no reason to relive the past. Not anymore. I need you and Nelle in my life. I'll die without you. Things can normal again. We can be a family again."

Kurt's stiff frame began to melt a bit. "You knew people would make the connection between what Sofia did to your family and what you did to her. The police would have motive to put a case together on you. The hospital deemed it an accident, but it would only be a matter of time before Sofia's husband found out what happened and pointed the finger at you. So you disappeared before anyone could put the pieces together. The potassium wasn't a mistake. You killed the woman who killed your brother."

Laura let go of Kurt's hands and turned away. "Would you kill for Nelle?" she asked. "If you walked into that house at Caroga Lake and saw Orton Bennett choking Nelle, would you kill him to stop him?"

"Of course."

"Well, there you go. You kill for the ones you love. Always."

"I'd kill to save Nelle's life. I wouldn't seek revenge after the fact."

Laura spun around and looked at her husband. "Bullshit. I know you. If someone hurt Nelle, you'd be the first in line to even the score. You think you can see this in terms of black and white, but when you live it like I did, you understand that it's all just gray. Some shades of right. Some shades of wrong. All mixed together. You might call me a killer, but is that really the entire story? Is that all I am?" She took a single step closer. "And what I did wasn't vengeance. It was necessity."

"I don't know what you are," Kurt spat. "I think you're Laura, but you're Betty. I think you're a great mom who likes to give of herself and volunteer, but you're an alcoholic pill-popper living this secret life where you wait for us to go to bed and get drunk in the dark. You get through your days on Zoloft and Xanax. I think you're from Florida and your parents are dead, but you're from Texas and you've been taking care of your mom upstate. Jesus, Laura. You talk about gray, but what I see is pretty black and white."

"Because you haven't been through what I have. It's gray. Trust me. I did things to get to Nelle that others would think are wrong, and I did them to protect my child. My dad did things to protect me. Things aren't black and white when you've been through what I've been through."

"What about Estrada?" Kurt asked. His voice got quiet, his eyes searching for the woman he'd known for the past two decades. "What if he digs around enough and finds what I found?"

"His case is closed. He has no reason to keep digging. We have the tape. There's nothing for him to find. It's over." Laura picked up her pocketbook and walked back down the small hallway toward the hotel door. "I love you, and I know you love me. We can put this all behind us and start fresh. I think we deserve it."

Kurt said nothing.

"I've been away from Nelle for too long." Laura wiped the remnants of her tears. "Forget the shower. I'm going to go back to the hospital. I hope I'll see you there, for her sake and for mine." She stopped at the door, but she didn't turn around. The air was heavy. "You know everything about me now. There are no more secrets. We can be the family we were before this all began. Betty Hamms has been dead for a while. Let her go."

She walked out of the hotel room and let the door close behind her, wondering what might lie ahead for her. For her marriage. For her family. For her life. But she was optimistic. The bond of family was always stronger than people gave it credit for, and she'd do anything for hers. Just as she'd done in the past. Just like she'd do again in the future should she need to. Things would be fine. They had to be. Family was a bond that could not be broken.

Family was everything.

CHAPTER FIFTY

MARCH 27, 2000

The emergency room at the Dell Seton Medical Center had been quiet for most of Betty's shift. There had been the usual visits that coincided with a Saturday night—broken bones from a drunken fall, cuts and bruises from a fight, respiratory infection from a flu that had been ignored for too long, a pulled lower back from lifting furniture—but these patients were quickly tended to and sent on their way with pain scripts or sutures or casts that friends and family would sign over the next few months. There was nothing too serious, and for that, she was thankful. This wasn't a mockup of a hospital setting at school, nor was it a rotation where the real nurses did the work and the students assisted while trying their best to stay out of the way. This was an entirely new world, and in this world, she was the real nurse.

It was almost ten o'clock. Two more hours until the midnight team came in. Betty had discharged a man who'd presented with chest pains and shortness of breath. That was scary, but she'd handled it. After a battery of tests, Dr. Decker, the attending ER physician, had determined it was an acute case of indigestion and wrote the patient a prescription for powerful antacids. Now she was helping a nurse assistant, Charlene, exchange the sheets on the bed with a new set of linens.

"How long you been here now?" Charlene asked as she unfolded a top sheet and spread it on the bed. Her hair was tucked up under a cap and her flawless brown skin practically glowed in the overhead lighting.

"Six months," Betty replied.

"Oh, you're still a baby."

"Trust me, I know."

Charlene chuckled as she folded the sheet at the corners. "Don't worry about nothing. The days start to blend in together and before you know it, you're pushing twenty years like me. Keep your head down, learn what you can when you can, and you'll be fine."

"Thanks."

"We're all heading to the diner after shift if you wanna come. I got the next two days off and I need my disco fries to set me right."

Betty took two pillows from the bin and placed them on the bed. "Thanks, but I need to get home and catch up on some sleep. I have a clinical paper due that I have to finish. Between these shifts and my classes, I've only been stealing a few hours of sleep here and there. I need real rest."

"You still in school?"

"Going for my MBA. Figured I'd get it over with now before things in life get really crazy."

Charlene sucked her teeth. "Girl, I hope you know I don't feel sorry for you. Only a fool signs up for her MBA right when she starts her nursing career. And your first job is in the ER? You're crazy. A glutton for punishment. In fact, I'd call you a fool, except I like you too much and I don't talk like that about people I like."

Betty pulled the top sheet on her side and tucked it under the mattress. "Thanks. I think. Just trying to plan the best I can."

"Nothing wrong with a little planning. But you also have to make sure you can keep up with all of it. The three hours of sleep. The constant craziness of the ER. All the codes and procedures and drugs and protocols you need to learn. Not to mention—"

Betty held up her hand, laughing. "No more, please! I can't take it."

Charlene was smiling. "I want to make sure you got your priorities right. Giving up disco fries to get a master's degree. I don't get it."

"That decision is harder than you think," Betty said. "Disco fries are one of my favorite things on earth."

Tricia Parks, one of the senior nurses, opened the door to the room and nodded toward Betty. "You got a phone call."

"Okay, thanks."

"Take it at the main desk."

Betty handed her sheet to Charlene and walked out into the hallway, picking up her pace as she made it to the central nurses' station. The receiver was off the phone's base, waiting on the desk next to one of the printers. She leaned over and picked it up, turning away from the others.

"Hello?"

"Betty."

The crackled whisper on the other end was faint, but distinguishable. It sounded pained. Hurt. Betty's grip on the phone tightened as she pressed the receiver closer and spun away from the others who'd gathered in the hallway.

"What's wrong?" she asked.

"I did it."

"Did what? Where are you?"

"I did it. I couldn't take it anymore. I had to fix things. I had to make things right again."

The whisper on the other end shook as it spoke, and although Betty couldn't see the tears, she could hear them as clearly as if she was standing right there. There was commotion behind her, but she dared not turn around. Let the others handle it. This was more important.

"Tell me what happened."

The crying on the other end was suddenly choked off, replaced by breath that was quick and panicked. Sounds of half-words and syllables began pouring forth, but there was no way to make out any of it. It was gibberish. Hysterical.

"Calm down," Betty said through clenched teeth. "What's wrong?"

"I... I did it."

"Did what?"

"I couldn't take it anymore. She had to die."

"Who?"

"Sofia Bennett."

Betty leaned against the counter, because if she didn't, she knew her knees would give out and she'd tumble to the floor. "Dad," she whispered. "What did you do?"

Her father's voice was foreign to her, weak and frightened. "I couldn't let your mother destroy her life anymore, and I couldn't allow her to go to the hearing. What if they took her away from us? I couldn't let that happen. We already lost Donny. We couldn't lose her, too. I knew I had to get rid of Sofia. If I got rid of her, there would be nothing for your mother to obsess over anymore. Sofia would be gone, and that's all your mom ever wanted. Now they can both be at peace."

The commotion behind her was growing.

"Dad, what exactly did you do?"

"I did what she did to our boy. I hit her with my car. Ever since your mother caused that scene at the Walmart, I knew Sofia did her shopping here in Austin. I followed her in a car they could never trace back to me, and when she was walking into the food store, I hit her like she hit Donny. But she's not dead."

"What?"

"I tried to get out and check, but people were starting to rush

over, so I had to drive away. I heard on my police scanner that they're taking her to your hospital. To your ER. To you."

One of the nurses behind the desk twirled her finger, telling her to wrap the call up. Betty nodded, wiping away tears that wouldn't stop.

"What am I supposed to do?"

"I need you to finish the job," her father croaked. "She saw me right before I hit her. She knows it was me, and if she lives, she'll tell them I was the one who hit her. I need you to do what I couldn't. For me and your mother. For Donny. For our family."

"Dad—"

"I need you to end this and keep my secret. I'll make the investigation go away. I have that power in my own jurisdiction. End this tonight, and I'll take care of everything else. Do this for us. I love you."

"I can't!"

"You have to. Our lives depend on it. Our family depends on it."

Tricia poked Betty's shoulder. "Let's go, we have a car accident victim coming in. ETA under one minute."

"Okay."

"Get the crash cart and get set up. I hear she's in bad shape."

"On it."

Betty hung up without saying anything further. She wiped the tears from her eyes and hurried down the corridor to retrieve the crash cart. She could see Dr. Decker waiting inside the bay doors. He was a picture of calm, gloved hands up and ready, his protective gown covering his dress shirt and tie. There wasn't a single hair out of place, his clean-shaven face stoic. He might as well have been waiting for a bus rather than preparing to save a life. He looked over at her and gave her a quick nod.

The ambulance bay doors opened as Betty passed the nursing station. Two paramedics ran in with a patient on a gurney.

"What do we have?" Dr. Decker asked, quickly sliding next

to them to start a cursory examination as they made their way inside the emergency room.

"Female, thirty-four. Hit-and-run. Multiple lacerations. Multiple fractures both upper and lower body. Possible internal bleeding. BP is 95 over 50. Heartrate is high. 120 bpm. We secured her with a cervical collar and put an eighteen-gauge needle in the A/C. Gave her two milligrams of Dilaudid IV at the scene."

"Put her in room two."

"Copy that."

The paramedics pushed the gurney into exam room two, and as Dr. Decker, Tricia, and the other senior nurse, Pat, followed, Betty got to the crash cart. The cart looked like a small metal dresser with a monitor and paddles on top. The six drawers were full of medicines, IV needles, bags, and various other supplies that were already unlocked and ready for use. She wheeled it into the room while the rest of the team focused on evaluation and treatment.

The woman was conscious, breathing rapidly, her eyes darting from side to side. She was groaning, seemingly unable to speak, but it was clear she was in a lot of pain, even with the drugs she'd been given at the scene.

"Name?" Dr. Decker called from over his shoulder.

"Sofia Bennett," the paramedic replied as he backed out of the room.

Betty looked at the woman who had changed all of their lives so permanently that cold and gray morning.

Dr. Decker nodded and bent closer. "Sofia, my name is Dr. Decker. I'm going to help you get through this. Can you squeeze my hand? Good. Hang in there."

Betty pushed the cart to the opposite side of the room and placed it next to where the IV station had been set up. Her father's voice echoed in her mind. He needed help. He'd helped her after the accident, and he'd never stopped loving her. Now she needed to return the favor. Her mother wouldn't rest until Sofia Bennett was no longer part of their lives. Without Sofia, there would be no hearing.

The speed with which everyone in the trauma room moved was like choreographed madness. Each instruction was immediately met with a reply and confirmation. Each movement, whether by doctor or nurse, was done without interfering with the other. This wasn't the first emergency Betty had been part of, but she felt as if she was floating above it instead of being a vital member of the team. She tried to block out the images and the memories, but they came, one after the other, convincing her that saving her family was the only option. It was the only way.

"Get the light over here. Good."

Sofia Bennett was bleeding from a wound on the side of her face as well as from her mouth. Her dark hair was moist with sweat and Betty noticed tiny pieces of glass stuck in her curls, shining in the overhead light.

"Pupils are responsive to light," Dr. Decker said aloud. "That's good. Give me a head-to-toe and look for deformations and blatant trauma. The paramedics said she had multiple fractures. If they saw them, we can, too."

Tricia and Pat moved in and began feeling around on the woman's body, searching with both their hands and eyes.

Betty's thoughts wandered. The accident. Donny's funeral. Her mother's hatred of her for not keeping a better eye on him. Her lies. Her father always on her side and never really knowing the truth. It could all go away if Sofia went away. She was the key to all of their suffering.

"I need a CT scan of her head and chest, a C Spine, and a CBC. Let's also get a CMP, type and cross for blood, and a PT/PTT. Let's also check the urine. We have bleeding from the mouth. Might've punctured a lung when the airbag deployed." Dr Decker looked up at Betty. "You with us?"

"Yes."

"Good. Give her two more milligrams of Dilaudid IV stat. We need to stabilize her, and I want her as comfortable as we can get her for now."

There were more calls of instruction from both the doctor and the two senior nurses, but Betty knew they weren't talking to her. She focused on Sofia. There was only one option.

Betty spun around toward the med cart and pulled the third drawer open. She should've grabbed a vial of Dilaudid, but instead she took a bottle of potassium from the drawer on the opposite side. She was new enough to make the mistake they warned her about over and over again in nursing school and orientation. It was a chaotic scene. She got overwhelmed. She could play dumb. She had to. And the tears would be real, no question.

She took two syringes full of saline, a needle, and an empty syringe for the drug itself. She unwrapped the syringe, screwed the needle on, and plunged the tip into the bottle of potassium.

"Hurry up with the painkiller!" someone cried.

"Coming!"

Her fumbling hands unscrewed the first syringe of saline and Betty screwed it into the IV that the paramedics had already prepped. She repeated the instructions she'd first learned in nursing school to calm herself.

Flush first, drug second, flush third. Flush first, drug second, flush third. Flush first, drug second, flush third.

"Let's go, Betty. We need that Dilaudid pushed."

"On it!"

Time eased to a crawl as Betty screwed the syringe into the IV line and pushed the potassium, knowing she was pushing as fast as she could without overwhelming the patient's system, but seeing everything happen in a kind of suspended reality. "Dilaudid is in!"

More personnel came rushing into the room. Betty watched them all as if they were characters in a movie. One man taking scans and X-rays. Dr. Decker bent over the patient, pushing against her skin, examining something. The other nurses floating around Sofia Bennett, continuing to examine, evaluate, and stabilize. Time wound back up again as soon as alarms began to go off. Everyone stopped and looked at the monitors.

"We have an arrhythmia on the monitor," Pat said.

Another voice from the back of the room. "She's going into V-fib!"

Dr. Decker ran over and stared at the heart monitor. Betty could see the lines of the patient's heartrate jumping up and down rapidly. Alarms continued to ring out.

"Heartrate is erratic!"

"She'd going into cardiac arrest!"

"Starting CPR!"

Dr. Decker leaned over the woman and began administering CPR while the other nurses ran around the gurney, calling in the code. Betty watched all of it, half-frozen, the syringe still in the IV, her thumb still on the plunger.

Pat rushed to the crash cart and snatched the vial Betty had used. She examined it, her eyes widening. "Oh my god. This is potassium. You pushed the wrong med."

"No," Betty replied, trying hard to act shocked and confused. Her head was swimming, her body trembling. "Third drawer. White label with the blue stripe. Dilaudid."

Pat turned the bottle around. "They both have a blue stripe. Dilaudid is dark blue. Potassium is light blue. You just pushed 20 mEq of potassium. You're killing our patient."

"Well... I..."

The senior nurse pushed Betty away and extracted the syringe, quickly flushing it with the second syringe of saline and screwing in something new she couldn't see.

"We got the wrong med pushed," Pat cried out. "The cardiac arrest is from giving potassium IV push."

"We've got no rhythm. Going into asystole!"

"Get the paddles!"

"Blood pressure plunging! Unable to get a BP!"

Betty backed herself into the far corner of the room, out of the way of the others, as she stared at the woman who'd stopped moving. Somewhere in the background, she could hear Dr. Decker's calls for intervention and Tricia crying out that the patient's heartrate was failing. Dr. Decker began shocking the woman while the monitors were beeping with alarms until it all became the single tone of a flatline.

Betty watched it all, her body numb, her mind flipping through images of Donny's accident and the days that followed like lights cutting on and off, one after the other. She fought to push those pictures out of her mind for the moment, wanting instead to stay in the present. This was for her family. This was to make things right again. She was the hero now instead of the villain. She was the one saving them all.

New thoughts began to emerge. There would be an investigation into this accident, and despite her father's ability to make a police inquiry go away, there would always be questions and conspiracy theories. Her mistake would forever be woven within the relationship between Sofia and Donny, and she'd never be able to shed the what-ifs.

She thought about her career—all the schooling and the promises of a life she'd set out for herself. In the blink of an eye, her parents had taken that away. Their weakness had left Betty with no choice but to save them. Now she'd be stained with the act of an innocent mistake looking malevolent behind the scenes. Someone would always find the connection, and her accident would always become a premeditated act in someone's version of what happened, but if she could get away, time and distance might be the very things to save her.

It was clear, right then and there, that contingencies would have to be made. Plans would have to be thought out. She could put on an act for the review board and the police and whoever else wanted to ask about what had happened in the short term. She could play the overwhelmed newbie nurse who was confused and gave the wrong med. And she could even acknowledge that Sofia's connection to her family had caused some of her bewilderment. But that connection between Sofia and Donny would always be there, which meant there would always be suspicion of premeditation. She'd need to figure out next steps for the long term, but that was for another day. For the moment, she cleared her mind with the sole intention of watching the woman who killed her little brother and destroyed her mother's psyche die on a blood-soaked gurney in front of her. Soon it would all be over. The pain. The suffering. It was justice and she was the hero.

No one could hear her from where she was standing. The team was too focused on trying to save the patient, and no one was looking at her. But she said it anyway. As easily as she could feel the sweat forming on her brow or her heart beating in her chest, she could feel the guilt worming its way into her. It would get worse as the years went on, but in that moment, she whispered the only thing she could as she watched Sofia Bennett take her last breath.

"I'm sorry. For everything. I really am a good person."

A LETTER FROM MATTHEW

Dear reader,

Writing is such a solitary thing, but what makes it fun and exciting is knowing someone out there will pick it up and allow me to take them on an adventure that they will want to talk about with friends and family. I'm so excited to have shared this book with you and want you to know how thankful I am to you for choosing to read *The Perfect Mother*. If you enjoyed it, and want to keep up to date with all my latest releases, I encourage you to sign up at the following link. Your email address will never be shared and you can unsubscribe at any time.

www.bookouture.com/matthew-farrell

I hope you loved *The Perfect Mother,* and if you did, I would be very grateful if you could write a review. I'd love to hear what you think, and it makes such a difference helping new readers to discover one of my books for the first time.

I also enjoy hearing from my readers—you can get in touch on my Facebook page, through Twitter, Goodreads or my website.

Thanks, and happy reading!

Matthew

KEEP IN TOUCH WITH MATTHEW

www.mfarrellwriter.com

facebook.com/mfarrellwriter2

twitter.com/mfarrellwriter

instagram.com/mfarrellwriterbooks

ACKNOWLEDGMENTS

I'm so grateful for the support I have around me, both personally and professionally, and would like to take a moment to thank those people who help in this writing endeavor:

To my agent, Curtis Russell, of PS Literary Agency, to whom this book is dedicated. I appreciate the partnership more than I can ever express. The honest feedback, the phone calls that always last longer than I planned, the fabulous edits, and the advocacy you lend to me and my work mean so much. Thank you.

To my editor at Bookouture, Kelsie Marsden. Your feedback has helped this book evolve into what it is today, but more importantly, your enthusiasm for it has gotten me so excited. I can't wait for my readers to dive into this one. Thank you for all you've done to make this story even better than I thought it could be.

To the support staff at PS Literary who are always pushing my work out through social media. I appreciate you helping to get the word out, each and every day.

To Kim Nash and the Bookouture marketing team. Thank you for helping to spread the word about *The Perfect Mother* and getting me and my book in front of readers, reviewers, and influencers. I couldn't do any of that without you.

To my team of police professionals, Investigator Brian Martin of the New York State Police, Manhattan, and Christopher Calabrese, Chief Inspector of the Westchester County Police. Thank you for sharing your insights on the inner workings of the police departments you work for and for responding to my texts about murder, protocols, and random procedural questions. If I got anything wrong, that's on me.

To the mother/daughter ER nursing team of Linda Pallo BSN, RN and Melissa Young BSN, RN. The ER scene in this book is, literally, the backbone of the entire story and it was critical to get everything as accurate as possible. I'm so thankful for your feedback and assistance with the procedures, meds, protocols, and everything else that went into making that scene as realistic as we could. Again, if I got anything wrong, that's a hundred percent on me.

To my wife, Cathy, and my daughters, Mackenzie and Jillian. Thank you for always being patient while I'm writing and supportive in this crazy new world as an author. Your enthusiasm is inspiring and I couldn't do this without you guys. I love you.

To my family, thank you for the support and for always being willing to spread the word about my books. You guys are the best.

To my readers, your support and willingness to get the word out about my books continues to fill my heart with joy. I cannot express how grateful I am that you've chosen my books to read and post about when there are so many options out there. Thank you, from the bottom of my heart.

Finally, a shout-out to Mom who is no longer with us. Thank you for sitting next to me each time I sit in front of my computer to write. I know you're there, pushing me and cheerleading along the way. You are, and will always be, my #1 fan. I love you and miss you.

Happy reading all!

MF

Printed in Great Britain
by Amazon